ALL THE SECRET PLACES

ALSO BY ANNA CARLISLE:

Dark Road Home

ALL THE SECRET PLACES

A GIN SULLIVAN MYSTERY

Anna Carlisle

CROOKED
LANE

NEW YORK

Published in the United States by Crooked Lane Books, an imprint of The Quick Brown Fox & Company LLC.

Crooked Lane Books and its logo are trademarks of The Quick Brown Fox & Company LLC.

Library of Congress Catalog-in-Publication data available upon request.

ISBN (hardcover): 978-1-68331-287-1
ISBN (ePub): 978-1-68331-288-8
ISBN (ePDF): 978-1-68331-290-1

Cover design by Lori Palmer
Book design by Jennifer Canzone

Printed in the United States.

www.crookedlanebooks.com

Crooked Lane Books
34 West 27th St., 10th Floor
New York, NY 10001

First edition: September 2017

10 9 8 7 6 5 4 3 2 1

1

Gin Sullivan was having the strangest dream. She was running along a narrow, rocky ridge, each footfall loosening clods of earth and pebbles, which tumbled and spiraled thousands of feet down through the open air. On one side, far below, wound the Monongahela River, its lazy curves and gray, opaque waters as familiar to her as the back of her hand. On the other side was a dark void, as echoing and lonely as it was bottomless.

Someone was pursuing her, but—with the strange certainty that sometimes accompanies dreams—Gin somehow knew that turning around to face her pursuer would mean losing her footing and falling to her death. She could hear brush breaking and rocks clattering behind her as the danger drew ever nearer, and now there was another sound, an insistent, rhythmic tone piercing the silence.

"Gin . . . Gin, sorry, sorry—"

Her eyes flew open as the familiar voice next to her ear sent the dream images splintering. The room was cloaked in darkness, but it was nothing like the terrifying void of the dream. As Gin blinked sleep away and shifted up onto her elbows, the faint moonlight coming through the windows illuminated the comforting landscape of Jake Crosby's bedroom.

There at the end of the bed was the roughhewn footboard built from lumber he had felled himself. There was his flannel shirt, worn thin at the elbows and softer with every wash, hanging off one of the posts. On top of the dresser, in a tarnished silver frame, was a photograph of the two of them taken nearly two decades earlier in the stands at a Trumbull High School football game.

And though she couldn't see them from the bed, she knew that her jeans and sweater lay puddled on the floor in front of that dresser . . . exactly where Jake had torn them off of her in a fevered rush last night.

"Gin, honey, go on back to sleep. I'll take this downstairs."

Jake reached across her for his phone—somehow, in the hours after they'd fallen into each other's arms, finally exhausted, she'd ended up on his side of the bed—and padded out of the bedroom and down the stairs. She could hear his voice, soothing and low at first, then rising in what sounded like alarm. For a moment, sleep hovered at the edges of her consciousness, but the interrupted dream lingered with its halo of anxiety, and finally she gave up. She rolled over and looked at the clock.

5:18 AM.

Gin ran a hand through her long, tangled curls and pushed back the covers, reluctantly getting out of bed. The cold air instantly raised goose bumps on her flesh as she dug running tights and a pullover from one of the drawers that Jake had cleared for her a few months ago when, without ever discussing how long she would be staying, Gin had moved into his house.

While she was making the bed, Jake appeared in the doorway wearing faded jeans and nothing else. His face was shadowed with the beard he shaved only once or twice a week, and there were fresh scrapes and bruises on his work-hardened forearms, a constant hazard of working in construction. He'd lost a little weight as winter set in and he raced to finish a major project; as a result, the muscles of his torso and abdomen stood out in high relief.

Gin tried not to get distracted by the sight as she pulled on the tights and smoothed the hem of her pullover over her hips.

"That was Gus," Jake said. Something in his words tipped her off—a carefulness that rippled the surface of his gravelly, sleep-thickened voice. "I need to get to the site."

"Is something wrong?"

"Yes."

The single syllable was clipped and hard. Fear pricked along Gin's skin.

"What?"

Jake grimaced, looking past her, out the bedroom window to the mist drifting past the trees, their branches black and leafless. "Fire. Bad one. Trumbull already responded, and Munhall and McKeesport are on their way."

"Oh, no," Gin gasped.

"Gus thinks we'll lose the Archer place." Jake grabbed for the shirt at the edge of the bed and pulled it on, buttoning it with practiced motions. "The roof's about to go, and the fire's in both floors."

Shock was followed by dismay. Over the summer, Jake had bought a parcel of land up on a ridge overlooking the river, a quarter mile out of town, when the elderly woman who owned it died and her estate was split up. He'd worked hard to get it permitted for three large houses of his own design, a project he'd been dreaming of for years. He'd put his best crew on the job, and they'd worked feverishly through the fall, Jake putting on his tool belt along with the rest of them, doing the work he preferred by far to the business aspects of running a growing construction company.

The land had been a good deal, but the bank had its doubts: the houses Jake proposed building were larger and grander than anything that had been built in Trumbull for decades. Jake was convinced that wealthy Pittsburgh families, especially the new denizens of the burgeoning tech economy, would be willing to make the half-hour commute to the city in exchange for the stunning views of the river, the nearby trails and forests, and the quaint downtown that was enjoying a fledgling renaissance. But most lenders couldn't get past Trumbull's reputation as a former steel town that had been plagued for decades by unemployment, crime, and poverty.

In the end, Jake had been forced to put up much of his own money to get the project off the ground, pouring nearly every penny of his savings into it. Gin knew that the future of his company depended on the successful completion and sale of the three homes.

She had visited the site half a dozen times at various stages of construction, basking in the pleasure of Jake's quiet pride as he pointed out the details of design and construction, the thoughtful nuances and distinctive, deceptively simple lines that had defined his reputation as a builder. She had believed in him before the first shovelful of dirt was dug, and her confidence only grew as the homes began to take shape.

The first of the houses had already been sold: Leon Archer was a consumer products executive who'd just gotten a very expensive divorce from his Philadelphia socialite wife. The "quiet life" he'd publicly stated he intended to pursue in Trumbull, according to the local gossip, was really a refuge to stash his mistress and their baby until the worst of the scandal had passed. Gin had never met the couple, but she knew Jake had spent many hours honing the details of the plans to Archer's exacting specifications. The house was meant to be spectacular, a showpiece that would bring more business Jake's way—and money into Trumbull, as well.

"You're insured." Despite her efforts, Gin's small voice came out sounding more like a question than a statement. After all, they'd never discussed it; Jake kept the details of his company close to the vest.

Jake shrugged miserably. "I mean, insurance isn't going to make me anywhere close to whole. The value wasn't in the land, the raw materials . . . it was more about the vision. That was my toe in the door, you know? Selling the dream. Archer's not going to want to wait around for me to rebuild from the ground up—that baby's due any day now. And without him in the picture, how am I supposed to talk anyone into buying a half-finished house with a burnt-out wreck next door?"

Gin knew what he wouldn't say: Jake had counted on the lure of Archer's quasi celebrity to bring buyers for the other two homes while there was still time to modify the plans with expensive finishes and enhancements that would drive the selling prices up. He had hoped to build one-of-a-kind homes that not only were nearly as large and impressive as the first but would showcase his distinctive style and drum up more business down the road. This was supposed to be the project that would finally let him focus on the work he loved every day, that would allow him to turn down the less desirable projects he took just to keep his crew employed and pay the bills. Demolition work, insurance jobs, commercial, and infrastructure . . . Jake had spent many years bidding on everything that came along just to stay afloat.

But if the prospect of Pittsburgh royalty living right next door evaporated, there would be little to lure the kind of wealthy buyers from the city who would pay a premium for a Crosby home.

Gin knew that practically the only family in Trumbull that could afford such a home was her own . . . and Madeleine and Richard Sullivan would never leave the old steel magnate's mansion on Hyacinth Lane in which they'd raised their family.

"Be careful," she blurted as Jake grabbed his boots from the closet.

"I will," he said, but he didn't look back before heading downstairs.

*   *   *

Gin spent the next hour drinking coffee and checking online for updates with the local news on in the background, knowing that Jake would call when he was ready—and that he wouldn't welcome a call from her until then.

At 6:30, she decided it was late enough to call her parents. She tried the house phone before remembering that Richard had finally made the transition to his cell phone in retirement. She was about to dial that number when she impulsively decided to drive over instead.

She took the ridge road, high above town, to the old "millionaires' row," where her parents' old stone mansion held pride of place at the end of the street. It was the most gracious of the fine homes that had been built a century earlier for the steel barons who ran the plants and factories along the bend in the river below, and Madeleine had grown up inside its walls, just as her own mother had. Gin walked through the formal parlor, past the dining room, whose walls were covered in sky-blue silk, and into her favorite room of the house—the kitchen, which her mother had recently redone with all the bells and whistles while keeping the original beams and stone floors and even the old stove. The effect was inviting and comfortable. Her parents were

drinking coffee at the kitchen table and sharing the newspaper, Richard in his Brooks Brothers robe and her mother
in a Lanz nightgown that looked almost exactly like every
other Lanz nightgown she had worn as far back as Gin could
remember.

"Is everything okay?" Madeleine asked in lieu of a greeting.

"It's fine," Gin said quickly—too quickly, a reflexive reas-
surance that she then had to walk back. "I mean, Jake and I are
fine, but he got some bad news. One of the houses he's building
caught fire."

"Oh, my God, I saw that fire on the news upstairs," Madeleine exclaimed. She kept a small television in her walk-in
closet; Richard believed it was uncivilized to turn on the
television before evening, but Madeleine overrode him in her
private quarters. "Up on Kitts Hill. I didn't make the connection to Jake's project—they just kept showing footage of
it from down by the bridge. It looked like a giant orange bon-
fire up there."

So at least the news helicopters from the city had stayed
away. And the police were probably preventing anyone from
driving up to the site—for the moment, anyway. There was
only one road up, a former fire road leading to the Rudkin
estate.

Gin knew that Jake wouldn't want his misfortune broad-
cast for the whole world to see. He had far too much pride.

"Let her talk," Richard said. "Sweetheart, how did it
happen?"

"Poor Jake. Sit down and let me pour you some coffee,"
Madeleine insisted.

"They don't know yet. At least, they didn't when Jake got
the call—which was over an hour ago. I was wondering . . . I
mean, is there anyone you could call, Mom? I've been checking online, but no one seems to know anything yet."

"Lots of theories masquerading as facts," Madeleine sighed. She had proved surprisingly adept at social media when she had ramped up her bid for mayor after serving two terms on the Trumbull city council. Now, just a few short weeks after being voted into office by a healthy margin, she seemed like an old hand. "I should be able to find something out for you once city hall opens. Look, you're going to find out soon enough, because the press release is going out today—we've named the new police chief. Though he won't know anything at this point."

"Who is it?"

"A guy from county, actually. Tuck Baxter. Have you ever run into him?"

"I don't think so." Gin had spent her entire career as a medical examiner in Chicago before returning to Trumbull the past summer; now she consulted part time at the county offices in Pittsburgh. The cases she worked on often brought her into contact with the county police, but the name didn't ring a bell.

"Word is he got himself into a bit of trouble up in the city," Richard said, folding the newspaper fastidiously. Gin knew her father golfed with a retired judge and several former councilmen, so she wasn't surprised that he knew details that Madeleine hadn't shared with him. Luckily, Richard—who'd retired only that year from a demanding career as a physician—was happy to cede the role of full-time professional to his wife, though the transition to retirement was proving a challenge.

"He's probably got his hands full anyway, getting settled in. And honestly, there probably isn't anyone left at the fire department to talk to either—I'm sure they're all pitching in."

"Jake said they called in a couple other departments . . ."

"As well they should," Madeleine said crisply. "Trumbull shows up for everyone. Let someone else help for a change."

This had been a central plank in her mother's strategy on the council: attract goodwill to the town by offering to share whatever meager resources they could. Before Gin returned to Trumbull, her mother had regaled her during their occasional phone conversations with stories of hospital drives and school fund raisers and downtown rededications in all the struggling river towns that had once been the backbone of American industry, shipping steel on huge cargo craft in the sluggish brown river waters. There had been a shared sense of struggle against the ruined economy's immutability, of bracing up against the never-ending storm.

Now that her mother's Hail Mary efforts to revitalize the town appeared to be working, however, Gin wondered if some of that fellowship was crumbling, a victim of envy. There seemed to be room for only one forgotten town to thrive so far, and Gin was torn between pride that it was Trumbull and fear that the changes wouldn't last.

"How's Jake doing?" her father asked, switching gears. "Lord knows he deserves a break."

"He's, um, worried, of course," Gin stammered. She couldn't admit that there was a side of Jake that he kept from her, facets that he hid, even now. "But you know Jake. He's strong; he'll find a way through."

"Of course he will. You both will," Madeleine said. "I'll walk down to the station as soon as I get in, and when I have anything to share, you know I'll call you right away."

"Thanks, Mom." Gin let out a frustrated breath. "I shouldn't get so far ahead of myself. It's probably under control by now."

"I'm sure you're right," Richard said mildly. "When are we going to get you two up to the city for a play?"

Gin didn't have the heart to admit to him that their season tickets to the theater would be wasted on Jake, who was not a fan. It was only recently that her father had warmed up to Jake, and she didn't want to jeopardize the thaw in their relationship.

"Tell you what, Dad," she said impulsively. "How about you and Mom come over for dinner instead? Maybe next Saturday? Jake will cook, and I'll sit around and let him wait on us."

"That's my girl," Madeleine said approvingly, flashing a smile. It was something of a joke between them, as Madeleine had been a homemaker until her forties, when she discovered an interest in local politics. "Does that work for you, Richard?"

Richard leaned contentedly back in his chair and folded his arms over his chest. "I'll have to clear my busy schedule," he said, "but I think I can fit you kids in."

Gin finished her coffee and declined an offer of a second cup. She was more concerned than she was letting on, but it would be pointless to worry her parents too. They walked her to the door and watched her get in her car, their arms around each other in a pose she'd seen them in many times before. Their hair was gray now, and her father had lost a fair amount of weight, but they had been seeing her off in just that pose for decades now.

"Love you, Virginia!" her mother called just as Gin was closing her car door. As Gin backed out of the drive, she thought about her mother's willingness to say those words, which her proper, buttoned-up family had eschewed all through her childhood. And she wondered why it was so hard for her to say the words back. Especially since she'd craved them so desperately for the first eighteen years of her life, when she would have traded her parents for ordinary folks in a heartbeat. Having a brilliant surgeon father and a former debutante mother who had inherited a steel fortune passed down from men who'd had the sense to get out in time, Gin had known status and wealth since birth—but it had come at a cost. With the single exception of Lily, her younger sister, they had all been distant with each other, almost cold—right up until the tragedy that tore them apart.

During Gin's senior year of high school, Lily had gone missing. No trace of her was ever found, and her loss became a painful wedge between Gin and her past, her hometown, her family. When Lily's body was discovered the previous summer, stuffed in a cooler near the water tower where the two had spent time with friends as teens, the old wounds were ripped open. Gin had taken a leave of absence from her job and come home to Trumbull, helpless in her renewed grief until she found an outlet in assisting in the case.

Now—with Gin's help—Lily's murderer was in prison, and Gin and her parents were doing their best to nurture the bond between them all. Her leave of absence had been extended indefinitely, and while Gin had not yet made up her mind to move to Trumbull permanently, the days passed without her making any plans to return to Chicago. The consulting work kept her busy and engaged for ten or fifteen hours a week. The rest of the time, she caught up on her reading, went for runs through the beautiful late-autumn mornings high above the river, and tried to enjoy her time with Jake without analyzing it or putting labels on it.

As Gin began the descent down the hill, she spotted the smoke, black and acrid looking, still belching into the sky. What did that mean? Why hadn't they been able to put the fire out completely? She considered driving straight to the site, but she knew that it would be crowded with emergency vehicles already, and besides, she wanted to run.

She drove back to Jake's house, where she pulled her hair into an elastic and splashed cold water on her face. She was glad she'd taken the time to go see her parents, something she'd promised herself she would try to do more often now that she'd moved home.

Her time in Trumbull had been good for her—despite the fact that she had no full-time job, no plans for the future, and no idea what she was going to do next week or next month. "Just for today," she whispered, echoing a sentiment that the therapist her mother had connected her with was fond of repeating, a reminder not to let her mind travel too far forward—or, more to the point when they'd begun their sessions, backward.

She pulled on her shoes and headed down the stairs, out the door Jake had framed with his own hands, and into a frosty, forbiddingly gray November morning.

And then she began to run.

2

Half an hour later, a weak morning sun was making an effort to break through. The sky was turning faintly pink where it met the horizon, and the weak light illuminated the wet pavement of the road that had been built alongside the railroad tracks. In daylight, Gin would have chosen a different route, running along the trails high above town, past thickets and meadows and ash heaps that had barely changed since her childhood. But sunrise came late this time of year, and Gin stuck to the streets of town, counting on the reflective striping on her jacket and tights to protect her from the occasional car or truck.

Maybe it was the eeriness of her dream that had triggered her introspective mood, or maybe it was worry about Jake's construction site, but Gin steered clear of the clean, well-lit streets near the town's center and ran through the neighborhoods not yet touched by the nascent redevelopment efforts. Broken glass and plastic bags and bits of colorful paper littered the streets; houses leaned into each other as though they were exhausted.

At the corner of Miller and Park, she paused almost reflexively to make sure no one was coming out of the liquor store. This corner had been the site of frequent robberies and at least two murders in the last decade, as her mother had dutifully reported. But the evidence of more hopeful times was all around: at a nearby house, children bundled into colorful puffy jackets followed their mother to her car, a heap that looked like it would take a miracle to start. A white truck adorned with the logo of an organic bakery in nearby Pittsburgh lumbered by, headed no doubt for one of the new restaurants that had sprung up downtown.

Here was where Gin usually turned and headed back toward home, along Hornbake Avenue, a long street that climbed up the side of the hill before leveling out in the newer housing developments built during the first hopeful wave of gentrification in the early seventies. This route allowed her to pass by Hyacinth Lane and see whether the lights were on in her parents' kitchen. Her mother was often out of the house early, but sometimes she would linger over coffee in an effort to draw Richard out of the funk that had held him in its grip since he'd abruptly retired after the discovery of Lily's body in June. Madeleine often beseeched Gin to "check in on Dad," even though neither of them believed she had the power to improve his mood any more than the mild antidepressant recommended by his psychiatrist. Gin was glad she'd taken the time to see her parents this morning, even if her motives had been selfish. She vowed to visit on another morning soon, once the current crisis had been resolved.

And here, on the northern edge of town, she was only a quarter of a mile away from Jake's jobsite. Already she could smell the smoke, feel it scouring her lungs; the sky above the ridge was dense with it, even though the winds were sweeping it away from town, over into the valley on the other side. The worry that had sent her out into the frigid morning had turned, with every footfall on the cracked and broken asphalt of downtown, into a sharper, keener emotion. Something between dread and panic.

Living with a man was not the same as knowing him—not, at any rate, the way Gin had once known Jake, when they'd been teenagers joined at the hip and anointed with first love, finishing each other's sentences and almost smug in the knowledge that nothing would tear them apart. How wrong they had been. Now, having found their way back to each other after a separation of almost two decades, Jake and Gin were more cautious. They each protected parts of themselves; they held back.

Something had been brewing even before this morning, but Jake hadn't told her what was at the root of his increasingly gloomy mood. She was nearly positive it had to do with money, with the calculated risks he'd taken with his business, not all of which had paid out. Each night at dinner, sitting at the kitchen table crafted from a single chestnut oak felled on his property, she tried to find the words to ask him how bad it had gotten and whether he would consider allowing her to help.

She never found the words. Instead, many evenings ended as last night had, when the pent-up questions and declarations and emotions translated into lovemaking that was needful, sometimes almost frantic. Each of them had grown bolder, each demanded—and gave—more and more. In fact, the longer they went without revealing their unspoken feelings to each other, the more they communicated in other ways.

Gin knew that Jake had the scratches on his back to prove it.

She started up the hill, pushing herself hard, trying to beat back her frustration by force. After all, she knew better; as a medical examiner, she had told countless families that the key to weathering difficult times was communication. She had seen marriages turn cold and empty without it. So why did the connection between her and Jake continue to burn so fiercely?

Was it love—or was it the sputtering end of a relationship on the brink of failure?

By the time Gin neared the top of the ridge, the chilly air was beginning to warm, the sun breaking weakly through the clouds. The road narrowed as it rose past the developed part of town, and she kept to the shoulder, ignoring the occasional icy spray from a passing car. Down below, morning traffic was beginning to clog the road to the bridge connecting Trumbull to Route 837, which led north to Pittsburgh; those lucky enough to secure jobs in the city were headed there now.

In a few more minutes, she'd arrived, breathing hard, at the cleared, flat, two-acre parcel where the three homes were in various stages of completion. The Archer home, situated in the best part of the lot with a view from the back windows out over the river valley and a large, gracious circular drive in front, was unrecognizable. The stench was nearly unbearable, but at least the flames had been doused, leaving a charred black steaming wreck. Bits of burnt debris and ash floated in the air, making Gin cough, and the acrid fumes stung her eyes.

All over the site, fire and police vehicles were parked, and responders milled around. In what had been meant to be the side yard of the ruined house, she could see Jake slumped dejectedly against the framed-out walls of one of the houses that was still standing. As Gin started making her way across the construction site, going slowly and carefully to avoid twisting an ankle on the rutted earth studded with charred and unidentifiable gobbets, two marked county cruisers arrived and pulled up next to the house in the circular drive that had been carved from the raw earth. A third arrived seconds later, rounding the top of the hill fast enough that its occupants were undoubtedly being jounced uncomfortably.

All three vehicles bore the seal of Allegheny County on its field of royal blue, an image that never failed to move Gin. She'd written a sixth-grade essay on the symbolism of the images dating back to colonial times—the sailing ship representing trade, the plow and sheaves of wheat representing the bounty of the earth. Nowhere, she had understood even then, was there evidence of the steel economy that would someday lift and then decimate the region's fortunes.

But now the beautiful image was nearly lost above the large stark letters spelling out "POLICE." Light bars flashed the strobing blue and white that signaled the kind of trouble Gin had hoped was finally in the past. And moving purposely through the smoldering fire site was a figure she recognized with an involuntary shiver of dismay: Detective Bruce Stillman, who'd been the senior detective in the investigation of the discovery of her sister's remains and the subsequent arrest and conviction of a woman who'd been a trusted family friend.

Stillman had shown little sensitivity to Gin and her family, despite the anguish they'd experienced at the discovery of Lily's body seventeen years after she'd disappeared. His partner, Liam Witt—who was considerably younger and less experienced, still in his first year as a detective when he'd worked on Lily's case—had been kinder but followed Stillman's lead in most areas of the investigation. Neither cop had much regard for Jake, who'd been their prime suspect nearly until the end.

The fact that Stillman and Witt were assigned to this case did not bode well for Jake, who would need the investigation of the fire wrapped up quickly so that he could file an insurance claim and start rebuilding as soon as possible.

Gin was certain that Jake had spotted her, though he managed only a brittle and brief smile. He gave the burned house a final, baleful glance and started toward her.

"Hey," he said, making another attempt at a smile, this one even weaker than the first. They stood together at a distance from the growing assortment of uniformed officers who seemed to be gathering next to a recently dug trench between the houses and the woods that came nearly to the edge of the clearing.

"I didn't want to call," Gin said lamely. "I knew you couldn't talk . . . I just thought I could come by and see."

Jake nodded wordlessly, the muscles of his face tight. He hadn't kissed her. But maybe that didn't mean anything; they weren't really the type to kiss in public. Not yet, anyway, though Gin had thought that might come in time.

He wasn't making this easier for her, she thought in frustration. Yes, of course the fire was a terrible blow; of course he was devastated. He might be thinking of the long and arduous road ahead of him. And yet. Wasn't that the whole point of loving someone, of making them your partner—not having to be alone in life's most difficult moments? Weren't they meant to face these challenges together?

Guilt pushed its way into Gin's thoughts—she had been the one to leave him the first time. And even if they'd still been kids, even if there had been terrible extenuating circumstances, maybe she wasn't entitled to expect Jake to trust her easily now that they were together again.

She pushed down all of her hurt, her negativity, and tried to come up with something encouraging to say. But as she was deliberating, a large van drove up, this one bearing the markings of the county crime scene investigation unit.

"Aw, *hell*," Jake muttered.

It wasn't a good development—the decision to call the CSI team meant that the responding officers suspected arson. "They can't think someone set it *deliberately*," Gin protested. "Who would do something like that? I mean, what possible reason could they have?"

Jake shrugged, using the motion to turn his body slightly away from her. "You know as much as me at this point."

Which wasn't true, not by half; but Gin could sense Jake's mounting despair and knew he wouldn't want to talk further about it—not with her, anyway. The firefighters had managed to extinguish the fire before it could consume the framed structures of the other two homes, which had suffered only some minor scorching when the wind carried the flames consuming the Archer home. Maybe they could be saved as they were—there were no finishes to absorb the smoke, drywall to crumble, carpet to sag, or wallpaper to peel away under the hoses.

But it was impossible not to gawk at what was left of the Archer mansion, which only two days ago had stood tall and glorious against a brilliant wintry blue sky, sunlight glinting off its windows and burnishing the polished hardware of its custom-made double entrance doors. What was left of the dove-gray siding was now peeling and blackened, the windows were shattered, and the brand-new roof was caved in. Where the firefighters had used axes to release some of the fire's rage, the raw splinters looked like fresh wounds. The smell of smoke and ash and melted synthetic materials and metal was both cloyingly sweet and throat-scrapingly acrid. A number of the responders had tied bandannas and handkerchiefs over their noses and mouths.

Gin's gaze fell on the detectives, who were conferring with several of the firefighters. As she watched, Stillman broke away and began making his way toward them, stepping carefully around charred debris and orange cones, a frown of distaste marking his otherwise blandly handsome features. Gin's heart sank.

Jake followed her gaze. "Is that . . ."

"Stillman and Witt," Gin confirmed with a sigh of resignation. "Of all the officers who could have turned out, it had to be them."

Stillman came up even with them before Jake could respond. The men acknowledged each other tersely. As far as she knew, there had been no contact between them since Jake was cleared. Some members of the investigation, including

Detective Witt, had attended Lily's memorial service, forming a respectful queue in the back of the hall and leaving before the reception; Stillman was not among them.

He'd done nothing technically wrong. Given the years Gin had spent working with the police on investigations of suspicious deaths, she knew that the best officers did not allow emotion or personal bias to stand in the way of investigatory zeal, and she didn't hold Stillman's dogged pursuit of the suspects in Lily's murder against him, even if he had been misguided and ultimately wrong; even if their interactions had proved him to be aggressive to the point of badgering.

What she couldn't forgive him for was never acknowledging to her family that he had been wrong when the real killer was revealed. Her parents deserved better. Jake deserved better. And maybe even she had deserved better too.

"What do you know about this place?" Stillman demanded without preamble. "I mean, how did you pick this particular site to put up your McMansions?"

Jake let the insult go by, though the twitch in his jaw gave away his anger. "I'm not sure exactly what you're asking. I'd bet you already know that I bought this parcel from Corinne Rudkin's estate after she died earlier this year. I can assure you that everything was done in compliance with every law and code and rule that the county threw my way. You can look at all the paperwork at the city offices. I'll even spot you the thirty bucks for the records fees."

"That right?" Stillman raised one bushy eyebrow, and the smirk that characterized most of their conversations settled onto his thin lips. "You got a hell of a deal, is what I heard. Have to say I wondered about that."

Gin sensed Jake stiffening at her side and touched his wrist, willing him to keep his temper in check. There were still those in town who'd love nothing more than to see Jake hauled off for fighting, just like when he'd been a moody high school student being raised by a single dad who just happened to be the local chief of police.

"Listen, Stillman, I don't know who set this fire, but I sure hope you track them down and prosecute them to an inch of their life. I've dotted every i and crossed every t on this project, and believe me, I have absolutely no motive to interfere with it. I've got pretty much everything I own tied up in these three houses."

Gin wondered if it was only her who noticed the faint cracking of his voice on the last few words.

"Calm down, buddy, I'm not here to waste my time on building codes," Stillman retorted. "Believe it or not, you've got even bigger problems than a firebug with an ax to grind."

His smirk widened as though he was enjoying this. She seethed; Stillman was the sort of person who thrived on the discomfort of others, who enjoyed making accusations with little regard to whether they were on the mark just to see people squirm.

"Spit it out," Jake said, his hands clenched into fists.

"The crew dug trenches out along the edge of the woods there." He pointed to the area past the houses where the officers were gathered along the mounded dirt. "I guess they were afraid that if that other house caught, it could jump to the woods. Anyway, they stumbled on something interesting. Buried only a few feet down—kind of surprising you didn't run into it when you cleared up here. If you'd built just a few feet over, you probably would have."

He paused, eyes bright with anticipation as he delivered the punch line: "Crosby, it looks like you built your little nouveau-riche neighborhood right on top of a burial ground."

3

The crime scene unit was carrying equipment from the van toward the cluster of officers at the edge of the site while the local cops helped mark off the area. Peter Haimes came puffing up the hill on his ancient Schwinn; the old man spent his days monitoring the police scanner and was usually the first on scene to view anything from a shooting to a traffic accident. It was only a matter of time before the looky-loos returned, the downhill neighbors who'd heard the sirens and come to see the firefighters in action, then wandered back down to town when it was contained. Once they realized that the fire had now turned into a crime scene, they would return in force along with many more.

Gin and Jake reluctantly followed Stillman.

"They had three other departments turn out," Stillman explained. "They had enough guys on the house, how it was explained to us, they had a bunch of them working to contain it in case it spread. Way the winds were this morning, they were most worried it could hit the woods over there." His finger traced the arc from the edge of the woods back toward the rest of the Rudkin land. Somewhere back there were the estate buildings—the main house, guest house, pool, and garages for the antique automobile collection that had been Howard Rud-kin's passion before he died a decade ago. Early in Gin's career at the Chicago ME's office, Madeleine had sent Gin an article from *Pittsburgh* magazine that showed Howard and Corinne Rudkin standing in front of what seemed like an entire fleet of old cars, their three teenage boys—the eldest barely old enough to drive—looking embarrassed in their prep school uniforms.

Corinne and Howard were both dead now, and the boys were grown. They probably had families of their own. The thought saddened Gin; it was a reminder of the inevitable march of time, the tarnish that faded even the brightest memories as they slipped into the past.

"Were they afraid it would carry back to the rest of the estate?" she asked.

"They were worried it would burn the shit out of fuck-all," Stillman responded disdainfully. "That's what firefighters tend to focus on."

"Hey," Jake snapped.

"Oh, excuse me." Stillman rolled his eyes. "I forgot there was a *lady* present. Pardon my French. The point is, they were digging that trench as a firebreak that turned out not to be needed. Only it was just sheer luck they picked that location. Got a few feet down and hit something they weren't expecting. Body decomposed beyond recognition in some sort of old military uniform. Good thing they didn't go at it with the pickax, or they would have done even more damage than they already did."

Gin was well aware of the friendly—and sometimes not-so-friendly—competition between firefighters and police, each of whom tended to view their own professions as the more dangerous and demanding, so she let the comment pass, but Jake muttered a curse of his own.

"Look, I'm sorry that this happened. I understand the need to figure out who the body belongs to and give it a proper burial and find whoever was responsible for putting him there in the first place. But look, it's not enough that my jobsite's burned down—now it's going to be tied up in the investigation too?" Jake was doing his best to control his frustration, but his voice bristled with tension. "Look, Stillman, like you said, if it had been found just a few yards over, it wouldn't even be on my land. I'm not asking to interfere with what you need to do, but you have to understand that I need to get my guys in here and start cleanup. I mean, leaving it like this"—he gestured at the still-smoking hulk—"is not only structurally dangerous, it's opening me up to attractive nuisance claims if you people can't keep the crowds under control."

"Oh, we can control the crowds," Stillman shot back. "It's just too bad you can't seem to control the dead bodies that always seem to end up connected to you."

"That's enough," Gin said, exasperated. Stillman had been among the officers who'd pushed hardest for Jake's guilt, but the rift between them went further back than that. Jake—raised by his father when his mother left the family when he was only a baby—had been a troublemaker in high school, and many in the county police department believed that his father had pulled strings to keep him from paying the consequences.

Gin knew that wasn't the case, but small-town politics were what they were. Stillman had been a cop for as long as Jake had been working in construction, and while Stillman's career had taken him to the county offices in Pittsburgh, he'd grown up in a river town just a few miles up the road. Until last year, their paths hadn't officially crossed, but each knew of the other, and neither had any reason to expect anything but the worst from each other.

Gin had no intention of playing peacemaker between two grown men. And besides, she had to admit, Stillman had a point. What were the odds that, less than six months after the discovery of Lily's body under the Trumbull water tower—where Jake and the rest of them had once gone to hang out—another body would be found buried just a few miles away, with Jake connected at least peripherally to the location?

"What do you know so far?" she asked, hoping to focus attention on the facts rather than the two men's tempers.

Stillman, who had been leading them toward the firebreak, stopped shy of the tape the officers had strung between sawhorses to isolate the scene. He turned to face them with his arms folded across his chest.

"What I know so far is that Crosby's got some questions to answer," he said coldly. "As for you, I understand that you're cozy with the ME's office and you've made a few friends up there. But unless there's something I don't know about that connects you to the dead guy, you can turn your little Spandex ass around and run back the way you came."

"I'm not 'cozy with' the ME's office," Gin snapped. "I'm officially consulting to them, as you know. My relationship with everyone on the staff is purely professional. As is my relationship to you," she couldn't resist adding.

She knew that there were still those who felt she'd overstepped professional bounds in her sister's case when she had asked to be allowed to sit in on the autopsy, and later when she and Jake had done their own investigating when the official case veered off in the wrong direction.

Still, without her specialized experience, critical evidence would have been missed and Lily's killer never found—which was why the ME's office had called upon her to help out on several more cases. So far, her consulting work had amounted to little more than a pastime; still, it grated to have her professionalism questioned.

"So they say," Stillman said. It wasn't much of a comeback, but then again, as Gin reminded herself, men who were put off by working with competent, strong women weren't often all that clever.

"The body is male?" Gin asked, refusing to take the bait.

"It's a goddamn decayed corpse," Stillman snapped. "It's got no parts left, if you catch my drift. Look, until I've got official notification that the ME's office has invited you into this one, don't start thinking you can walk into my investigation and go nuts with the theories and the amateur detective work."

"How about this," Gin said, finally having had enough. "Since we're both on the county payroll, I suggest we exhibit a spirit of cooperation. Since this is a decomp case, I'm bound to be called in sooner or later—so you might as well let me do my job."

"Maybe he's right," Jake spoke up. He'd been watching them spar, glowering, his hands jammed in his pockets. "I don't think you should be part of this case, Gin. It happened on *my* jobsite—it's a conflict of interest."

Stillman looked at him in surprise but nodded. "Yeah, since we're going to have to clear you, Crosby, it won't look good for you to be banging anyone involved with the case in any way."

Even for Stillman, the comment was vulgar. Jake's face darkened with fury. "I'll forget you said that," he said in a low voice, "but you'd better learn to tone it down, my friend."

Stillman turned and swung his leg over the crime scene tape, effectively putting a barrier between them. The two technicians had suited up and were kneeling next to a long mound of dirt next to the unfinished trench. One bent to peer into the hole as the other set up lighting equipment.

"Wait—don't let them disturb the body," Gin said.

"Don't worry, they're just setting up for photos for now," Stillman said over his shoulder. "Believe it or not, none of us want to contaminate the scene."

A man in a county windbreaker jogged over. He looked vaguely familiar to Gin: lean and rangy, several inches over six feet tall, with sandy hair cut military-close. His eyes were a startling clear green, and his jaw was chiseled as if from stone. Only the faint lines around his eyes hinted at his age, which Gin took to be midforties; he had the physique of a younger man.

"You Crosby?" he said, stepping over the crime scene tape as though it wasn't even there.

"I'm Jake Crosby."

"Tuck Baxter." He offered his hand, and Jake stared at it a moment before shaking it.

"You're the new chief?" Gin asked.

Baxter stared at her thoughtfully for a moment, as if deciding whether to answer her question. Finally, his features relaxed.

"Sorry," he said. "I should have introduced myself properly. It's my first day on the job, though, and I've got a few other things on my mind. If you don't mind my asking, how did you know? As I understand it, the press release is going out this afternoon."

"News travels fast in a small town," Gin said. "But I should explain that my mother is Madeleine Sullivan. She's—"

"—the mayor," Baxter finished. "She was on the search committee. I interviewed with her several times. Sharp lady."

"Jake," a voice called, and everyone turned toward the road, where a man in a weathered barn coat and Steelers cap had gotten out of a white Silverado parked next to the collection of official vehicles.

"Excuse me," Jake said. "That's my foreman. I need to talk to him."

"Not so fast," Stillman said, holding up a hand to stop him. "I've got questions for you."

"And I'll answer them," Jake said tersely. "But this is my goddamn livelihood at stake, and that's my goddamn employee, and—"

"I've got questions for him too," Baxter said. "Besides, there's not much either of you are going to do here at the moment, from the looks of it."

"I've got this, Baxter," Stillman said. "It's our scene now. You're not county anymore, in case you've forgotten."

The way law enforcement was structured in Allegheny County, local police focused on peacekeeping efforts, including traffic control, domestic disputes, and minor infractions; their involvement ended at more serious crimes, when the county police came in and took over. In cases of murder, arson, rape, assault—anything bigger than a simple robbery or drug charge—they stepped aside, participating to the extent that the county requested.

In Trumbull, when Jake's father was the chief, their cooperation had been mostly uneventful. As gangs and the drug trade infiltrated the town over the years, Chief Crosby worked closely with the county, helping out wherever he could, giving them space to work and manpower to augment their own.

"Good." Baxter looked at Gin. "I know about your work. The Srinivasan case—that was mine, last one I worked on before my transfer. You did some good work for the department."

Gin nodded. The cause of Eric Srinivasan's death would have remained a mystery if it weren't for her input. The young man's moderately decomposed body had been found in the marshy end of a pond in a remote area of North Park, where he'd sometimes gone to fish, and no one on the county ME's staff had been able to identify the cirrhosis of the heart, given its state. When Gin was brought in to review the autopsy results, she was able to identify the heavily scarred tissue from photographs. Reviewing his medical records revealed that he'd likely suffered from a rare heart condition that led to its failure.

For Gin, it had been a relatively easy catch—but that was because she'd had experience that none of them had had: a six-month tour volunteering with the Red Cross, exhuming mass graves in Srebrenica where victims of Bosnian ethnic violence were buried. There, she had helped exhume hundreds of bodies and learned more about decomposition than she ever would have in an entire career at Cook County.

She didn't like to talk about it with anyone but her colleagues. Most people tended not to understand.

"Thank you, but—"

"So if you want to take a look, I'm sure the county would be obliged," Baxter said. Evidently he wasn't one of those who were impressed to the point of volubility by what she did. "Detective Stillman, you can make that happen, can't you?"

Stillman looked at Gin with obvious distaste. "I'll consult with Captain Wheeler on that."

"She'll be fine with it, Bruce," Baxter said with an exaggerated show of patience. "Just tell her you talked to me. Interdepartmental cooperation—there's apparently been too damn little of it since you lost your old chief. When the mayor interviewed me, she let me know it was one of the city council's top priorities."

"Thank you," Gin said stiffly.

"Tell her hello, won't you," Baxter said as he began walking toward Jake's foreman's truck. "I'm looking forward to working with two generations of the legendary Sullivan family."

4

"I just want it on record that this wasn't my idea," Stillman said. They had been joined by one of the techs, who'd handed Gin booties, gloves, and a hair net, which she put on with practiced ease. For twenty years, since the first day of medical school, donning the gear had been as much a part of her day as brushing her teeth. "All that's going to happen, with you getting involved so early, is the site's going to be compromised that much more."

"This isn't my first crime scene, you know," Gin sighed. She considered calling him "Bruce," as Baxter had, but she got the feeling that would only further antagonize him. "In fact, I used to get called to them regularly in Cook County. They seemed to think I was capable of behaving myself."

"Well, that was when you were officially on staff. In my book, that's a different story. I personally would never have given an outside consultant the kind of latitude you evidently believe you have. Opens the department up to all kinds of liability."

The thing was, he had a point. Gin herself wasn't sure she would have approved a similar arrangement back at her old job. A key part of the job of medical examiner—one that took up far more time than the average lay person ever realized—was to testify in court. If any of the cases she'd consulted on went to court and she was called as a witness, there would be a nightmare course of legal hoops to jump through to get her testimony accepted into the record.

"Fine," she sighed. "Look, I'm here to help, okay? Baxter clearly thinks I might be an asset to the case or he wouldn't have asked me."

"Baxter doesn't work for the county anymore," Stillman pointed out. "And as I'm sure I don't need to remind you, arson and murder cases are under county jurisdiction. Baxter's just the liaison."

And he stepped on your insecure little toes, Gin thought to herself.

"Gin. Glad you're here." Fred Rappaport, the county coroner, emerged from the tarp that had been set up near the scene, where he'd been consulting with one of the technicians. Detective Witt was with him. "This one might be right up your alley."

"Hi, Dr. Sullivan," Witt said, dusting grime off his pants. "I talked to Jake earlier. Hell of a thing to happen here."

Gin was grateful for the effort Witt made to be civil. "Thank you. It took us both by shock, obviously."

"These are quite possibly the oldest remains I've ever dealt with," Rappaport said, evidently relishing that fact. Though short on social graces, Gin had found him to be knowledgeable and thorough. "Dry as a box of sawdust—barely any skin fragments left. Can't wait to get them on the table."

Gin was surprised; it was generally almost impossible to determine the age of skeletal remains with only a visual assessment. "Advanced decomp, obviously?"

"Oh, my, yes. They're taking soil samples now, but it's pretty obvious that these evergreens are old growth."

Gin knew what he was implying: The forest was thick with hemlocks, which—in addition to being the state tree—grew best in acidic soil. And acidic soil provided ideal conditions for decomposition of organic matter . . . including the human body.

"Not much left but the bones," Witt concurred, without bothering to mask his relief. He was well known in the department for his unease in the autopsy room; he had yet to develop the hardened tolerance for the grislier aspects of the job that the more senior detectives possessed. Gin suspected he took a fair amount of ribbing for his sensitivity.

"I'd like to take a look," she said. "Are you ready for me, Fred?"

"Sure thing, doll. Let's not make it a party, though— the team's trying to reconstruct the upper soil layer near where they were digging. Kind of hard to tell what it looked like before they went at it with the axes and shovels. Best if we stick to where they've marked off, but there isn't much room."

"No problem," Witt said. "Glad to let you handle it."

"I'll wait for your findings," Stillman said, obviously irritated to be excluded.

"You'll get them as soon as the captain does," Rappaport said. When they were out of earshot, he added, "What an insufferable asshole. Good cop, though."

They arrived at the edge of the trench, which had been widened by the investigators to unearth as much of the body as possible without disturbing it further. The techs had moved out to the perimeter, where they were taking samples and measuring the depth using a variety of specialized tools; with their white hooded jumpsuits reminiscent of space suits, they gave the raw, scraped earth a surreal, lunar look.

A quick glance revealed the skeletal remains, draped in ragged shreds of rotted clothing, with bits of dried skin tissue clinging to the bones here and there. The body was lying on its back, with its arms at its side; whether they'd been arranged there when the body was first placed in the hole, or whether they had originally been placed in another arrangement and shifted when the earth was shoveled on top, it was impossible to say.

There was always a moment when Gin viewed the remains from a case where a body was discovered in a decomposed state in which she was transported back to the days she'd spent on the other half of the world, working to untangle the identities of the cruelly murdered and abandoned men and boys who'd died, sometimes hundreds at a time, in the most inhumane circumstances. The work she and her colleagues had done in Srebrenica was not something that they spoke of often once they returned home, and in fact, the work itself had been conducted in silence more often than not, conversation saved for later when they returned, exhausted and dirty, for a few hours of sleep before another dawn.

But the images haunted all of them. Days, weeks, even months would go by when Gin gave barely a thought to the hundreds of bodies she had helped disinter and identify. But then a case would come across her table that would bring it all back again.

A body buried in soil will give itself over to the earth at a rate determined by many factors: the minerals in the soil, its humidity and alkalinity or acidity, the average daily temperatures and rain- and snowfall levels, microorganism populations, insects and fungus, surface disturbances from human or animal interference, or even earthquakes and avalanches and floods. The daily dramas that disrupt the lives of humans when they are alive can also alter the course of the dead.

In Srebrenica, Gin had worked in pits that were filled with bodies twisted together like scraps of yarn, like bits of sodden paper, like a junk drawer full of spare parts. No analogy could capture the terrible spectacle of so many dead in their peculiar embrace. Most of the victims had been tossed into their graves with no ceremony at all, dropped or pushed or thrown, then moved with earthmoving equipment. The human mind simply seemed incapable of accepting it, and in short order, it went from trying to slot the images into some—any—other pattern to giving up and treating it all as almost meaningless, no more structured than pebbles in a jar or paper balled up and tossed into a trash can.

Somewhere in her third or fourth day in the mass graves, at a site where bodies had been moved months after their death in an effort to deflect attention from the atrocities by their perpetrators, Gin had been trying to make sense of the various partial skeletons, sorting them into likely matches, when she had the strange sense that she was performing a familiar exercise. And then it came to her: She and Lily had once owned a dog-eared set of cards that were a simple memory game for children. They laid all the cards facedown and then turned them over two at a time, looking for matches—two apples or two boots or two goats. Gin had liked the game because it was highly structured and gave her a sense of accomplishment when she succeeded; Lily had hated it because it forced her to sit still and focus. Many times the game ended when Lily gave up and pushed all the cards together into a messy pile, then ran away, leaving Gin to tidy up.

In that pit, she had been playing a grislier version of that game, trying to match femur to femur, ulna to ulna. But reducing it to a logic puzzle had been her coping strategy. Seeing the bones painstakingly extracted from the earth as objects imbued with no more meaning than those cards had allowed her to do her work without breaking down.

She'd never told her parents about the experience, nor had she told Jake. They didn't ask: it was almost as if people were afraid to open the door to what she had seen and experienced. It was only among her colleagues that Gin could be frank; she answered their questions as honestly and completely as she was able, and in the answering was some sort of healing—at least, those were the moments that allowed her to let out enough of the horror of her mission that she could continue doing her work.

All these years later, however, the sight of a body that had been buried in the earth threw her right back into the detachment she had cultivated to survive. It was an assemblage of parts, their features merely clues to be prized apart.

Later, in preparation for the autopsy, she would read all the case notes. There would be information about the discovery of the body, the damage that might have inadvertently been done by the firefighters and other responders. By the time she arrived, they had done what they could to secure the scene, and the investigators who arrived with their van full of equipment would have taken exquisite care to disturb as little as possible as they uncovered the rest of the body. Dirt would be whisked away with brushes finer than the ones Gin used to apply her makeup; every bit of decayed clothing would be marked, photographed, and bagged. What she saw had been curated as carefully as a museum exhibit, which further helped depersonalize it.

As soon as her brain had processed that first glimpse, it began clicking through observations like an old-fashioned camera's shutter clicking through its shots. The body was somewhere between five foot seven and five foot ten, by her estimation, a guess that had a large margin of error, as Gin had difficulty judging the height of a body laid out horizontally. It had been fully dressed, at the time of death, in a shirt or jacket and trousers; this observation was supported by the little fabric that had survived, which was draped and twined around the bones. There was no evidence of shoes or socks. There was no obvious damage to the body, though much would have to wait to be determined in the autopsy, but the skull had been shattered in front, the maxilla and mandible splintered, with bone fragments still protruding from the ramus of the mandible and underneath the anterior nasal spine.

"He took one to the face," Fred said cheerfully, if unnecessarily, pointing to the gap between skull and spine. "Hell of a blunt force to do that."

"He?" Gin echoed. She made a point of trying not to make assumptions, no matter how well supported they seemed to be by the circumstances of the death.

"We'll have to wait until we get him back to be sure, but I'll bet you lunch on the Strip," Fred said. He took a long, pointed plastic tool from his belt and carefully lifted the clothing shreds from the skeleton's pelvis. Gin knelt down and examined the area and nodded.

"I won't take that bet," she said. "I think you're right." The sex of a skeleton could be determined by the subpubic angle, which in this case was less than ninety degrees, based on her quick visual assessment. "But what makes you think the remains are so old?"

"Well!" Fred knelt beside her, and they stared down the trench together. "Take a close look at the clothes and see if you can guess."

Calling them "clothes" was a stretch, as all that was left were a few patches of fabric clinging here and there to the bones. These shreds were the same dun color and dusty texture of the skeleton itself; everything in the trench, in fact, was the uniformly indistinguishable shade of the soil.

"Obviously natural fiber," Gin said. Synthetic fabric—which included fabric that was blended with nylon, polyester, or other fibers—would last as long as plastic, which was to say, thousands of years. "Given the weave and the texture, I'm guessing wool?"

"Good guess," Fred said smugly. It wasn't the first time he'd invited her to guess at his conclusions, a game he seemingly never tired of.

"Okay, I agree that suggests age," Gin said. For the past fifty years, most Americans wore at least some synthetic elements daily, whether it was a polyblend T-shirt, the lining of a coat, the soles of shoes, or the elastic in a waistband. "But I'm not sure how you get past a few decades."

"Keep looking. Here, use this."

Fred handed her his flashlight, which Gin used to slowly and methodically view the body. Besides the damage to the skull, there was no obvious injury to the skeleton. The long bones of the arms and legs were intact, as were the broader scapula and sacrum. The exposed sternum and rib bones were visible on their bed of matted clothing fibers and soil.

Gin shone the light slowly around the perimeter of the body, examining the soil. It was crumbly, with tiny roots, decayed plant matter, and worms and insects. Farther down, it formed clumps and clung to rocks. Whoever had dug the hole had been lucky not to run into any larger rocks—or else he or she had removed them.

The beam of her flashlight glinted off a stone near the skeletal arm. Gin peered closer.

"Warmer . . . warmer . . ." Fred said.

"What is that—a button?" The object was covered in grime and dirt, but protruding from the back was what might have been a shank. The exposed metal shone dully.

"Bingo! Here, look at this one." Fred took the flashlight from her and shone it on another, which had lodged between a rib bone and a fold of fabric. The outline of an eagle was faintly visible on its surface. "Tell you what, any history buff worth her salt would recognize it—every Union enlisted man's uniform had buttons just like that."

"You're saying . . . you think this is a Civil War soldier?"

"Well, it's his uniform, anyway. Tell you what, let's double down—if I'm right, you buy a six pack of Leineys."

Gin laughed; Fred's fondness for Leinenkugel beer was matched only by his enthusiasm for professional hockey. During the season, he'd been known to wear a Penguins jersey to work on Fridays.

"Sorry to disappoint you, Fred, but I'm not much of a gambler. Good catch, though—I'll be interested to see if you're right."

"Oh, I'm right," Fred said confidently. "See this here?"

He pointed to a narrow metal scrap in the dirt next to the skull. It was about an inch and a half long with holes in the ends.

"What is it?"

"Can't be completely sure, of course, but I think it's the tab for attaching the shoulder scales to the uniform."

"Shoulder scales?"

"They were a brass plate you'd wear over your shoulder—the idea was if someone came at you there with a sword or whatever, it would give you a little protection from the blow."

"Wow, you really know your stuff," Gin said.

"Yeah, well, it's a hobby of mine. I've got my great-great-grandfather's uniform up in the attic. I did some research on it a while back—turns out the family legends about him being a war hero were a little exaggerated, unfortunately. He didn't even make it through a single winter before dying from an infection he got from cutting his finger on a sardine tin."

"Maybe that's what happened to this fellow," Gin said lightly, straightening up. She'd seen all she could for the moment; any further investigating would have to wait until the crime scene unit had finished photographing and processing the scene and the remains were transported back to the morgue.

"Maybe so, but getting clobbered in the face didn't help."

They both stared at the ruined lower jaw for a moment. Without the typical leering grin that gave skulls a characteristic appearance of—depending how one interpreted it—mischief or amusement, it looked jarringly incomplete.

"Where are the teeth?" Gin asked after a moment.

"What? They're . . . well, what do you know," Fred said. He prodded gently at the earth under the skull, where the spine was still partly covered in soil. "I suppose they might be buried still, along with the rest of the mandible . . ."

"Maybe," Gin said. "Although look along the edge of the maxilla there." She pointed to the left, less-damaged side of the skull, where the roots of a few teeth were still lodged in the bone. "Judging just from what I can see from here, it almost seems like the teeth were all knocked out. Which would take more than a single blow, or even half a dozen." Something, she didn't add, that might be undertaken by a killer who didn't want a dental identification made.

"I noticed that too," said a hesitant female voice. Gin turned to see a female technician standing behind them, her hood pushed back from her long, glossy, dark ponytail. "I was thinking maybe we'll find them in the soil below."

"At least a few of them, anyway," Gin concurred. Teeth were even more durable than bone, often the last of the remains to disintegrate—but they could also easily become dislodged and lost during the excavation process. "I'm Gin Sullivan, by the way. I hope we're not getting in your way."

"I know who you are," the young woman said solemnly. "I've seen you around the county offices. My name's Katie Kennedy. I'm so sorry about your sister . . ."

"Thank you," Gin said, more brusquely than she intended. It was still difficult to talk about that loss, even with a stranger who was trained in working with victims.

"You're consulting on this case, then? They called you in fast."

"Well . . ." Gin was reluctant to explain the personal connection. "We'll see—for now, I'm just taking a look."

"Well, I'm glad you're here, anyway. There's not going to be a whole lot to work with. I mean, we'll do what we can, but between the damage the firefighters did and the age of the remains, it's going to be tough. Of course, I guess you're used to that. I mean, with the, uh, mass graves."

The girl was blushing, and it took Gin a moment to realize that her discomfort came from admiration as much as shyness.

"Every case is different," she said warmly. "And the work you're doing is invaluable. I'll see you up in the city, okay?"

"Okay, sure." Katie brightened. "Bye, Dr. Sullivan."

"Call me Gin."

"You've got a fan," Detective Witt observed when she made her way back out of the taped-off area.

"Well, given your partner's opinion of me, I could use one."

Witt chuckled. "Ah, don't let Bruce get you down. He just doesn't like outsiders coming into our cases."

"Is that what you see me as? An outsider?"

Witt shrugged. "I mean, you nailed the Dempsey thing . . . I guess it comes down to whether you can keep delivering."

"Okay, noted," Gin said, allowing a smile.

The Dempsey case was the only time she and Witt had worked together since she began consulting. Several years earlier, a dog that got loose from a backyard had made a grisly discovery in a culvert near a field owned by a farmer named Raoul Dempsey: fragments of a human tibia bone. An investigation had led to the discovery of additional bone fragments—but had stalled because there wasn't enough to identify the victim.

Gin was invited to review the evidence by an investigator assigned to cold cases. After spending an afternoon in the lab with the bone fragments under a microscope, she'd noticed what the medical examiner had missed: the diaphyseal cortical bone was too thick to be human in origin. Further testing revealed it to have come from a pig—and follow-up investigation of the original case notes revealed that one of the sons had buried the pig bones as a prank.

"That was an easy one," Gin said, smiling.

"Yeah, no kidding. Liquids and smells—that's what gets to me," Witt admitted. "First time I ever attended an autopsy—you've probably heard about it—I almost passed out. I came home and called my mom and told her I was never going back."

"That's not the hard part," Katie said. She'd joined them, leaving the protected area to the forensic photographer. "I mean, not for me, anyway."

"No?" Gin noticed the keen attention Witt focused on Katie and wondered if the pair were interested in each other. Romance bloomed in the strangest circumstances, in her experience; even during the devastating work in Bosnia, or maybe because of it, some of her colleagues had found comfort in each other's company.

"You don't mind the, uh, blood and guts?" Witt said admiringly.

"No, not really. I saw a lot during my training, you know. If I was going to be put off by that sort of thing, it would have already happened before my first day on the job."

Gin understood the distinction the girl was making. During medical school, she'd seen plenty of people quit when confronted with the realities—decomposition, decay, malodorousness—of the job. Some people, herself among them, were able to make their peace; others were not.

"So what does bother you, then?" Witt asked.

Katie hesitated before answering. "Well, to be honest, it was the idea that we might never find answers. My very first case was this little baby someone left in a public restroom in a park. The restroom was supposed to be closed for the winter, but people broke in and used it to get high . . . anyway, the baby had been dead for a few hours by the time we were called in. It was probably born premature because the mother was using. My supervisor, the detectives, everyone worked all night long, and then once we were sure we'd gotten everything we could from the scene, we were all standing around the van, trying to warm up. It was a cold,

41

cold night, and they'd brought in a portable heater that they were running off a generator. It was loud, and you almost had to yell to be heard. My boss looks back where they've got the baby loaded up in the ambulance, and I don't think anyone else heard her, but she said, *It'll be like she was never even born.* And it just seemed so . . . sad."

"I get that," Gin said. "It can be really difficult."

"But this guy?" Witt said. "If he's really been lying there for a hundred and fifty years, it's not like there's anyone left alive who would care."

He gave a little wave, directing his smile at Katie, and headed off toward the porch of one of the unfinished houses, which Stillman was using as a temporary command center. Gin and Katie watched him go, Katie smiling wistfully.

Impulsively, Gin put voice to the thought nagging her, glad to have someone to bounce her thoughts off. Unlike when she'd worked in the busy Cook County office, where she consulted with her colleagues on a daily basis, her consulting work was mostly conducted alone, and she missed having people to discuss her cases with.

"The thing with the teeth—that makes it hard for me to believe the body's Civil War era."

"You mean, because of dental records?"

"Yes. There's evidence of odontology as far back as Roman times, but it didn't become widespread until the nineteen-sixties and seventies. And it took a while for criminals to catch on that destroying teeth—and fingerprints, for that matter—could destroy evidence."

"You're saying that there was no reason for the murderer to knock out the teeth if the victim was killed a hundred and fifty years ago."

"That's right. And there's something else too. The body was only found a few feet down. Given the natural shifts in soil, slope, erosion, and so on—especially in a forested area

like this one—it strikes me as odd that the body wasn't discovered until now."

The two of them were silent for a moment, looking out at
the woods behind the freshly dug trench. Wisps of mist hung
in the barren branches of the trees, giving the whole scene a
melancholy, eerie cast.

"This probably sounds ridiculous," Katie admitted, keeping her voice low, "but sometimes, when I'm out on a scene,
I almost think—I mean, not *really*, of course—but I get
the feeling that the answers are there, desperately wanting
to be found. Like if I just try hard enough—"

She broke off, blushing.

"I know what you're talking about," Gin said. "I feel it too.
Almost as if the dead can hear us. That they're . . . encouraging us."

"That's it, exactly."

"That's what makes you good at your job, Katie."

"Even if it's not scientific . . . ?"

"I look at it a little differently," Gin said. "There's so much
that science can't explain. So many questions that go unan-
swered. I like to think that people like you and me work in
that place in between mystery and truth. That by being open
to things that don't fit into what we know, we create the possibility of discovering something new."

"Wow, that's—" Katie said.

"Probably a little overthinking," Gin laughed. "I should
probably spend more time in the lab and less attempting to
practice philosophy."

But as she said good-bye and turned to go, she cast a final
glance into the woods, where the swirling mists looked like
specters hiding in the trees.

5

By the time the body had been extricated from the earth, carefully loaded into the van, and driven away, it was already after noon, and a weak sun had burned off the earlier gloom, offering a temporary respite from the frigid cold. Gin conferred briefly with the detectives, going over what they'd learned so far.

Jake was gone. Gin hadn't noticed him leaving, and the fact that he hadn't said good-bye caused a spike of annoyance. For all she knew, however, he might have tried; she'd been focused on the body and on observing the strict protocols of crime scene preservation. Having participated in the disinterring of literally hundreds of bodies, Gin had seen too much evidence rendered useless out of carelessness or ignorance to let her own vigilance ever lapse.

Fred stopped to talk on his way to his car. "Long day," he said. "Given that I've been here since before dawn. I'm starving. Want to get a cheesesteak?"

"I'm afraid I'd better get back to Trumbull," Gin said. "Another time, okay?"

She started walking down the hill toward the road, no longer feeling like running the two miles back to Jake's house, when a car pulled up beside her.

It was Baxter, the new chief, driving what looked like the former chief's old Explorer with new Trumbull police decals freshly applied to each side. He leaned out the window with his forearm resting on the edge.

"Glad I caught you," he said. "I talked to Chozick—it's official, they want you to pitch in on this one."

"I'll be happy to. I have to admit, though, I'm surprised to hear it from you," Gin said. "Given that county's got the case now."

Baxter shrugged. "Chozick and I get along. I figured I'd save a step and go straight to the source. This is my beat now, after all."

"So you'll be . . ."

"Respecting the chain of command." Baxter winked, giving the impression that he intended the opposite. "And looking out for the people of Trumbull. And, of course, offering the department's assistance where needed."

"Sounds like you've already made yourself at home here."

"Trying, anyway. Need a ride? I think I'm headed your way, considering the only way to go is down."

Gin deliberated; as much as she could use the lift, she wasn't sure she was ready to have any significant interaction with the local police. Jake's father had served as the chief of police for decades before being killed in the course of the investigation into Lily's death only last summer. Without him at the helm, the small department had struggled to keep up with day-to-day operations, even after the county took over the investigation. Gin knew it was painful for Jake to drive past the humble municipal building complex that housed the police department over which Lawrence Crosby had presided for so long. And she had unconsciously been avoiding it herself. The memories of the hours she spent inside, both trying to remember everything about the worst days of her life, and defending herself and her family from any suspicion of being involved, might never scab over enough to make it easy to be near it.

Of course, the department would rebuild. Gin knew it was unreasonable to wish for things to stay the same. She of all people—as one who helped usher others through the loss of those they loved—knew that life had to go on somehow. Eventually, considering the size of the town, she was going to have to come to grips with the past.

That . . . or run away again.

"I think I'll walk," Gin said, more forcefully than she meant to. "But thanks."

"Hang on a second—listen," Baxter said. "I know not everyone's happy the appointment went to me. There were more than a few people throwing their hats in the ring, and that's a credit to your mom and the rest of the council. They've done a hell of a job turning this town around, and that's not an easy thing to do—not in this county, anyway. I consider it an honor that they offered me a shot. And I'm going to give my best back." He exhaled as though it was a speech he had practiced.

"Well, thank you for being so candid," Gin said. "And, in turn, I'll say that I'm sure you know all about what my family's been through this year, and I, um . . ."

Was she really going to say it? It wasn't like Gin to share her emotions with people she'd just met—or with anyone at all generally. But today had been a roller coaster, starting with Jake's terse reaction to the early morning call, to seeing the smoking hulk of what had been his dream project, to confronting the sight of a dead body—nothing new to Gin, it was true, except that this one had been discovered uncomfortably close to her own life.

And there was something about Tuck Baxter—the way he looked directly into her eyes when he spoke, the plain economy of his words, the casual way he handled the familiar vehicle, as though he'd been driving it for years—that made him seem . . . safe.

"I appreciate the fact that you didn't say you were sorry for me the minute you met me," she said in a rush. "I've had about enough of that to last a lifetime."

She felt her face heat with embarrassment, but Tuck merely raised an eyebrow. "I don't often have women thank me for being tactless," he drawled, "but I'm glad. It'll make things easier. I'm not surprised, anyway—your mom's a straight shooter, and I value that. So listen, I'd like to talk to you about something else—unrelated to the case, or to city government."

"Oh?"

"The Wings, actually. I hear you're in preseason."

Gin blinked. "How do you know about that? Did my mother seriously make you listen to the boring details of my life?"

Baxter shrugged, grinning. "Nah, I'm just a huge fan of girls' basketball. Thinking you might have what it takes to take them all the way this year."

"All the way to county finals?" Gin rolled her eyes. She had agreed to coach only when it became clear that if someone didn't step up, there wouldn't be a freshman team this year—and it gave her a regular means of being in touch with Olive Hart.

Olive, a precocious and good-natured fourteen-year-old, was the daughter of Gin's childhood friend Christine—the same woman who was revealed to be Lily's murderer and was killed by her own brother in a tense standoff. Gin had been trying to be a positive presence in the girl's life ever since Christine's death.

"I don't know where you got that idea, but we'll be lucky to field a complete team if I can't talk a few more girls into taking part."

"Well, I think I can help you out there."

"Listen, Chief, no offense, but I don't think I've got a uniform in your size."

She was rewarded with a slow, lazy smile and a very unofficial wink.

"Not me, Coach. But my daughter, Cherie, has her first roundball, and we've been practicing for weeks. Say you'll give her a chance on the team, and you'll make her the happiest kid in town."

*   *   *

Gin called Jake's cell phone twice on the walk home, but he didn't pick up either time. She didn't leave a message; if he hadn't texted her by now, he was busy enough with other things that an interruption would not be welcome.

She was torn between worry and irritation. None of the morning's events were Jake's fault, which somehow almost made it worse. He was unfailingly considerate of her feelings and had done his best to make her transition back to living in Trumbull an easy one. He'd listened when she needed to talk about Lily's death, about her father's withdrawal and depression, about her sense of aimlessness. He'd offered emotional support when she said she wasn't ready to work full time again yet. He seemed to innately know when to be tender, when to try to cheer her up, and when to leave her alone.

But now that he had problems of his own to deal with, he wouldn't let her in, wouldn't talk to her about what was going on. The easy conversations had turned into long silences. He stayed away longer and longer, making excuses to stay late on his jobsites.

Maybe they'd moved too fast. The day after Lily's funeral, Gin had come over to Jake's house with a suitcase full of dirty clothes, and when he opened the door, she'd burst into tears.

She couldn't even get the words out—that she couldn't stand to stay in the house she'd grown up in, in the stifling atmosphere of her parents' grief and the memories that haunted every room—but he had simply held her for what seemed like hours and then, when her tears finally dried up, picked up her suitcase and carried it to his bedroom without a word.

In the days that followed, he'd held her, listened to her, cooked for her . . . and made love to her, over and over, telling her without words that he would be there for her no matter what. They'd learned each other's bodies all over again, but the rhythm of being together fell instantly into place. The few relationships they'd each had in the intervening years suddenly seemed as fleeting and inconsequential as dandelion silk floating away on a summer breeze.

It felt, in short, like returning home.

After a month of wearing the same suitcase full of clothes—and after she'd been offered the ongoing consulting role with the county medical examiner's office—Gin spent a Saturday with her mother in a tony Pittsburgh department store, selecting a wardrobe of simple, well-cut clothing that was both timeless and flattering. She spent more on those purchases than she'd planned to, but her expenses were few, and besides, there suddenly seemed no reason not to dip into her substantial savings.

"I'll build you a walk-in closet," Jake had offered, only half joking, as he helped her carry in her purchases, "and if you want to redecorate or something, we can talk about it."

She didn't want to redecorate. She loved everything about the home Jake had built, from the hand-carved stair rail and heart pine floors, to the rustic fittings on the cabinets he'd made himself, to the woolen blankets and handwoven rugs that provided elements of color and design, to the simple rooms. The things she had owned in the past no longer held any appeal for her—furniture that was only a step above the castoffs she'd collected during her med school days; business clothes she no longer had any use for; the scrubs she'd worn as an intern; the evening clothes she'd bought while dating her last boyfriend, an attorney with a packed social schedule.

She made a quick trip to Chicago to her apartment in Hyde Park and returned with the few clothes she'd decided to keep and two cardboard boxes, mostly filled with books. She was touched that Jake had cleared a shelf for her books while she was away; she'd teared up when he presented her with the ornate jewelry box inlaid with mother-of-pearl that had belonged to his mother. But when he asked her why she didn't simply give up the apartment in Chicago, she found herself holding back, unable to put her reasons into words. It wasn't that she longed for the life she'd had before—with its grueling schedule and the hustle and bustle of city life—but she wasn't ready to close the door on it forever either.

She put her few pairs of earrings in the box and lined up her books on the shelf, and then they'd gone back to living their new life together. The subject of the apartment didn't come up again, and each month, Gin wrote the rent check and put off making the decision for a little longer.

Now Gin pulled into the drive and parked in the spot Jake had cleared for her, its edges lined with railroad ties salvaged from the rail yard downriver. His truck was in the other spot, but even before she opened the front door, she could sense that he was not home. Jett, his aging border collie mix, whined in greeting and began the painful process of getting up from her bed.

"Where'd he go, girl?" Gin asked, kneeling to pet the old dog. She smoothed back her silky ears and allowed her to nuzzle her wrists, but the dog whined again and padded over to the back door.

Gin fetched the leash from its iron hook and took the dog out back, where the rear of the house was set into the crest of the hill. The ridge was lined with evergreens, forming a forested backdrop that served to heighten the spare beauty of Jake's design. The woods continued down the backside of the ridge and through the paths and hills that several generations of steelworkers' children had wandered, and it was on these paths—largely abandoned now—that Jake and Gin often walked Jett.

The old dog pricked up her ears and sniffed, and then Gin heard it too—a faint, rhythmic sound.

"He's chopping wood, isn't he?" Gin sighed. Jett waved her tail in agreement, and they set out, following the sound.

They found Jake half a mile away in a clearing where a large, ancient oak tree had fallen, crushing several smaller trees and saplings under its weight. The tree would provide several seasons' worth of firewood for anyone willing to haul it away. And Jake was willing. At least, in certain moods he was; the hard physical labor of splitting the logs seemed to be a form of therapy for him.

For a moment, Gin stood at the edge of the clearing and simply watched him methodically stand up the sections of the tree that he'd previously cut with a chainsaw, using the stump as a chopping block. He'd then raise the ax behind his head before swinging it smoothly down, the force splitting the wood cleanly in two, the pieces falling to the ground.

There was already a sizeable pile of split wood. Jake had worked up a sweat and taken off his shirt, despite the fact that the temperatures were only in the upper thirties. The muscles of his chest and arms glistened, and his face was set in concentration, his jaw firm and his brow knit. With each stroke of the ax, the force of the blow rippled through his taut body.

Jake seemed to sense her presence, the ax faltering on the upswing, and he let it fall to his side, dropping it blade-down on the sodden blanket of leaves.

"Hey," he said quietly.

"Hey, yourself. I hope . . . I hope you don't mind that I came to find you. If you'd rather I give you some time alone . . ."

"No, Gin. I'm done here."

"Work off all your frustrations?" Gin tried to inject a note of humor into her voice.

"Well, I gave it a shot, anyway." He pulled his shirt on, picked up his old canvas barn coat, and slung it over his arm. Then he hefted the ax, and they started down the path toward the house. "I'll come back up here on Saturday to fetch the wood."

"I'll help." Jake kept an old wheelbarrow repaired and oiled for tasks such as these. "It'll be fantastic exercise."

"Actually, I can probably come back and take care of it in the morning. I won't be working. We're officially shut down until they sort this mess out."

Gin had guessed this was the source of his grim mood. "Did you hear from Asher?"

"From his attorney. Not a bad guy, really—he could have been a jerk about it, but he just said he was sorry but his client couldn't wait, not with a baby coming. He said they wouldn't pursue a refund of the deposit money, thank God. He even said Asher would write me a reference, if I wanted him to."

"Well—that's good, then."

"Yeah, and the deposit wasn't anything to sneeze at. It'll pay the grocery bill for quite a while. But the first payment on the construction loan's due next week. Unless I line up buyers for the other two houses fast, I'm not going to be able to pay my guys by the end of the month."

"You'll find buyers. Jake, those homes are beautiful. Even if you can't rebuild right away, once you clear the site, people won't even care that a fire took place there." She didn't mention the body; people might well balk at its presence. She knew there were laws requiring disclosure of deaths occurring in homes being sold, and these disclosures often had the effect of significantly lowering the price buyers were willing to pay. A similar bias could well turn people off of Jake's project—but that was a bridge to be crossed later.

Gin had an idea. "I don't know why I didn't think of this before: What if I help? I could do marketing—talk to local agents—maybe make some contacts in the city."

"Gin, you don't know the first thing about real estate. I mean, don't take this as a criticism, but you've never even owned a house."

"I could learn," Gin said stubbornly.

Jake stopped and took her arm, turning her so she was staring up into his expressive eyes. "Woman, you're the smartest person I know. And I have no doubt that if you set your mind to it, you could become a real estate tycoon. But these are *my* problems, and it's my job to solve them. And besides, don't you have other things you'd rather do?"

Gin tried to ignore the sting. Jake didn't want her help. She took a deep breath and forced a casual tone. "Speaking of that . . . they've asked me to consult on this case."

His grip on her arm loosened. Just like that, the atmosphere between them changed, and he stepped away. "I shouldn't be surprised. Well, I guess I ought to be grateful; if you're on the job, I know it'll get done right, and maybe you can even speed things up a little. I guess you probably can't tell me anything, right?"

"You know I can't talk about the case," Gin said. "And besides, I won't know anything for certain, really, until the autopsy."

"And when will that be?"

Gin shrugged. "I'm not sure. It's not my decision to make. I'll call Stephen when I get home and see if he can pull the case."

Stephen Harper, a staff forensic pathologist, had been the lead on Gin's sister's autopsy, the first case she'd sat in on at the county medical examiner's office. It had been a highly unusual situation—family members were almost never present at autopsy, no matter their qualifications—and it was Harper's kindness and willingness to speak on her behalf that had paved the way for her to participate. Since then, the two had worked together on various cases.

The relationship was strictly a professional one—Harper was happily married, with small children—but Jake had chafed silently whenever Gin mentioned the man's name. Now the set of his jaw became even fiercer, and he folded his arms and glared at the ground.

"What's that going to do, Gin?" he demanded. "Can Harper make this thing go away? Can he at least sign off on the paperwork so I can get back to work?"

Gin stared at him, startled by the venom in his voice. "Jake . . . this 'thing' is a human being. He deserves our best efforts to discover how and why he died."

"Come on, Gin, he's been in the ground for over a century, from what I pieced together up there. Anyone who cared about him is dead. I don't mean to be insensitive, but I really doubt he'd mind."

"That's nowhere near certain. There's no solid evidence that dates his remains more than a few years old."

"Okay, but still. It's not like his loved ones have beaten a path to Trumbull, wondering what happened to him."

"Jake . . . you have to know that I care very much about you and your work," Gin said carefully. "But I can't take shortcuts or rush our report just because it would be expedient."

"'*Expedient*,'" Jake echoed hollowly, and Gin wished she could rephrase. When she felt unsure of herself emotionally, it was her habit to retreat into the safety of clinical language, to speak like an academic rather than acknowledge how vulnerable she was at the core.

But to Jake—a man who worked with his hands, who preferred action to talk, who never minced a word when he could help it—she knew she sometimes came off as distant and even condescending.

"Jake . . ."

"Whatever, Gin," he said stiffly. "Never mind what I've got riding on this. I feel for that poor guy, I really do. I'm sorry for whatever happened that ended with him in that hole. But he's dead, and nothing you do's gonna change that. Frankly, when I go, if someone sticks me in the ground up here, overlooking the valley, I'd count myself lucky—but you got to do what you got to do, I guess."

Gin was torn between wishing she could bridge the gulf between them and objecting to his words, just as he'd taken offense to her own. "I know very well that nothing I do will change the fact that he died," she said. "But there's value in discovering how it happened. Otherwise, what would you have us do? Just—just chuck him in a dumpster? Fill up the hole with concrete so you can build an outdoor barbecue over it?"

"I know what I do isn't as important as your work," Jake shot back. "But it puts food on my table. Look, Gin, you made it clear when you moved in that you don't want me taking care of you. Fine. I get it. But I still have to take care of myself. So while you and your pal Harper shut down my site so you can poke around a body that's been lying there long enough to turn into dirt, I'll be trying to figure out how to pay my bills when I don't have any houses to sell or crew to build more."

He started down the trail without looking back, holding the ax handle in a tight fist. Gin desperately wanted to race after him, to try to make him understand.

But the problem was that he did understand, maybe all too well. They were standing on opposite sides of a divide that neither could cross.

6

Despite the fact that Gin had felt him toss and turn during the night, Jake was up and gone by the time she woke at seven. She drank the rest of the coffee that was left in the pot and forced down some toast, then dug up a presentable sweater and skirt and boots with enough of a heel to make it look like she was trying. She pulled her hair back into a large tortoiseshell clip, letting the curls cascade over her shoulders, and applied her makeup with care, using concealer to try to banish the dark circles under her eyes.

When she was finished, she stepped back from the mirror and squinted at her reflection. She had changed since leaving Chicago, and it wasn't just the fact that the pallor that resulted from spending so much time in the lab had given way to healthy color from the time she spent outside, going for hikes with Jake or running along the trails that crisscrossed the hills above town. She'd let her hair grow longer, mostly due to the fact that her regular hairdresser was hundreds of miles away, but also because her mother had offered to make her an appointment with her own stylist, and Gin had no intention of adopting her mother's sprayed, every-hair-in-place style.

But the biggest changes couldn't be attributed to a haircut or a tan or a new cosmetic. Gin thought she looked . . . more like herself. Relaxed. Rested. And until the recent distance between her and Jake, mostly contented.

She tossed a few things into her good handbag, the one she'd purchased because it was large enough to bring home case files in and sturdy enough for crowded L trains, and headed for Pittsburgh.

The temperature had dropped overnight, and the road was made treacherous by patches of ice. Gin drove carefully, and by the time she arrived, it was two minutes before the appointed starting time of ten o'clock. She didn't recognize the receptionist and had to dig for her identification and then wait for her to call to check that she was expected, so by the time she'd made her way down the hall to the morgue, everyone was already assembled for the autopsy.

Stephen Harper and his boss, head medical examiner Harvey Chozick, had taken their positions on either side of the body. Stillman stood behind them, and as far away as he could get in the corner of the room, Witt stood with his hands jammed in his pockets, his complexion only faintly green. Two technicians joked quietly in the rear of the room, where they would stay unless asked to assist, which in this case was unlikely: there were no organs to remove and weigh, and there was no point in sectioning the skull in order to access the brain, which had long ago liquefied and drained out. No brute strength would be required to crack the ribs, and no dexterity with a bone saw would help. Having set up the room in advance, their tasks were likely over until the autopsy was finished, when they would prepare the body for burial or cremation, but that task would be simplified as well: there were no tissues to be sewn shut, no cavity to be packed and prepared, and no once vital organs to carefully replace.

Stephen Harper noticed Gin first and gave her a little wave. His face was partially covered by a mask, but his warm gray eyes managed to convey a smile anyway.

"Hello, Gin, so pleased you could come," Harvey Chozick said. Like Stephen, he was generous with his praise for her contributions, even when they amounted to little. Gin suspected there might also be some posturing taking place for the benefit of the detectives, whose presence was generally tolerated with a measure of distaste in high-profile cases, where the integrity of the pathologist's findings was constantly under scrutiny.

"Hello, everyone," Gin said brightly, taking her place a couple of feet from the end of the table, where she could observe but would not be in the way. She had to resist apologizing for her tardiness; it only amounted to a few moments, and she knew her presence was already viewed as unnecessary and even potentially disruptive, at least by Stillman.

She washed and gloved as quickly as she could, but when she was finished, Stephen was already going through the preliminary observations. He recorded these into a small digital recorder, which would be transcribed and formatted into documentation to be included in the case files.

There was a unique rhythm to the opening notes of the autopsy, the stanzas of which varied little from one department to another, and Gin allowed herself to be lulled by the familiar language, concentrating not on the overall description, which she herself could have supplied from her initial view of the body, but on Stephen's small tics and gestures in the belief that she could divine what else he was thinking by reading between the lines. In theory, autopsy was a place where participants would merely catalog the evidence in front of them. But Gin knew that intuition played a far greater part in a skilled pathologist's toolbox than he or she would ever admit.

Stephen, in her estimation, seemed slightly tentative as he worked through the initial analysis, reading the data in a sober, quiet voice as he measured the various bones and described the matter clinging to them. The shreds of clothing were removed, bagged, and labeled with information about where they were found in relation to the rest of the remains, giving the techs something to do, and the growing pile of evidence on their cart began to look like a clearance bin at Filene's Basement.

Stephen made his way up the body, leaving the skull for last, reading off the measurements of various bones. When he arrived at the pelvis, he pointed to the pelvic inlet, an opening in the center of the bone. "I'm satisfied this was a male."

"I concur," Gin said.

"Wait," Stillman said. "How do you know?"

"The pelvic inlet—this hole here—is narrower in a male. Also, the sciatic notch is narrower. And finally, do you see the angle where the two pubic bones meet in front? It would be a lot wider in a female."

"There's nothing else that tells you it was a man?" Stillman asked, sounding almost affronted. Gin braced herself for a tasteless joke, but Stephen cut him off; he'd endured Stillman's presence in other autopsies and, as he had confided in Gin over coffee, decided that the best way to handle him was to ignore his goading.

"Minor skull differences," he said mildly, "but this is all we need for a conclusive determination. Now, let's move on to the condition of the bone surface. I notice faint lateral grooves along the diaphysis," he said, peering closely at a humerus. "One to two millimeters deep—none reaching the medullary cavity."

He looked up at Gin and raised his eyebrows, questioning. She cleared her throat and leaned in at the unspoken invitation, careful not to touch anything, even the steel table; her consulting agreement specified that she was to observe the autopsy being conducted by staff, and it prohibited her from handling the remains, unless a formal request was made and approved by the chief medical examiner.

"Rodents, I'm nearly sure," she said. The grooves—really little more than scratches—had probably been made in the early months that the body had lain in its earthen grave, when there were still remnants of tissue for scavengers to feed on. She'd seen the damage that gnawing could do; entire sections of bone could be consumed if small animals were determined—and hungry—enough. But the depth at which the body had been buried had probably kept the damage to a minimum.

After the bone dimensions had been recorded, Stephen made an estimate of height. "Five nine, perhaps five nine and a half," he noted, within Gin's preliminary estimate.

"What about size?" Stillman asked. "Was he a heavy guy?"

Again, Stephen looked to Gin, but this time, she gave him a slight nod to encourage him to answer the question himself, as the data was fairly standard.

"It's generally difficult to assess weight from skeletal remains," he said. "Other than a slightly wider femur, resulting from carrying a significant load, we expect to see little difference."

"So for all you know, he could have died of starvation?" Witt asked. "There's no way to tell?"

"Yeah, well, there's the tiny little fact that he had his head caved in," Stillman quipped, causing Witt to blush.

Gin felt sorry for the junior detective, who had impressed her as earnest and dedicated in their interactions. "It's a good question," she reassured him. "And yes, bones are affected by malnutrition. When we get samples under the microscope, we'd expect to see poor mineral density. The skeleton of a malnourished person will also have poor cortical strength, so we'd expect to see a greater incidence of fracture."

"What about this guy?" Stillman said. "Any fractures? Could you see them if they were healed?"

"The answer to that question is a little vague," Gin said. "Bones do heal, just like other tissues in the body, and over time, evidence of injury becomes less pronounced. A major break could leave evidence of the break line, or the bone could even heal crookedly. One thing I noticed"—she stepped forward and indicated a very faint line extending at an angle at the upper portion of the right wrist—"here, along the right distal radius, this may be evidence of a break that occurred years before death, given how the tissue has healed."

"Colles fracture?" Stephen suggested, obviously embarrassed that he hadn't noticed it.

"Yes, I'd say so," she said, "but don't worry, it would be easy to miss, given the fact that it healed so cleanly."

"But it didn't have anything to do with what killed him," Stillman pointed out. "So he broke his wrist—that didn't put him underground."

"No, I suppose not," Gin allowed. The transcriptionist would record only the key details of their recorded conversation, but she was still irritated at Stillman's comments. When law enforcement officers attended autopsies, they were trained to ask only clarifying questions about the evidence, not to draw conclusions of their own. She had made herself available after dozens of autopsies to go over evidence and, in many more cases, had appeared in court to testify in civil and criminal cases, where her opinions as an expert witness were admissible.

"Okay, let's move on to the skull." It was resting at the head of the table but had become fully detached during transport and so had to be supported with a white, Teflon-like plastic stand. The injuries the jaw had sustained somehow looked even more pronounced without the context of the spine and the rest of the skeleton, giving the appearance of a fright mask made to cover only the eyes and nose. Some of the bone shards Gin had noticed during her examination of the remains before they had been moved were missing, but she assumed they were in the evidence bags on the counter.

"We see extensive fragmentation of facial bones due to impact trauma to the face. Cranial bone fragments are missing, including teeth and segments of tooth-bearing bone. The majority of the mandible was not recovered."

"The mandible—that's the chin, right?" Witt asked. "And the lower teeth."

"That is correct."

"So if it was somehow smashed clean off—"

"That would be difficult to do," Stephen said, "if I understand your meaning. No matter how hard the blow, the tissues connecting the bone would probably keep it in place, albeit being quite damaged."

"You're saying if someone hits me hard enough, even if it pulverized my jaw, the skin and gums and what have you will keep it attached," Stillman said. Briefly, Gin indulged that image; she could tell from Stephen's effort to suppress a smirk that he was doing the same.

"Well yes, more or less. If these remains weren't buried, I'd be unsurprised that the mandible is missing, because a scavenger could easily detach it and carry it elsewhere to feed on, especially if tissues had already begun to decompose. But since the body was buried, that is unlikely."

"Could it have been buried, then dug up and moved?" Witt asked. "And maybe the jaw became detached then, and the teeth fell out?"

"I'll defer to my colleague on that one," Stephen said. "She has more experience with that scenario."

"In short, no," Gin said, hoping she wouldn't have to go into detail describing what happened to bodies that had been buried twice. Due to their decomposition, in her experience, they came apart and became mixed up in their second grave, which led to exhausting analysis to try to sort out individual sets of remains. "The state and position of the body as discovered indicated it was placed there after death and before decomposition."

"So what happened to the teeth?" Stillman demanded.

"I would say that they were deliberately knocked out," Stephen said. "See the jagged edges of the maxilla, here, and how the ramus broke off almost cleanly here at the zygomatico-maxillary suture. There's also damage to the nasal bone and septum, here, which might indicate a misplaced blow. That's just speculation, of course."

"Can you tell what was used to do it?" Witt asked, moving forward to better see.

Stephen shook his head. "Could be just about any heavy, blunt object. A hard enough blow to just the teeth could knock them loose from the alveolar bone, but this damage is even more severe. A more precise tool wouldn't have caused all this peripheral damage." He looked to Gin.

"I agree," Gin said. "This is consistent with a deliberate effort to remove the teeth."

"But . . . I don't get it," Witt said. "Why would anyone do that during the Civil War? I mean, nowadays, a crook might be worried about dental records, but they didn't have those back then."

"Who knows?" Stillman shrugged. "People are crazy."

While Gin occasionally agreed with that assessment, she was still troubled by the missing teeth. "I think we need to hold out the possibility that this man died much more recently than the 1860s. Given the preliminary evaluation of the conditions, a body could decompose to this state in as little as a couple of years. Are there plans to evaluate the clothing?"

"Of course," Stillman said. "It's going straight to the lab when we're done here."

"Didn't they recover some buttons?" Witt asked.

"Yes, they're over here." Stillman went to the counter where he picked up a plastic tray; as he carried it over, the metal contents rattled. "We recovered six of these."

Everyone peered at the buttons, which all bore the same eagle design that Fred had pointed out to her. One had been cleaned, however, and the dull patina of the brass made the design stand out in high relief.

"Those are probably worth something," Stillman said.

"There's also these." Stephen fetched another tray containing two of the metal rectangles like the one Fred had showed her. "Not sure what they are, though."

"I have to give credit to Fred Rappaport, but he says those were used to attach a shoulder plate." Gin repeated what the coroner had told her. "Were any other ornaments or metal pieces found?"

"No, nothing that was turned in here," Stephen said. "But anything organic—leather, silk embroidery, cotton thread— would have decayed at the same rate as the wool."

"And they didn't have zippers then," Witt added. "They didn't start using them until the 1920s. I did a paper on them in middle school."

"Of course you did," Stillman said sarcastically. "Probably joined the sewing club then too."

Witt shrugged far more graciously than the taunt warranted, and Gin wondered how he endured his more senior partner's running commentary day after day.

"I think that's all we have for you," she said. "Unless you have anything to add, Stephen?"

"No. At this point, we'll wait for the soils report to come back, as well as any findings on the textile samples. I do take your point regarding the teeth and the possibility that the body's not nearly as old as the uniform suggests. The truth is that we really don't have enough here to determine the age of the body yet.

We'll hold off on issuing the certificate—maybe the investigation will turn up something conclusive."

Stillman frowned. "Wheeler's going to want that as fast as she can get it. She's getting a lot of media pressure."

"There's *always* a lot of media pressure in cases like these," Gin muttered. She knew she ought to keep her mouth shut, but this had been a pet peeve of hers since her very first year on the staff in Chicago. "But we can't afford to cave to it. Until we know if there were other factors that could help us pinpoint the cause and time of death, it would be irresponsible to release any conclusions."

"Well, in that case, call when you know something," Stillman said. "I'll let her know you're busting your hump, okay?"

He lumbered toward the exit, and Witt followed, offering a quick thanks as he headed out. Stephen waited until the door had closed behind them, snapping off the portable dissecting lamp that had illuminated the remains.

"Sometimes I wonder what would happen if we ran this place the way those guys think we should," he said.

Gin laughed. It was a relief to be able to speak her mind without the officers there. "Well, we'd clear cases a lot faster," she said. "We might even be able to give Captain Wheeler the answers she needed in the time frame she asked for—just as long as no one cared if we ever got anything right."

7

After she'd helped organize their findings while Stephen put away his tools and the techs covered and removed the remains, taking the various bagged samples with them to be sent to the forensics lab, Gin said her goodbyes, promising to be in touch. Stephen was headed to the daily briefing, in which he and his colleagues would discuss their findings and offer each other input on any open cases, as well as discuss any bodies that had been brought in since the prior day.

Gin missed those sessions. She'd been lucky to serve under a respected chief, Reginald "Ducky" Osnos, who had also mentored her since her first day on the job. Ducky had been tolerant of his staff's mistakes, generous with his advice, and patient with their caseload. He'd also been exacting, demanding, and famously difficult to impress—but the hours that she and the other pathologists spent together, practicing a craft that few understood, had made her proud of the work she did.

Now, as a contract consultant, she was neither fish nor fowl in a sense. She could offer opinions, particularly in matters where she had deep expertise, primarily decomp cases. But the department was in no way bound to listen to or act on her advice, and they could take her off a case at any time without cause. She felt vulnerable in the presence of the detectives, particularly Stillman, knowing that if he decided to push hard enough, he could easily have her excluded.

She knew Captain Wheeler only slightly. Her impression of the captain was that she was extremely dedicated and just as ambitious. Gin had heard rumors that Wheeler was planning to parlay her term as captain into a run for city office, and as the daughter of a mayor, she knew just how many irons she must have in the fire—and how many people she would have to answer to if she was to amass the influence she'd need to be elected.

When Lily's remains were found, seventeen years after her disappearance, it had been a media sensation; the public had clamored for answers. In an era of social media explosion, it was no longer just the traditional news outlets that exerted pressure for justice on the county police department. Jake had nearly fallen victim to the circus, and her father had been arrested and held on a lead that turned out to be false.

Gin and Jake had survived it all . . . but she wasn't sure they could do so again. If Jake were dragged into the investigation of the body merely because it was found on his land, it would mean more of the public scrutiny that he detested and quite possibly a negative effect on his business.

These depressing thoughts were going through her head as she walked into the bright midday sunshine of the plaza in front of the medical examiners' offices. Like the building itself, the plaza was constructed of blocky sections of concrete, with very little grass or ornamentation, but that didn't stop workers from using it to enjoy their lunch breaks in warmer weather. Now, with the temperatures hovering around freezing, there was only one person sitting on a bench, a man in a parka and ball cap hunched over his phone.

As Gin approached, he stood up. "Hey, Gin."

It was Tuck Baxter, his uniform shirt obscured under the bulky coat. At the last moment, Gin recognized the logo on his cap as being that of the Penn Quakers and couldn't help laughing.

"Seriously?" she said, pointing at the cap. "You don't even know if your daughter will like basketball enough to join the team."

"Oh, I'm fairly certain she will. And I'm ready to sign on as number-one fan."

"We could use a few cheerleaders," Gin laughed. "What are you doing here, anyway? Missing your old job?"

As soon as the words were out, Gin regretted them; if there was bad blood between Tuck and the county department, he probably didn't want to be reminded.

"Something like that," he said mildly. "Truth is, I was hoping they'd let me sit in on the autopsy. When that didn't happen, I figured I'd wait for you and see if I could learn anything. What do you say, there's a decent falafel joint down the street—I'll buy."

"I—um—" Gin was torn. Her stomach had been growling for the last half hour, and she could use someone to bounce her ideas off of. But the case officially belonged to the county now, and it was their decision how much or little to involve the Trumbull police.

In a case like this, they would rely on local police for crowd control, access to local facilities and contacts, and—depending how long it took to solve—resources like office space and services for a command center and media outreach. Depending on the complexity of the case, they might borrow manpower for interviewing witnesses, checking databases and records, and even search and rescue.

But neither Gin nor Tuck had the power to make any of those decisions.

"Why do you care?" she blurted. "I mean, this is an anomaly. Other than my sister's murder, Trumbull hasn't had an investigation like this in years. You could spend all your time on the drug problems, the break-ins and robberies, things like that—and still keep busy every day of the week."

"Yeah," Tuck agreed. "And I will. It's not like I'm trying to stir things up or anything. I think I have a good grasp of what the job entails, and I plan to do it to the best of my ability. It's just . . ."

His voice trailed off, and he stared up at the ugly building, scratching the back of his neck.

After a few moments, Gin began to wonder if he was going to finish the thought. But he finally dropped his hand and looked directly into her eyes.

"I left on a bad note," he said. "I wasn't fired, and I wasn't exactly asked to leave—not publicly, anyway—but people certainly knew I was pushed out. I don't like that. I think I was right. I think other people were wrong. Some of those other people are more wrong than the rest—wrong and possibly crooked. I got caught in a mess because I didn't keep my mouth shut, and I got hammered for it. I don't mind—I wouldn't respect myself if I'd stayed silent—but I don't like taking someone else's fall." He regarded her steadily, then added, "See what I'm saying?"

"Um, no, not really. But that's okay. I accept your—your mysterious motives. It's just that I can't really tell you anything that I find out about this case. You've got to know that, right?"

"Let me ask you something," Tuck said. "If something is going to become public knowledge anyway, eventually—and if you accept my word that I take my oath seriously and would never do anything to undermine an active case—then wouldn't it make sense to keep me in the loop? I mean, just in matters that could affect the town I'm supposed to protect and serve."

Gin was caught off guard: the brand new chief of police was asking her to confide in him—when she hadn't even known him long enough to decide if she trusted him.

"And besides," he added, "you've already compromised your ethics, wouldn't you say? I mean, given that you're involved with a suspect, shouldn't you have declined to consult on this one?"

"Jake's a *suspect*?"

"Well, I don't know that, officially," Tuck admitted. "But if I was running the case, I'd be looking hard at anyone who worked on that site, who had twenty-four-hour access to it."

"You—you wouldn't say that if you knew him. Jake would never . . . He isn't capable of . . ." Gin grew increasingly flustered.

"Hey, don't sweat it. It's just checking boxes. And I don't care who's running a case—there's a certain amount of questions you have to ask yourself at the outset that you already know the answers to." He narrowed his eyes, and Gin resisted the urge to fidget under his intense gaze. "At least, you think you know the answers. But then again . . . sometimes, you prove yourself wrong."

Gin didn't respond to the insinuation—if that's what it had been. And a moment later, he grinned, and the intensity left his expression. "Hey, Liam."

Gin turned to see Detective Witt approaching. He gave a friendly wave.

"What are you doing over here, Baxter? Miss me?"

"You know it. Actually, I miss the food. There's nothing in Trumbull that compares to the Strip."

"My mom would be very disappointed to hear you say that," Gin said lightly, matching her tone to his. "She worked hard to bring Jezebel's and Sea Mist to town. They've both gotten great reviews by Pittsburgh bloggers, you know."

"Sorry, sorry," Tuck laughed, holding up a hand in surrender. "I was basing that comment on the greasy spoons out where my daughter and I were staying while we looked for a house. But we move in on Friday, so I'll spend the weekend trying out the local fare. Deal?"

"Deal," Gin agreed. "Where did you find a house?"

"Right on Spruce—found a two-bedroom rental less than a mile from the station, actually. Can't beat the convenience, and Cherie can walk to school."

"Aw, that's great, man," Witt said. "How's she adjusting?"

"Eh, you know kids," Tuck said. "Generally bounce back like rubber bands. And I've got a lead on a basketball team that might try her out. Coach is supposed to be a bit of a dragon, though."

Witt laughed. "Hey, listen, Stillman said he'd call you later to let you know what we need. There are some people he wants to interview, and he needs the names of the firefighters who responded. He was also hoping you could help us get in touch with the Rudkin brothers who sold that land to Crosby."

"Sounds good. I'll poke around and see what I come up with."

"Great. We'll try to stay out of your hair after that. I know you're trying to get settled and all." Witt gave Gin an assessing glance. "Just don't steal our talent, okay?"

"Who, Gin here? Not a chance." Baxter winked at her. "I've had to revise my opinion somewhat."

"Oh? What exactly was your opinion?" Gin inquired.

Baxter shrugged. "Wasn't sure. I figured your mom oversold you—she seems to think you're a genius. Far as I can tell, you fall a bit short of the mark."

"You . . . what?" Gin stammered.

"You parked in a red zone. That *is* your Touareg, isn't it? Looks like they're giving you a ticket now."

"Oh, no!" Gin looked down the street where she'd congratulated herself on finding a spot within a block of the facility. As the sun melted some of the snow and ice that the plows had pushed up onto the curb, she could see that the curb was indeed painted red.

"Too late now. I'd just wait and see if you can explain in traffic court. Maybe you could wear a tight skirt and cry or something."

Gin bristled. "I'm going to assume that you already know how offensive that comment was."

"Oh, yeah?" Baxter's smile was easy and confident. "Which part?"

"I've been to seminars in Cook County where I learned that in order to stay above any suggestion of harassment, it's best to say nothing at all."

"Yeah, well, I must have missed that one. Anyway, I guess you could file a formal complaint."

"I'll keep that in mind," Gin said drily. She was nearly positive that Tuck Baxter was teasing her.

"I was talking to Stephen, and he told me he actually read some paper you wrote when he was in med school, that you know what you're talking about."

"You know Stephen Harper?"

"Gin, I'm not sure what you've heard about me, but I've worked for the county for almost twenty years. I was in homicide for a while before I got moved to property crimes."

This was news to Gin. "But I never heard your name during my sister's investigation."

"I'd moved on by then."

"Shit went downhill once you left," Witt said. "You used to keep things interesting, at least."

"Yeah, well, sometimes you have to buckle down and do the job they give you. Anyway, this chief position was just the exit I needed, even if I'm going to have to turn over every case with teeth to you guys, just so I can spend all my time settling domestics and directing traffic on the never-ending road construction."

Witt chuckled and offered his hand. The two men shook, and Gin and Tuck watched Witt walk to his vehicle.

"So Trumbull's your idea of exile," Gin said when he was out of earshot.

The sharp stab of resentment surprised her; she'd never felt defensive of the town in the years she'd been away. In fact, she'd told plenty of people that she came from a dying town of 6,000 people, that there was no reason to return, that it was a miracle the other 5,999 people hadn't left too.

But hearing the same sentiment from Tuck Baxter made her want to convince him that Trumbull was worthy of his admiration.

"I'll keep an open mind," Tuck conceded. "But listen. I could really use a win on this one . . . I need to prove that I can do more than just run a fourteen-person force writing tickets and chasing misdemeanors. I need to show that I can handle bigger things."

"To yourself? Or to Captain Wheeler?"

"Let's just call that part of what I don't want to talk about."

Gin considered for a moment. The investigation was firmly in the hands of the county now. But as in her own sister's investigation, the official version didn't take into account the reality of the way things happened in a small town. Locals might be leery of opening up to officers they didn't know, especially if they got a whiff of city-bred impatience.

"People here are going to think that you getting the chief job was a promotion," she said. "Chief Crosby was a much admired figure. From what you're telling me, you feel that the opposite is true."

"Look, I'm not trying to criticize the job my predecessor did or suggest that what my guys do isn't important. I paid attention when your mom talked about the problems facing this place. And despite what I said a minute ago, I know it's going to be a challenge to keep up with the kind of crime that a clash between poverty and gentrification tend to bring."

"But it's just not worth *your* time," Gin observed coldly.

"Look—what do you want me to say?" Tuck shrugged. "I was raised in West Philadelphia, back when it wasn't safe to walk to your car. My dad saw more action as a night security guard at a warehouse than I did in my first few years on the job. My mom kept one gun in a kitchen drawer and another in her makeup table. I have a certain . . . need for adrenaline, you might say. And an extremely low tolerance for bullshit."

Gin watched him for a moment, trying to figure out where he fit into the world she knew. She had met more than a handful of renegades during her career, men—and the occasional woman—who worked in law enforcement because they craved the kind of excitement that came from high-speed pursuits and breaking up street races and gang disputes. They tended not to last long—and they usually went out on injury or disciplinary measures.

But Tuck didn't seem like he fit into that category. He seemed neither reckless nor out to prove something. He seemed, in fact, like someone who meant to leave his mark on the world—and fair warning to those who would stand in his way.

"Well, you're going to have to be careful," she said. "People are watching you. They're going to be looking for you to make missteps."

"Like your boyfriend?"

Gin felt her face grow warm. "Not him. I mean, Jake's stubborn, but he's fair."

"I read your whole case file. Not just the new entries . . . I read the whole thing, all the way back to when you were in high school. I know you were involved with Crosby back then. I know your father accused him of your sister's murder, that it ended a thirty-year friendship with his father."

"You didn't need to read the file to learn all that. There are a lot of people in town who would have loved to tell you all about it."

"Yeah, well, that's why I'm talking to you. You may have noticed I'm a fairly direct guy. I figure you could help me get the lay of the land. Advise me."

"On how to make people like you?" Gin gave him a thin smile. "I'm afraid I'm not going to be much help to you there. I'm not exactly Miss Congeniality myself."

"But you can help me avoid the pitfalls." Some of the confidence evaporated from Baxter's eyes. "Look, consider yourself a consultant, maybe. Help me understand the way things work around here. Help me learn to love this place—at least as long as I'm here."

He focused his gaze on her, his bottle-glass-green eyes alive with emotion. He was standing a little too close, and Gin felt exposed, like he guessed things about her that she wasn't ready to admit even to herself. Something dangerous arced between them, an awareness that stemmed from the emptiness she had been feeling ever since Jake started shutting her out.

But that was ridiculous . . . she and Jake were having ordinary couple problems; that was all. They were both under a lot of stress, and all they needed was for things to settle down, maybe take a few days off and go away somewhere. She ought to be with him now, figuring out how to help him navigate the crisis he was in—not offering her assistance to a man whose involvement could only spell more trouble for Jake.

"That doesn't sound exactly proper," she said firmly. "And I need to remind you that my loyalties lie with Jake. I won't do anything to expose him to more suspicion."

Baxter raised an eyebrow. "That's a pretty bold statement, Gin. Especially if the body buried on land he currently owns turns out not to have been dead for a hundred years after all."

Gin was caught off guard. Word that the uniform was Civil War era had rocketed around the Trumbull grapevine, despite the medical examiner's decision to wait on the death certificate. It made a good story, after all. And it had deflected suspicion from Jake—giving him a break he badly needed.

"What makes you think that? After all, Fred Rappaport himself said that—"

"Don't be coy, Gin," Baxter said. "Condescension doesn't suit you. I've had a fair amount of training. Look up my resume, if you like—I got a minor in forensic science from Penn State. I also still have friends in the ME's office. So I know that any conclusions about the age of that body are premature, to say the least."

"Okay, fine," Gin allowed. "But you can't be implying that Jake's a suspect—"

"Now that's a hell of a big jump to make. Still, that fire didn't start itself. All I meant was, considering there's an active investigation, you were probably right, and I should probably try making friends somewhere else."

The feeling that took hold of Gin felt suspiciously like disappointment, even though she'd been the first one to raise a red flag.

"You might try to stay in touch with my mother," she said. "I'm sure she would be happy to meet with you and advise you on . . . procedural matters. She has an exceptionally highly developed sense of civic responsibility."

"Duly noted. But there's still that other thing . . . strictly not job related. Unless your mother's also coaching a basketball team, you're still my best bet. For Cherie's sake. Tell you what—if you'll agree to it, I'll pitch in when I can. And we'll have a rule—no shop talk. No talk about work at all, just focusing on the game."

Gin laughed. "Oh, all right. We're meeting up at the Shoney Middle School gym this afternoon after school lets out." She eyed his crisp shirt collar, which still bore the faint outlines of the packing folds. "And wear something you can run in."

8

Gin stopped by the house to change clothes and grab a bite to eat before heading over to the middle school. Jake's truck was gone, and he hadn't left a note.

If Gin had to guess, she supposed he was probably at the office he leased in a modest brick one-story building down by the old processing plant that had once housed the steel company surveyor's office. As part of her mother's redevelopment scheme, it and a couple of other buildings had been converted to office spaces, outfitted with high-tech amenities and contemporary furnishings, and advertised to firms that were seeking less expensive space than was available in the city. Madeleine had exceeded her own goals for the fledgling office park: over 70 percent of the spaces were now occupied by tech startups and biotech consulting firms and the headquarters of a chain of gluten-free bakeries.

Madeleine had given Jake a great deal as one of her first tenants. His office was small, but it had floor-to-ceiling river views in two directions and featured the original hardwood floors, buffed until they were gleaming, and the original surveyor's cabinet, which Jake had refinished and used for his client files.

Just maybe the office had been a form of apology for the years when nagging suspicions of Jake's guilt in their daughter's death had prevented Madeleine and Richard from mending fences with him.

But that was their business, not Gin's. She could stop by the office, see Jake for herself, try to break down the chill that had formed between them . . . but there was a part of her that was still too irritated that he'd put her in this position.

After all, with the jobsite shut down at least temporarily, there was no reason he couldn't be the one helping out with the girls. He knew how important the volunteer position was to her. Jake had played a few years of basketball before getting kicked off the team, and he could run passing practice or lead drills or at the very least help out with team meetings. The fact that he hadn't volunteered to participate didn't help her mood.

Gin took Jett for an easy run along the ridge, cutting her speed to accommodate the old dog's pace, and made sure she had clean water and a fresh chew toy, then drove to the middle school. She'd arranged in advance to meet Olive by the stands, and she could make out the girl's long, swinging ponytail and hot-pink high-tops from across the parking lot.

"Hey, Lefty!" she called after she'd gotten her equipment bag from the trunk and jogged over.

Olive rolled her eyes and flicked her ponytail over her shoulder. "Stop trying, Gin, it isn't happening. Besides, Lefty's a boy's name."

"Not necessarily. You could be the first . . ." Noticing that the girl was preoccupied with something going on by the gym, she followed her gaze over to the double doors, where the rest of the team was gathering. Four girls clustered around their gym bags and backpacks, talking and laughing. Several paces away, a girl stood alone, watching them, a brand-new ball in her hands.

"Gin," Olive interrupted. "Did you really tell Cherie Baxter's dad she could be on the team?"

So that was Cherie. Gin's heart slipped a little: the girl looked frightened, her big brown eyes uncertain and her mouth pulled into a tremulous pout. "Sure, honey, why wouldn't I?"

"Uh, because she's going to be *terrible*?"

"I hate to break it to you, not-Lefty, but you're pretty terrible yourself. No offense, but you and all of your other teammates are pretty much unformed lumps of clay. At this point, any one of you could break out of the pack and become the star, including Cherie."

"Gin." Olive glared at her witheringly. "I'm not trying to be mean, but she's *special*. And not in a good way. Not in an athletic way, anyway."

"I'm afraid I don't understand," Gin said. "Can you be more specific?"

"Just talk to her, you'll see," Olive said. "But look. I'm nice to her, okay? So don't make me like be her partner or whatever, like I know you're probably going to. Please? I've got enough social issues of my own without that."

She sounded so adult that Gin was torn between amusement and concern. She knew that Olive was receiving therapy to help her deal with her mother's death, but the middle school social landscape was difficult enough even without additional complications. The tangle of emotions surrounding Christine's role in Lily's death would have been insurmountable if two innocent children weren't involved. The town, showing their best side, had rallied around Olive and her little brother, Austen; their father had been offered support from all sides. The kindness of friends, neighbors, and strangers, as well as top-notch counseling assistance, had given Olive and Austen the opportunity to return to school without suffering censure because of what their mother had done.

But Gin knew how cruel kids could be even in the best of circumstances, how the importance of belonging could overshadow the efforts of teachers and parents. She understood the ease with which an awkward child could be shunned. She and Lily, lucky enough to have been born into one of Trumbull's most prominent families, further gifted with social ease and pleasing personalities, had taken their luck for granted. And Gin was determined that, now that she was an adult, she would try to help those who hadn't been as lucky.

"Let's just go and say hello," Gin suggested. "And then maybe you can introduce her to the rest of the girls."

Olive groaned. "That's exactly what I *didn't* want you to do," she said. "At least promise me that I'm not going to have to carpool with her."

"We'll see," Gin said, leading the way. Out of the corner of her eye, she saw Tuck Baxter getting out of his car. He was wearing athletic pants and a faded gray sweat shirt with, improbably, an image of a *Star Wars* stormtrooper on the front. The sweat shirt had been laundered to faded softness and outlined his muscular torso. Gin cleared her throat and turned her attention back to the girls.

Nanette Springer had joined them, consulting a clipboard in her hand and sagging under the weight of her own bag. Her twins had potential to form the backbone of the team; Cora and Carla were sturdy, tall girls with a fondness for running, so Gin was hoping she could turn them into skilled players.

"Hey, Nanette!" she called. "We'll be right there."

Olive, resigned to her fate, went over to speak to Cherie Baxter and her father. Gin followed a few paces behind.

"Hi Cherie, I'm glad you decided to play on the team."

"Okay," the girl said shyly, toeing the dirt with her foot.

"I'm Olive Hart," Olive said.

"I know."

"I'm Tuck Baxter." Tuck grinned, putting an arm around his daughter. "And I'm real glad to meet some of Cherie's friends."

"Cherie's dad might help me run the practices when he has time," Gin said. "I'm counting on him to get you in top shape for the season."

"Do you want to come over with the rest of us?" Olive said in a voice that held very little enthusiasm while pointedly ignoring both adults.

"Okay," Cherie said, a crooked smile blooming on her face.

"You can leave your things here. We'll get them when they make us start. That's a nice ball, by the way," she added grudgingly.

"It is?" Cherie said. The ball was lying on top of her brand-new gym bag, but now she picked it up and twirled it on her palm. It looked comically oversized on her small hand.

The two girls wandered over to where the others were standing. Gin couldn't help noticing that Olive walked a few paces ahead, as though she didn't want to be seen with Cherie. Tuck watched them go, his smile slipping.

"That was nice of Olive," he said, turning back to Gin. "Cherie . . . she's had a hard time."

"I'm sorry to hear that," Gin said diplomatically.

"She's globally delayed—born with fetal alcohol syndrome," explained Tuck. "Her mother hasn't been a part of her life, so it's just been me and her ever since she was two months old. There's nothing she can't do if she puts her mind to it—that's what I always tell her. It might take her longer, and she might have to do it her own way, but she'll get there. But . . . ever since she started middle school, it's gotten harder. The girls hit puberty and . . . well, it hasn't been easy for her to make friends."

"This team is inclusive," Gin said, suddenly aware of how much she intended her words to be true. "I hope that playing basketball will be a good experience for everyone, including Cherie."

Tuck's phone buzzed, and instantly he tensed up, dropping his easygoing smile.

"Gotta get this," he said, turning away. "Work."

Gin left him at the edge of the court and joined the girls. She'd been glad to have the practice on her calendar as a distraction from her relationship issues as well as a chance to get a little exercise and spend time with Olive. And now that she had met Cherie, maybe she could play a small role in helping the girl fit in. Gin smiled to herself, remembering how earnestly her mother had tried to rope her into all of her volunteering jobs when she was a teen; like most adolescents, Gin wanted nothing to do with her mother's agenda. But now that she was an adult, it looked like she was heading down the trail blazed by her mother, getting involved in the town's future.

She would have to remember to thank Madeleine, one of these days.

Gin corralled the girls who'd showed up for the practice, noting that there were eleven of them—more than enough to field a team. Already the practice was going better than she'd dared hope. She got the girls to stand in a circle and started an ice-breaker exercise involving tossing the ball from one girl to another and calling out their names. She was happy to see that Olive threw the ball to Cherie, who almost fumbled it but broke into a huge grin when she managed to hang on.

Someone tapped her on the shoulder as she was cheering.

She turned to find Tuck standing there with a grim expression. "That was a courtesy call, from the county. I'm sorry to be the one to have to tell you this, Gin . . . they've picked Jake up. They're talking to him over at the station for the moment."

"Jake?" Gin's mind reeled, trying to take in this new development. "But why?"

Baxter was already shaking his head. "Maybe this wasn't such a hot idea. You know I can't . . . Look, I only told you as a courtesy. I need to get over there, though. I'm damn sure not letting them shut me out on this. Do I need to drop Cherie off at home on my way, or . . . I hate to ask, but do you think there's any chance that someone could drive her? She seems to be having so much fun, and—"

"I'll make sure she gets home," Gin said woodenly. She needed a moment to process her reaction to the news, but it wasn't fair to make Cherie suffer the fallout of events that had nothing to do with her.

"Thanks, Gin. Look, I know this is . . . complicated, but I really appreciate your help with her. This is the happiest I've seen her since school started. If you can just make sure she gets into the house, she'll be fine on her own, but I'd sure appreciate it if whoever drives her sticks around to make sure she locks the door after she goes inside."

"Tuck, I'll take her myself." She felt almost insulted that he would think she would do anything less. "I'll text you when I leave, but I'll walk her in and make sure she's settled for the night. Is there something I can do for dinner?"

"She knows what to do. We cook on the weekend, and all she needs to do is heat up leftovers. She'll clean up too." He hesitated, suddenly seeming unsure of himself. "I give her fifty cents to clear the table and load the dishwasher. And another quarter if she lays out her clothes for tomorrow."

"Seventy-five cents? I think I can spot you," Gin said. "But if I were you, I'd hope the union doesn't find out about those wages."

Tuck looked like the weight of the world was pressing down on him, but he managed a fleeting grin. "I never said I was an easy man to work for."

"Just go," Gin said, returning the smile. "It's handled."

Instead of responding, Tuck shook his head and headed for the doors at a jog.

Gin turned back to the girls, who were doing a drill where they tossed a ball back and forth and then up the court. There were more dropped balls than clean catches, but the girls cheered each other on either way. Nanette shouted encouragement to each girl no matter how they performed, but she was keeping a surreptitious eye on Gin the whole time.

Gin gave her a little wave and took her place in the center court, ready to go after the many dropped and missed balls. No sense giving Nanette any reason to suspect anything was amiss—Gin would simply compartmentalize for all she was worth, and after practice, she'd damn well get to the bottom of the situation. Jake could have been picked up for a variety of reasons, many of them perfectly innocent. In all likelihood, they simply wanted his version of events since he took possession of the land.

She slipped her phone out of her pocket just in case—but there were no calls or texts. She jammed the phone back into her pocket with more force than necessary.

"Who's ready for side-to-sides, girls?" she shouted.

9

Two hours later, she finally pulled up at Jake's house after presiding over postpractice snacks and driving Cherie and Olive and one other girl home. She made sure that Cherie was set for dinner (homemade macaroni and cheese in a microwavable container, precut carrots and cherry tomatoes in a dish in the fridge, and a homemade brownie wrapped in plastic with a Post-it note with a heart drawn in Sharpie, a detail that made Gin feel unaccountably wistful). She turned back Cherie's neatly made bed, wrote her phone number on a lined pad on the kitchen counter, and told Cherie to call if she needed anything at all.

Now she was back home, and she shut off the car's engine and sat in the driveway.

If Jake had been charged with anything, she was certain he would have called. Of course, he knew she had practice that afternoon, so he was probably trying not to bother her. Now that she was home, she could see that the house glowed with lights, and his truck was pulled up in its usual space, as though nothing was amiss.

Relief flooded her—mixed with a lingering sense of unease. Why hadn't he let her know what had happened? Her hand was stiff on the door handle, and as she made her way to the front door, her gym shoes making crunching sounds in the slush that had melted during the day only to refreeze, her irritation grew.

Inside, the house was filled with savory aromas. Something simmered on the stove, and Jake was grating fresh parmesan.

"Hey," Gin said casually, dropping her coat and purse onto the hall table.

"Where were you?"

"Basketball practice—remember?" she said. "The Wings kicked off their season today. All over the district, all the other seventh-grade girls are shaking in their shoes." She kept her tone light, but she was surprised—and maybe a little hurt—that he hadn't remembered.

"Oh, yeah. Sorry."

"Jake . . . I ran into Tuck Baxter. He told me you were picked up and questioned."

Jake froze, his hand on the lid of a pot, and took a deep breath. "I didn't want you to worry. Besides, I wasn't arrested or anything. Dinner's almost ready—I was afraid you were going to miss it."

"That smells amazing," Gin said, not sure what to make of his defensive tone.

"Well, don't get used to it—pretty soon it's going to be Hamburger Helper around here. Or else maybe I'll get a job at McDonalds, and we'll get by on chicken nuggets." He gave a pan on the stove an unnecessarily hard shake.

"Oh, Jake. Come on, it's not that bad."

Gin wasn't used to seeing him like this. For a kid who'd had a lot to overcome—never knowing his mother and having a cop for a dad who showed no mercy when Jake got into trouble, which he did a lot—he'd never been one to admit defeat. As a troubled adolescent, it had been all too easy for him to assume that the world was gunning for him; he'd compensated by looking for trouble before it could find him first. Still, he'd always been determined to meet his problems head on, to be bigger and tougher than the challenges facing him.

But right now, the look on his face was a mixture of shock and despair. And his words sounded more like someone who was giving up than someone who was going to stand and fight. Now that his father was dead, perhaps he'd decided he had no reason to keep fighting so hard.

Which made it all worse. *I'm here*, Gin wanted to say. *You have to get through this for me.*

Faced with seemingly insoluble problems, Gin had been trained to turn to logic. Maybe it was the natural domain of an eldest sibling, especially one who'd born the yoke of responsibility and high expectations in an extraordinarily high-achieving family.

"Don't get ahead of yourself," she said. "The discovery of a body may make the jobsite an active crime scene, but it won't be forever. Based on my experience, you may be looking at a week or two at the most. Look, everyone understands that you have a business to run."

"Which won't matter if I'm in jail for arson."

"That's—" Gin stopped herself. She was going to say it was ridiculous, but on the other hand, Jake had spent decades trying to clear his name for another crime he had nothing to do with. He had every reason to assume that the process would not favor him. "That's very unlikely. The county has an arson specialist on staff; once they process the evidence, they're bound to discover it was an accident."

"Actually . . ."

Something in his tone made her skin prickle. *Please*, she thought. *Please don't let this turn out to be deliberate.*

"They found traces of an accelerant. They rattled off some chemical compound I've already forgotten, but Baxter seemed to think it could have been brought here intentionally by someone who knew what they were doing. And the thing is, I've practically been spending every waking hour in that house, so it doesn't look good for me."

Gin could attest that he was telling the truth: as the Ashers' house neared completion, Jake had obsessed over doing the finish work himself and checking every detail that his workers were responsible for. Asher had agreed to let prospective buyers of the other houses tour his home while it was being completed—Jake thought he was the sort of man who enjoyed the attention, even if by proxy—and Jake had been counting on using the house to drum up interest. Later in the month, a local magazine was set to do a feature layout of the home once the couple's decorator had had her turn inside; it was to be the new Mrs. Asher's "coming out," a cementing of her new status, and she'd zealously sought out the media attention. Jake had been keenly determined to make sure every detail was perfect for the magazine piece.

"I would have known, Gin," he said tightly. "Accelerant in large enough amounts to do that kind of damage? I'd have smelled it the minute I came through the door. Which means that whoever brought it there did it that night, right before the fire. Apparently the cops think it might have been done in an effort to stop the project so the body wouldn't be discovered."

"That makes no sense," Gin said. "If their aim was to destroy evidence, why start a fire so far away from the body—and why did they wait so long? For that matter, why not just dig it up and move it?"

"I don't know, Gin," Jake said tightly. "You're the expert here. I would think that if someone came and dug a huge hole next to my project, someone would notice. I mean, it's not like you could drive a Cat up there and excavate without anyone seeing you."

"They probably dug that hole by hand in the first place. They could have dug it again. One person could do it in one night. Two people could do it in half the time."

"But there'd be evidence left behind, wouldn't there?" Jake persisted. "I mean, you've told me that the fluids drain out of the body. Unless they were going to take all the dirt underneath, wouldn't there be some indication of what had been there?"

"Give me a second," Gin said. She needed to run through the scenario in her mind, just as she would if she was in the autopsy room back in Chicago. "If there were bone fragments left behind, they could perform DNA analysis on them, but if the body truly is Civil War era, DNA sampling would be meaningless. I mean, what would you compare it to?

"But if the victim died more recently, then yes, possibly. But that assumes the murderer was careless enough to leave behind part of the remains. And I would think that someone willing to take the risk of retrieving the remains would be very careful to get all of them."

"But what about the seepage? I mean, there's DNA in all of that, right? Couldn't they just sample the dirt underneath?"

Gin shook her head. "It's not like body fluids just stay unchanged in the soil. When a body breaks down, it alters the chemistry of the soil underneath. The nutrients and minerals attract insects and maggots and rodents. It's like there's a food island for certain species—the soil would be organically rich. And then you have to factor in what's left behind—dead insects and fecal material from larger animals—all of that would alter the composition of the soil. So no, it isn't reasonable to expect to get any useful evidence from the soil."

"That's . . . that's disgusting," Jake said.

"More to the point, it isn't very helpful." Gin sighed. "Honestly, it just throws more complications into the issue of the age of the remains. If someone really was trying to prevent their discovery, that makes it more likely that they were contemporary. And that the murderer is not only still alive but still keenly worried about being found out."

"Okay, so who would ever bury a body up there in the first place?"

They were both silent for a moment, thinking.

"There's always the Rudkin brothers," Jake said. "Or more specifically, Griffin Rudkin. He's got a pretty notorious record."

Griffin Rudkin, the youngest of the three brothers, had torn through his adolescence on a string of spectacularly bad behavior, flunking out of Penn and getting arrested for cocaine possession and, after his parents cut him off financially, selling coke and other drugs. For a while in the nineties, it had seemed like he was in the paper every other week for crashing a car or breaking up with a model or showing up drunk at the black-tie fund raisers for the organizations his mother supported.

His name had eventually stopped appearing in the news, and there were rumors that he was in prison or rehab or dead, and eventually he was forgotten. In fact, he had been in the news only once more that Gin was aware of.

"Didn't his mother leave him out of the will?" she asked. "I feel like I read that he was estranged from her."

"That's how I ended up with the land in the first place."

"I thought you picked it up at auction."

"Well, yes, but the reason it was sold at auction was that Corinne Rudkin's will specified that Griffin's third be sold immediately upon her death and the proceeds were to go to one of her charities." He grimaced. "Honestly, I don't feel great about getting my hands on it that way. There's a lot of bad blood in that family, and well, I guess it seems kind of tainted."

"Was Griffin angry about being left out?"

"No idea. I met the other brothers—Randy and Keith, they had to sign papers at the closing—and they seemed okay. I mean, we didn't talk about Griffin, obviously, but they wished me luck with the project and all. It was decent of them, because they could have objected to housing going up so close to the main estate."

"How close is it?" Gin said.

"Just under a quarter mile. The main road to the house is off of Chilipin, on the other side, and the ridge blocks line of sight—but still, before I began the project, there were no other houses for almost three quarters of a mile in any direction."

Gin considered that for a moment. "The brothers were stuck with the terms of their mother's will," she said slowly. "But they may not have been happy about it, despite what they told you. Maybe they figured it would be easier to block the project than to stop the sale."

"You mean, by burning it down?" Jake frowned. "I don't know, seems like a hell of a stretch. Griffin, on the other hand . . ."

"If he felt that he was cheated out of his share, he might resent anything being built on land he thinks should be his. Is that what you're thinking?"

"That's about the size of it."

"But angry enough to kill someone?"

"Well, I guess we should see if either of his brothers has mysteriously disappeared."

"It's worth looking into, anyway."

"You're going to call Stillman?"

That was the logical thing to do, but given their contentious relationship, Gin had little hope he'd be receptive to her ideas. "Maybe. I'll sleep on it."

"Okay." While they were talking, Jake had spooned stew over polenta in large soup bowls and set them on the table. He poured wine into two glasses and handed one to her. "Better eat while it's still hot."

Gin had just taken her first bite when Jake snapped his fingers. "Oh, I forgot to tell you. Gus and his wife are coming over to dinner tomorrow."

Gin swallowed. "Oh," she said. "That should be nice."

"Try not to sound so excited."

"No, sorry, I am. It's just—"

What, exactly, had caused the spike of dismay at the news? Gin had been thinking for a while that they should entertain, meet other people. And this was a perfect opportunity. Maybe it would be just what she needed to get out of the mild doldrums that held her in their grip all during the autumn.

"Let me help," she said instead, aiming for an enthusiastic tone.

"I already did the shopping today. Thought I'd smoke ribs. You can make the salad, if you want."

"That sounds great." She forced a smile. "It'll be nice to meet his wife. I could use some more women friends."

"Atta girl," Jake said, lifting his glass in a mock toast. "You guys can get to know each other while Gus and I drown our sorrows and smoke cheap cigars."

"Jake . . ."

"Kidding, Gin. Look, let's just take one evening and forget everything else, okay? I promise not to mention anything having to do with the project."

"And I promise not even to think about dead bodies all evening."

As they touched glasses, Gin had a sinking feeling it was a promise she wouldn't be able to keep.

10

The next day, Jake went to check on a small project one of his crews was wrapping up in Clairton. After breakfast, Gin called Baxter but reached his voice mail.

"Could you call me when you have a chance? I've got . . . something I want to run past you."

After she hung up, she stared at her phone for a moment, thinking. The image she used as her wallpaper was an old photo of her and Lily from when they were in their early teens. They'd been at the beach, and Lily had found a starfish, which she'd wrapped around her fingers. She was holding it in Gin's face, while Gin shrieked and tried to get away. Her father had caught the moment on film.

There was something in the sibling bond, a need to antagonize, that was the other side of the coin of deep love. She thought about Griffin Rudkin, abandoned and shunned by those who'd loved him most. What would a blow like that do to a person? What could it drive him to do?

She tapped Griffin's name into the browser on her phone and narrowed the results to the last year. The few mentions were all in articles about his mother's death, and most were a single line about the three brothers who'd survived both their parents.

Finally, she found what she was looking for. "Son Griffin, forty-two, owns a small business in Tarryville." A quick search revealed that the business was called Mike's Bikes; Griffin evidently hadn't changed the name of the shop when he bought it. He looked like an older version of the boy who'd posed in the family picture that had run in the paper when his mother Corinne died. He stood in front of a refurbished old Vespa with an elderly man in bike shorts and a plaid shirt—Mike, perhaps. Both men looked somber in the photograph.

Griffin resembled his brothers in the sense that he shared the same receding dark hair, the same rounded chin, and the same sharp-planed brow. But there, the resemblance ended. He was dressed in a frayed flannel shirt over a pair of cargo shorts and leather huaraches. He had allowed his hair to grow past his shoulders in an untamed style reminiscent of a seventies shag. He was wearing small wire-framed glasses that gave him an air of a poet or a philosopher.

He certainly didn't look like a murderer.

But Gin knew that looks were deceiving at least as often as not. She'd examined elderly spinsters with livers destroyed by secret alcoholism, thugs with fingertips flattened from practicing piano. To really get a handle on whether Griffin could be guilty, she would have to talk to him in person.

Which she could do . . . in the space of a half-hour drive.

Gin checked the website again and found that the shop opened at 10:00 AM. It was already nearly nine. And the hours stretched between now and the dinner party with very little to fill them.

She could—should—visit her mom and dad. Gin made a regular habit of popping in on her mother in her modest office at the city building, but she saw much less of her father. He had retired abruptly after Lily's murder had been solved and her remains buried; he barely went out at all, and while he said he wanted to take a little time to "rest" before setting up a regular routine, he seemed to spend most of his time reading in the small den off the kitchen. Gin was worried about him, but she wasn't ready to face the possibility that Richard needed more support than he was getting. In fact, she and her mother both seemed to feel that way.

A visit would be a good thing. She could pick up a bucket of chicken—Madeleine wouldn't have to know—and some root beer and talk to him about his plans for his plot in the community garden or his thoughts on the NFL roster.

But her mind kept wandering back to Griffin. She could be there and back in less than a couple of hours; she wouldn't even have to say anything to him if it didn't feel right. There was an organic market in Tarryville that had an exceptional assortment of cheeses; she could pick some up, with some olives and rosemary crackers, as an appetizer for tonight. And she was nearly out of her shampoo, which they sold at the Aveda store in Tarryville but nowhere in Trumbull.

Gin washed her face and arranged her hair under a narrow pale-pink headband. She put on jeans and a peach-colored cardigan over a lacy camisole, took a chance on wearing suede boots, and headed out the door.

She was doing errands for dinner, that was all. And if she found herself near the shop, well, it wouldn't hurt to stick her head in the door.

*   *   *

Tarryville was known for its annual holiday decorations, and when Gin pulled up in front of the old-fashioned apothecary—it still boasted malts, shakes, and counter service—she sat in her car for a moment, enjoying the sight of a young couple working together to hang long swaths of greens over the door of a pet shop. The young man kept moving the ends, and the young woman kept changing her mind, until finally the young man got down off the ladder and pulled her into his arms and kissed her.

It was a scene that could have come out of a Norman Rockwell illustration, and Gin felt a pang of longing watching it. Why couldn't she and Jake have that kind of uncomplicated love, soaking up the simple joys of just being together? Why couldn't they settle into quiet lives together without tragedy and drama hounding their every turn?

It was a pointless train of thought, and Gin gathered up her purse and got out of the car. She walked slowly down the main street of town, browsing in the windows. She stopped to listen to an a capella group of carolers performing for the lunchtime shoppers and admired a pair of earrings in a jewelry store. Finally she came to the end of the street, where a row of half a dozen colorful, gleaming scooters, several with big red bows on the handlebars, were parked in front of Mike's Bikes.

Inside, a man with a strawberry-blond braid down his back and enormous holes in his earlobes fitted with onyx rings was showing a huge, powerful-looking motorcycle to a short, broad middle-aged man who looked like he would have trouble even getting up on the seat.

"Excuse me," Gin said. "Is Griffin working today?"

The salesman looked up and smiled.

"Today, tomorrow, every day. Go on in back, through that door."

Gin threaded her way through the rows of motorcycles and racks of accessories and into a large workshop that smelled pleasantly of rubber, tobacco, and coffee. Griffin Rudkin was seated on a stool in front of a workbench, eating a sandwich and tapping at a tablet. When he saw her, he hastily turned off the screen.

"Hey," he said, swallowing his bite of sandwich and chasing it with a sip from a big water bottle. "Just give me a second here."

He had cut his hair since the photo had been taken, and it was now very short, almost shaved, except for a fringe along the top. He wore rows of what looked like rivets in both ears, and he was wearing a black Henley shirt over heavy engineer jeans and black boots. He'd lost weight too, and the skin under his eyes was pouched and sallow. As if to underscore his pallor, he coughed, a long series of hacking coughs that made Gin back up.

"Sorry. Getting over something. Okay, what can I do for you?"

"My name's Brynn Walker," Gin said, using the name she'd come up with earlier while researching the Rudkin family. Using a combination of web searching and Facebook, she had discovered that all three boys attended the same private school in Pittsburgh. One of the elder brothers now served on its board, and his Facebook page featured lots of photos of him at various fund raisers and alumni events. Griffin hadn't been in any of them. "I'm with *Pittsburgh* magazine, and I'm doing a feature on Marshall Academy for Boys. It's kind of a nostalgic, 'where-are-they-now' piece we'll run the week before Christmas, and—"

"No, you're not."

Gin paused. "Excuse me?"

"Lady, you might be writing an article, and it may even be about me, but I'm pretty sure it has nothing to do with the Marshall Academy."

"I—I'm not sure what you mean," Gin stammered. "I don't—"

"Look, let's just drop the ruse, okay? Ask what you want to ask. I probably won't answer, but go ahead and give it your best shot." He took another drink of water, setting the bottle down unnecessarily hard. "I would have thought the story would have died down by now, though. I mean, it's done. The vultures have picked over the bones. Let it go, you know what I'm saying?"

"Vultures?" The reference to bones had caught her attention.

"You social media people and reporters and whatever you are. It's like you've got some sort of sick fascination with dysfunction. But like I've told all the other people who want to talk about my family, we were just like everyone else. Fucked up. I mean, the whole institution . . . shit." He got up off the stool and began pacing, stabbing the air with his finger to make his points. "I knew my mom had written me out of the will for years, so all this about me losing my shit about it, uh . . . no. I hadn't spoken to her in almost three years when she died, so how could we have had these big fights everyone seems to think we had? And that thing with Keith . . . I mean, in the first place, no one ever pressed charges. And in the second place, I mean, come on. I'm doing fine. I have everything I need. There's nothing—believe me, *nothing*—that my brother has that I want, and I only went there that day to talk to him."

"Listen, whatever you think I—I'm not here to write a negative piece about you," Gin said, scrambling to switch gears. She obviously hadn't searched deep enough to discover the family discord. "Wouldn't you like a chance to tell your side?"

Griffin laughed bitterly. "My side? Well, that would be a little tough. See, when my brothers brought me their bucket of blood money, they had this fancy little document their lawyers drew up. I'm not allowed to say anything about that." He made a gesture to simulate zipping his lips, then throwing the key away.

"You . . . signed a nondisclosure?"

"They didn't want negative publicity. Randy's going through a divorce, and his wife's got her eye on his inheritance. Which is kind of fucking huge, considering they only had to split it two ways."

"But they paid you something . . ."

"I used the money to buy this place," Griffin said flatly. "And look, I'm not complaining, but it wouldn't even be a pimple on the ass of what my brothers have in the bank."

"But they didn't inherit everything," Gin said. "Some of the land was sold off."

"*My* land," Griffin said. "My tract. It was the smallest one, but I never minded that. I used to go up there to fly kites. You can get them flying out over the point, with the river below—most beautiful sight you'd ever see. Look. I don't even care that she didn't leave it to me. I've got a life here—I've got no need to go back to Trumbull. But to sell it to some developer who's just going to put up cheap houses, I mean . . . shit."

Gin felt defensive of Jake even as she weighed Griffin's obvious resentment. But she didn't disagree with him. "That must have been difficult."

"Difficult? Oh, no, no. She was making a point. My mother was vindictive. You won't read that in the papers, but it's true. When I had some trouble a few years ago, I just needed a little to tide me over, and she . . . she wouldn't give me *anything.* So I was like, I did what I had to do, you know, I was mostly couch surfing. But in between, I was living in my car. I was *homeless,* man. So you know what she did with the money from the sale of the land?"

"No . . ."

"It all went to her favorite charity. It's this foundation that lobbies to get antivagrancy measures passed. Antihomeless, is what it is, but they don't come out and say it. It was my mom's way of trying to clean up trash. Because that's what she thinks I am." As he spoke, he got more agitated, seemingly not even aware that he'd switched to speaking of his mother in the present. "Okay, so now you know. You got what you came for. But I need to get back to work now. Bikes don't fix themselves, you know?"

"Okay . . . sure." Gin couldn't leave without trying to find out how deep Griffin's obvious anger at his family went—was it enough to propel him to sabotage Jake's project? And with his deep connection to the land, could he be connected in some way to the body found there? "I just have to ask, though. Do you get up there much?"

He watched her for a long moment, his eyes narrowed. "If you're asking did I go up and torch the place, you know, I kind of wish I had. But no. I was at home, minding my own business that night. Reading Tolkien, if I remember right. Look, I don't know who you really work for or what your angle is. But there isn't any story here. All I want from my family is for them to leave me alone. And that goes for you too."

He turned away and picked up a wrench. As Gin turned to leave, however, he didn't move, just watched her go with the heavy tool in his hand.

*   *   *

Gin spent too long trying to find the ingredients for the salad she'd hoped to make. The first place she tried didn't have chicory, so she took a detour on the way home to an organic market and then got caught in rush-hour traffic. There was an accident that closed all the lanes but one, and so by the time she arrived home, it was already after six—and their guests were expected at 6:30.

"Sorry, sorry," she said, coming through the door. Jett wagged her tail and struggled to get up to greet her. "I just need to wash these greens, and I can throw together the rest when we're ready to eat."

"Where were you?" Jake asked.

"Long story. I'll tell you later, okay?"

She'd been looking forward to a long, hot shower and time to blow-dry her hair and iron it flat. It had been a while since she'd really taken the time to look her best, and tonight had seemed like the perfect opportunity. Instead she was going to have to rush just to make herself decent.

"You look fine," Jake said, reading her thoughts as he stirred a pot on the stove. "Gus and his wife are really down to earth, you don't need to dress up for them. Look, I just needed a chance to talk to him—away from the cops and the reporters and everything. Besides, it's only a matter of time before they bring him in for questioning too."

"But neither of you did anything," Gin protested. "So you have nothing to worry about."

"I wish I had your confidence in the justice system," Jake said. "But Stillman's already decided to go after me, for no good reason other than he couldn't pin anything on me last time. And Baxter's got it in for the county—he's dangerous because he's flying under their radar. Cutting corners and trying to go around the system—it's going to be way too easy for Gus and me to get caught in the crossfire. And when that happens, the simple fact that we're innocent isn't going to mean a whole lot."

"All right," Gin said, gritting her teeth. She didn't have time to argue this with him now. "I'm just going to rinse off and change clothes, and I'll be back down."

"Look, it'll be a nice evening," Jake said, softening. "We should be celebrating. They've got a baby on the way. Gus has been waiting a long time for this—his wife has had a lot of trouble getting pregnant, and at their age, this might be their last chance."

Gin bit back her annoyance. "All right," she said. "But you're going to have to entertain them until I get back."

*   *   *

By the time Gin came back downstairs, she was feeling more presentable, if not more sociable. Her jade-green blouse and tight-fitting jeans were recent purchases made on the shopping outing with her mother; Madeleine had an eye for color and a fondness for fashion, and the outfit complemented Gin's coloring and figure. She'd tamed her hair as well as she could with a few swipes of her flatiron and dabbed on some makeup, and when she walked into the kitchen, she was able to conjure a warm smile.

"There's my girl," Jake said, hooking her belt loop and pulling her close beside him. "Gin, you've met Gus, right? And this is Marlene."

Marlene Sykes was a petite blonde with a full, curvy figure. Gin guessed she was close to forty, but she had the ombre dye job and fastidious makeup of a younger woman. She wore high-heeled boots and an arm full of bangles that jingled when she shook Gin's hand.

"It's nice to meet you, Gin," she said softly, handing her a pan still warm from the oven. "I made you some banana bread."

"It looks delicious. That will be perfect for breakfast."

"You've got such a beautiful home."

"Oh, it's not—I didn't have anything to do with this," Gin said, wondering what Jake had told his foreman about her. He'd hired Gus Sykes on the recommendation of a former employee who'd worked with him in the past; for their part, Gus and Marlene had moved to the area so Gus could get a better job. Jake paid his employees well—it was, in his estimation, the best way to keep good staff—and he believed it had paid off, since his workers were fiercely loyal.

Being out-of-towners made the Sykes the rare Trumbull citizens who might never have heard of Gin's family or the misfortune that had plagued their lives—or the very unorthodox path her relationship with Jake had taken. Which felt oddly freeing.

"I only moved in with Jake recently," she explained. "He's been a bachelor for a long time—long enough to decorate this place all by himself."

"You did good, man," Gus said, laying a palm flat on the paneled wall, admiring the grain and finish. Gin could tell that was a high compliment, but she also guessed it had more to do with workmanship and little to do with aesthetics.

Jake set out plates of crostini and roasted peppers and almonds, and Gin, who hadn't eaten since a piece of toast early in the morning, found that a little food restored some of her energy and allowed her to enjoy herself. She helped Jake serve dinner, setting out bowls of buttered haricots and mashed potatoes while he brought in the ribs that had been smoking all day.

The meal was a success, the pile of ribs transformed into a stack of bones and nearly all of the side dishes gone too. Gus spoke easily, laughing often and making a point to include Gin in the conversation. By contrast, Marlene barely said a word and mostly pushed her food around on her plate. Whenever Gin directed a comment or question her way, she seemed almost startled, and occasionally, she glanced at her husband with what looked like apprehension. All in all, it added an unsettling element to the dinner.

When the dishes were cleared and Jake had served up big bowls of peach ice cream over homemade brownies, talk turned to the topic they'd seemingly been avoiding all night.

"Detective Witt called me today," Gus said, almost apologetically. "I basically repeated everything I told the responding officers the other day. That I headed to work early because of all the copper thefts they've been having in the city."

Gin looked at Jake sharply. "What copper thefts?"

"Oh, it's nothing much; it happens everywhere," Jake said, giving her an uneasy glance.

"Not like this, it doesn't," Gus said. "I mean, copper's attractive to thieves, but what's going on in the city—it's organized and systematic. It's almost like they've made an industry of it. They get in and clean out a site, and it's been hard to catch them because they're so organized and because they're smart."

"You have to know what you're doing," Jake said. "Ideally you'd want to get it before it's installed, obviously."

"I knew it was just a matter of time before they start going farther afield once the easy pickings were gone up in Pittsburgh, and sure enough, they hit a place up outside Donora last week. They like to hit these places early in the morning because the odds of a random sighting are lower. Statistically, there are fewer people on the street between two and five than any other time."

"What is it even worth?" Gin asked. "I mean, how much could you make from raiding a site?"

"In the thousands, for sure," Gus said. "And that's a backroom deal. You'd have to have someone set up to take it off your hands. That's another reason it's gotten so organized. So anyway, I was up—I've been having trouble sleeping lately, I'm getting old—and I figured I'd park my truck down on the road, sit up there in the house. I had a thermos of coffee and my iPad loaded up with audiobooks."

Gin looked to Marlene. "Is that hard?" she asked sympathetically. "Having him out of the house so much?"

"What? Oh—no, of course not," Marlene stammered. "I know it's important for him to do a good job at work."

Gus gave her a curious look, one eyebrow raised. There was definitely a strange current between them. "Anyway," he finally continued, "so that night, or I guess I should say morning, the minute I started up the hill, I knew something was wrong. I could smell the smoke before I saw it, but I still don't understand how no one had called it in yet."

"My best guess is winds were heading northeast," Jake said. "That would have blown the smoke over the ridge, toward the estate."

"And there's no one living there right now?" Gin asked.

"Might be a caretaker," Jake said. "And it ought to be easy enough to check what the winds were doing that morning with the weather service. Too bad the cops all have their thumbs up their asses."

"Jake," Gin cautioned.

"Sorry." Jake had had a fair amount of wine with dinner, and the glance he gave her was a little bleary and faintly belligerent. She didn't often see him like this—Jake wasn't much of a drinker—and she didn't like it. "But it's true. County's just covering their asses. Wheeler's got her eye on the election. And Baxter? Shit, he's got some sort of personal grudge."

"Oh, yeah?" Gus asked, interested. "Like what? Didn't he just get the job?"

"You could ask Gin's mom," Jake said, not looking at her. "She's the one who hired him."

"My mother did *not* hire him. She served on the committee." Gin rose, stacking dessert plates a little too carelessly, fueled by her irritation, so that they clattered against each other. "But sure, let's go ahead and blame her."

"Okay, look, I'm sorry," Jake said. "I didn't mean anything."

"No, of course not," Gin said. Maybe she'd had too much wine too; and now she was making her guests feel uncomfortable. "I guess we're all just on edge about the situation. Let me start the coffee."

The kitchen was open to the dining area, with its huge rustic table lit by iron pendant lights turned down low, so that everything was lit with a golden glow. As Gin stacked dishes in the sink and made coffee, she listened to the others discuss the fire.

"Maybe we should ask around ourselves," Gus said. "Or we could go up to the main house and see if it looks like someone's living there, keeping an eye on things."

"Yeah, I had that same thought," Jake said. "Don't see how it matters, though—failing to report a fire isn't a crime."

"Not unless you set it yourself."

"Yeah, true."

Gus frowned and pushed the ice cream around in his bowl, turning it into a chocolate-studded soup. "Anyway, back to that morning. I put the pedal to the floor once I smelled smoke in the air, and when I came around the bend—shit. I mean . . . you can probably imagine. Tore me up. I knew we weren't going to be able to save it, not with the roof already gone. I spent about five minutes running around trying to figure out if there was anything I could do to stop it from spreading before I came to my senses and realized I needed to call it in, and then I just . . ."

He glanced at Marlene, who seemed to shrink backward in her chair.

"I just prayed, man," Gus said quietly. "Sat down on a paint bucket and prayed my heart out. Seems like it took forever for the first truck to get there, but they told me it was only seven minutes."

Gin watched Jake's face as Gus told the story. Nothing he was saying was new, and he'd probably given the same version of events to the cops, but this was the first time he and Jake had discussed that morning together.

"When Witt called you, did he say anything else?" she asked. "About—about whether they've got any more leads?"

"He brought up your name more than once, Jake," Gus said apologetically. "He pretty much admitted that county fucked up, picking you up like that. I mean, do a fucking Google search, you know? Every contractor truck in town's gonna have traces of accelerant."

"Did he mention what it was?"

"Yeah. Toluene."

"Shit."

"What's toluene?" Gin asked.

"It's a solvent, but it's in all kinds of shit. Paint strippers, lacquer thinners, Valvoline—people even add it to their gas tank to clean out the fuel line," Jake said. "They're starting to regulate it more—besides the fact that you could use it to make homegrown explosives, it's carcinogenic. Really nasty stuff."

"Yeah, but you can still buy it by the gallon at Sherwin-Williams."

"Hell, you wouldn't even have to do that. The coke processing plant would probably give it away."

"Sounds like that would make it hard to trace, if it's that common," Gin said.

"Exactly," Gus agreed. "Stillman must have known that too. I think he was pissed that Baxter shot off his mouth before he had a chance to try to get something else on you. He seems to have it in for you—any idea why?"

Jake glanced at Gin and immediately away, and Gin wondered how much Jake had told him about their past. "I'm not . . . There are a lot of people in this town who probably wouldn't mind seeing me get tripped up."

"I'm sorry," Gus said. "And Gin, I'm really sorry about your sister. Jake told me."

"Thank you," she said quietly, setting out a pitcher of cream and the sugar bowl before pouring coffee into four mugs. "But it was all so long ago."

There was an awkward silence as they sipped coffee, and Gin wondered if they were all thinking about the past, about the way small details add up to create an unstoppable wave. Joy, tragedy, revenge—the outcomes of human actions were difficult to predict and impossible to prevent.

She was also confused by the interaction between her guests. Gus—on the surface, at least—was a warm and considerate man, if a little rough around the edges. But Marlene was acting almost fearful of her own husband. Maybe it was simple shyness, manifesting as social discomfiture. Gin hoped so, for both of their sakes.

"Well, at least we have our health," Jake finally said in an effort to lighten the moment. Everyone laughed, but as they raised their mugs in a toast, she wondered how long it would take before the next unexpected turn of events shattered this fragile peace.

11

The next day was Saturday, but Gin was unable to sleep in, wakened by uneasy dreams she couldn't remember. She was fighting a slight hangover in the afternoon when she went to pick up Olive to take her to practice.

"Thanks so much for driving her," Brandon said. "Come on in. I've been after Olive to get her things together all morning, but she only just now realized she can't remember where she left her shorts. Sorry to make you wait—you've really gone above and beyond."

"I drive right by here, Brandon," Gin said. "It would be ridiculous for us both to make the trip."

"I'll make it up to you at the postseason party," Brandon said. "We'll have it here—the kids can go nuts in the garage."

After Brandon and Christine's divorce, he had turned the garage into a "man cave" with foosball, air hockey, a big-screen TV, and a game table. It was getting a lot less use these days now that Brandon was a full-time parent, but he'd good-naturedly given up his weekly poker game and let the kids take over the room. Austen was apparently becoming quite a pool shark, and the beer fridge now contained root beer and orange soda.

"That would be great, assuming I'm able to keep the girls interested that long," Gin said. "We're kind of building the team from the ground up."

"Hey, as long as they have fun, right?"

"Exactly. By the way—Olive's really showing a lot of promise."

"I doubt that's true," Brandon said. "But you're kind to say so. And even kinder to spend the time with her."

"How has it been going?" Gin asked gently.

"It's been . . . hard." Brandon glanced up the stairs to make sure Olive was still out of earshot. "The therapist says she's doing great, and she likes the other kids in the support group in the city . . . but I know there are things she used to talk to Christine about that she'd never talk to me about. Especially since she's getting, you know, *older*." His grimace reflected the challenges of a girl arriving at adolescence.

"Is Diane able to help at all?" Gin asked delicately. She'd seen Brandon's girlfriend at the funeral and heard through the grapevine that she'd been a huge support to Brandon throughout the events of the last few months.

Brandon shook his head. "Diane is great, but she's really cautious about overstepping. She grew up with a stepmom who pretty much came in and took over the household and . . . well, she says she wants the kids to know that they're in charge of the timetable. I mean, not that we have a timetable, or anything, but—"

"I think I understand," Gin said. "I mean, I can't understand, not really, but it makes sense. It sounds like you chose well. Diane's got a generous heart."

"Yeah. You know, I'd been thinking it would be nice for the four of us to go out sometime. Like a double date. Except—then I thought maybe that was weird . . ."

Gin felt a rush of affection for him. "Aw, Brandon, everything about this situation is weird, not to mention downright tragic. But the way I see it, all we've got is the future—might as well make the best of it, you know?"

Brandon gave her a grateful smile. "That sounds like something I'd see on Facebook with a picture of a turtle or something, but yeah, I agree. Maybe when things settle down with the investigation . . ."

"I'm afraid it might take a while," Gin said and explained about the newest developments in the case.

"Jeez, that's all Jake needs," Brandon said, running a hand through his hair. "Like it isn't enough to be trying to hold onto the business."

"Yeah . . . wait," Gin said. "What do you mean, hold onto the business?"

An odd look came over Brandon's face. "Damn, I'm sorry, I shouldn't have said that."

"I mean, I know he's got his own money tied up in this project but—have you heard something, Brandon?" Gin felt her face color. "I know I shouldn't ask—or maybe I ought to be asking him, but . . ." She felt like she was backed into a corner. She didn't know how to ask what she wanted to know without sacrificing Jake's privacy or letting on that the pair were having problems.

"No, it's okay," Brandon said. "It's just . . . I know a guy at the bank. Kind of an asshole, actually, can't keep his mouth shut when he's been drinking. I ran into him at McNally's, and he says Jake leveraged everything to get that land. Contractors have historically been considered high-risk borrowers, so his rate isn't great. And to make things worse, his bonding company has a priority lien on accounts receivable."

"Oh," Gin said, her heart sinking. "Can you tell me what that means in English?"

"It's complicated, but it means that if he defaults on the loan, any future payments go to the bonding agent, and he stands to lose his whole investment."

"I didn't know," Gin said. "I wish . . . I just wish he would have told me. There's—there's got to be a way I could help."

"Gin." Brandon touched her shoulder. "A guy like Jake, he's not going to want you to think he can't handle it. He's a hard-headed man. A little advice: don't push him on this."

"You're saying that from experience, I guess?"

"Hell yeah. I'm the same way. Or was, until all this therapy I've been having."

Olive came bounding down the stairs, her hair pulled up in a ponytail, her shorts in hand.

"Where were they, tiger?" Brandon asked.

"Nowhere, Dad."

"They were exactly where I said they would be, right?"

"Maybe."

"And if you'd folded your laundry like I asked, they never would have gotten buried under there in the first place."

"Whatever, Dad. Gin, can we go?"

Brandon gave his daughter a quick kiss on the forehead. "Do everything Gin says. She's the boss."

"No she isn't," Olive said, dashing for the door. "She's just the coach. I'm going to be team captain, and then *I'll* be the boss."

"Well, it seems like you've got the dad thing under control, at least," Gin said, following Olive out.

"Like I said—therapy," Brandon laughed, walking her to the door. "I'd suggest Jake give it a try, but . . ."

"Like you said," Gin said. "He's a hardheaded man."

*   *   *

Brandon came for the last fifteen minutes of practice, driving the minivan for which he'd traded his Dodge Charger when the kids came to live with him full time. Gin had her hands full when he got there—not with the practice but with an uncomfortable situation that she'd inadvertently made worse.

Olive had invited a few girls for a sleepover, and Gin made the mistake of mentioning it in front of Cherie. Olive shot her a warning look, but by then it was too late; the girl eagerly asked if she could come.

"Sorry, my dad won't let me have any more kids than I already invited," Olive said before running down the court, leaving Gin to handle Cherie's disappointment. Her face crumpled, and she began silently crying; the other girls edged away from her and whispered.

Gin was nearly certain that Brandon wouldn't have wanted to exclude Cherie, but it wasn't her place to try to fix the situation. She did her best to comfort and distract the girl, but the more she talked, the harder Cherie cried. "I want to go to the sleepover," she kept repeating. She only stopped when Brandon joined them, silenced by his presence.

"Whoa," Brandon said, grinning. "Was there a casualty on the court?"

Gin tried to signal him with a subtle shake of her head, but Brandon, unaware of Cherie's challenges, continued to joke with her for a moment before going down to help out at the other end of the court. By the time practice was ending a few moments later, Cherie had wandered off to the bleachers, where she was slumped despondently.

Gin drew Brandon aside. "Listen, I just want to give you a heads-up about something," she said, explaining what was going on.

Brandon frowned. "That's not okay," he said. "It's not like Olive to deliberately hurt a classmate."

"I don't think she did it on purpose," Gin said quickly. "I just think . . ."

Before she could finish her thought, Olive and a few of the other girls came running over, their equipment bags slung over their arms.

"Okay, Dad, ready to go," she said, not looking at Gin.

"Great news," Brandon said in a firm voice. "Cherie's going to be able to join the sleepover too."

Gin's heart sank. She knew Brandon's intentions were good, but the look of horror on Olive's face revealed just how much she hoped to avoid being associated with the developmentally delayed girl. She remembered Olive's words from the other day—*I've got enough problems already.* And now Gin had made everything worse.

Olive shot her a baleful glare, but she didn't contradict her father, instead allowing Cherie to catch up with her and the others as they walked toward the exit.

"Could you let Baxter know she'll be with us?" Brandon asked. "I'll drive her home tomorrow."

"Sure," Gin said, hoping Olive wouldn't feel betrayed—and that she'd make sure no one was cruel to Cherie.

"And about that other conversation . . ."

Gin winced, remembering their discussion about Jake. "Yes?"

"Just wanted you to know you can always call me if you need more love life advice." With that, Brandon winked and followed the girls out.

"Want to explain that?" Nanette asked good-naturedly. "Is Brandon Hart available for marriage counseling? Because I need someone to explain to Tom that Pirates season tickets are not an appropriate gift for our fifteenth anniversary tonight."

Gin laughed; Tom Springer adored his wife, and she knew the question was tongue-in-cheek. "I'll take care of this, Nanette. Go on home and soak in a bubble bath, have a glass of wine, and by the time Tom takes you out to celebrate, you'll have forgotten all about the Pirates."

"You sure?" Nanette tossed her a stray ball that had rolled under the bleachers. "Honestly, if you don't mind, I could sure stand a little extra time to shave my legs. My mom's picking up the kids for the night, and—"

"Say no more," Gin said. "I've got this."

By the time Gin finished collecting the practice balls and locking them into the equipment room, all of the girls had been picked up and the sky was darkening fast. A chilly wind kicked up leaves and sent them scuttling along the edge of the gym, lending a lonely air to the empty grounds. One of the parking lot lights was flickering, heightening the eerie, abandoned feeling of the place, and Gin walked quickly to her car.

She got in her SUV and turned on her radio for company, picking up a jazz station from the city. The mournful notes of a trumpet echoed her melancholy. She was worried she hadn't handled the situation with Cherie well. But she was even more upset about what Brandon had told her about Jake. How were they going to navigate this latest crisis together? Other couples got to go through a honeymoon phase of getting to know each other, each person putting on their best face and trying hard to make a good impression. But Jake and Gin already knew each other at the deepest level. At least, Gin had thought they did . . . until this latest revelation.

Gin had money. She'd been well paid in Chicago, and her needs had been few. A workaholic, she'd never taken luxurious vacations, never even bought a house. The momentum of her last relationship had seemed likely to sweep her along into the next stage of life—marriage, a home, maybe even a baby—but that relationship had come to an abrupt end when Gin had returned to Trumbull.

Now she was barely making a dent in her savings. Jake had refused her offer of paying rent, and while she tried to contribute in other ways, like buying groceries, their life together was simple. There were no expensive nights at the opera or fine restaurants, no housekeepers or gym memberships, no need for fancy clothes. She didn't miss any of these things, and she would gladly help Jake with whatever difficulties he found himself in.

But Brandon's words replayed themselves in her mind. *Don't push him on this*, he had cautioned, and Gin knew he was right. Jake's pride ran deeper than it did for most other men. He'd had to learn to be tough at a young age, and everything he'd gotten in life, he'd earned the hard way.

It was nearly dark outside, and Gin's stomach growled. She thought about picking up dinner at a downtown bistro that specialized in organic comfort food, but the last time she'd done so, Jake had looked at the receipt and scoffed. "Thirteen dollars for macaroni and cheese? I'm obviously in the wrong business."

Tonight wasn't the night to rehash that discussion.

She turned out on the road, driving carefully to avoid the cones that had been set up along the stretch of road due to a repair project. Erosion was threatening the hillside into which the school was set; the road was being shifted several yards and new guardrails would be installed at the edge. The drop was a steep one, down a sheer rocky cliffside. The road took several hairpin turns to get to the bottom, and Gin quickly realized that she should have taken the longer route, even though it would have added nearly a mile to her drive. With only her headlights to illuminate the road, the going was treacherous.

Parents had been complaining about the construction since the beginning of the school year, but tonight hers was the only car on the road. Far below, she could see the glowing line of headlights of cars heading to the city for a Saturday night's entertainment.

Maybe she and Jake could use a night out. She could dress up; they could have a cocktail at one of the trendy bars downtown before trying out a new restaurant. Someplace with candles and tablecloths and fresh flowers on the table. Somewhere they could forget all about their problems for a night and just focus on each other.

She had gone only about a quarter mile when a car appeared behind her. It came up surprisingly fast and flashed its brights, nearly blinding her as they bounced off her rearview mirror. She braked hard, hugging the edge of the construction zone to allow the impatient driver to pass her. She was dangerously close to the edge, but allowing the other motorist to pass would ensure that at least they wouldn't collide.

She glanced in the rearview mirror again and realized that there was only one beam—the other car was actually a motorcycle. She had reduced her speed to less than twenty miles an hour, but rather than passing her, the motorcycle was coming dangerously close to her rear bumper, tailgating. Gin could make out few details about the rider or the motorcycle other than that the bike was large and the rider seemed to be clad head to toe in black. As she tried to keep her eye on both the mirror and the road in front of her, the bike surged forward again, pulling up next to Gin's side of the car. For a second, they were traveling abreast, and Gin glanced over, taking her eyes off the road for a second.

Something hit her windshield hard, splintering it. Gin screamed and twisted the wheel, reflexively slamming on the brakes. But rather than finding purchase, she felt the wheels lose their grip and begin to spin out. She gripped the steering wheel fiercely and tried to steer through the spin, the terrifying sensation of her wheels skidding over the icy patch. The construction barriers loomed in front of her, and then she'd plowed through them, shards of splintered wood flying through the shattered windshield and hitting her face and arms. Gin could hear her own screams and feel the rush of icy wind on her face as the edge of the road rushed up to meet her front bumper and froze in the awareness that she was about to go over the edge, that her car was about to tumble like a tossed pebble down the rocky cliff.

Behind her, she was dimly aware of a second impact, of the scrape of metal on ice and asphalt, and wondered if it would be the last sound she would ever hear. Images of her parents, her sister, and Jake tumbled through her mind like a kaleidoscope, and then—suddenly, inexplicably—the car shuddered to a stop at the edge, and Gin was staring out the open windshield at nothing but charcoal-gray sky.

She put her fingertips to her face, and they came away slick with blood. More blood seeped into her eyes, and she smeared it desperately away. Her arms didn't seem to be hurt—her seat belt had held her in place, preventing her from hitting her head on the dashboard—and nothing felt like it was broken. But despite the fact that her foot was pressing the brake pedal down hard, the car groaned and slipped, tipping a few degrees forward, and Gin realized that the front wheels were resting dangerously near the crumbling edge.

She had to get out. Frantically she released the seat belt and opened the door, her fingers clumsy on the handle. As she twisted in the seat, the car pitched even farther forward. It shuddered to a stop only to start slowly sliding again, the sound of the tires on the ice the only sound in the frigid night.

Nothing was going to be able to stop it—the car was going over.

12

Gin took hold of the window frame and heaved herself out with all of her strength, pitching her body out onto the ground just as the front wheels lost their battle with the earth, grinding forward in a spray of scree and mud before finally losing the battle completely and plummeting over the edge. The back wheels missed Gin by inches, splattering her with icy sludge, and she pulled herself into a fetal position, protecting her face with her arms. She could feel the impact of the car through her body—once, twice—as it smashed against the protruding rocks before coming to rest hundreds of feet below.

The sudden silence was broken by a clatter a few yards away. Gin forced herself up onto her knees in time to see the rider disentangle himself from the motorcycle downed right in the center of the road. Had the object that struck her windshield bounced off and hit the rider? Had they both been the victim of some random accident—or, as Gin struggled to make sense of the last few moments, had the motorcyclist been responsible for running her car off the road?

The rider seemed dazed, but as Gin watched, he managed to drag himself out from under the bike, grunting with the effort. There were rips in his leather jacket and black pants and one glove had come halfway off, but once the rider managed to free himself from the bike, he began crawling away. After a few feet, he struggled to his feet and started to run, a compact figure with his head down, staggering at first before managing a limping jog. He disappeared almost instantly into the gloomy forest lining the other side of the road.

The silence returned, blanketing the scene. Gin rolled slowly and painfully to a sitting position, taking inventory of her body before trying to stand. Both arms felt bruised; a splinter of wood was embedded in her palm. Her forehead stung where something had struck her. But thankfully, none of her injuries were life-threatening or even serious.

She stared over at the wrecked bike, traced its tire tracks to where they practically joined with her own. Then she did a double take: lying in a glittering field of broken glass in the road, right next to the crashed motorcycle, was a tire iron.

It had to be the object that had struck her windshield. And it hadn't been an accident at all.

The motorcyclist had deliberately smashed it.

She thought of the repair shop she had visited yesterday, of the simmering anger in Griffin Rudkin's eyes when he talked about his family and losing the land he thought he would inherit.

Of the heavy wrench in his hand as he watched her go.

Could he have been so concerned about her investigating him that he would have resorted to trying to harm her, to either incapacitate her or scare her away from writing the story she was pretending to be working on?

But she had given him a false name. How would he ever have found her? Could he have somehow followed her back to Trumbull? She hadn't noticed anyone pursuing her, but then again, she hadn't been looking.

Another set of headlights lit up the scene, the car rolling to a stop. The door opened and a woman in a puffy parka got out, slipping and nearly falling on the ice before grabbing the car to steady herself.

"Oh, my God," she called. "Are you all right?"

"Yes," Gin replied. "I'm fine. Please be careful, it's icy so watch your step." The last thing they needed was both of them flattened on the ice.

In seconds, the woman reached her side and knelt down beside her. "Why on earth would you go for a ride on a night like this?"

It took Gin a moment to understand that the woman thought *she'd* been on the bike.

"No, no, I—my car—it went over."

The woman's eyes widened. There was something familiar about her; curly mahogany-colored hair cascade out from under a cherry knit cap, and expressive brown eyes showed concern.

"But—but you're the only person here," she said gently. "Did you maybe hit your head? I feel like I should hold up fingers and ask you how many, but—I'm sorry, I took CPR, but at the moment, I can't remember the first thing. Give me a second; I'll remember."

"I truly am fine," Gin said impatiently. "Just minor cuts. But my phone was in the car—could you call the police?"

"The police?"

"The motorcycle—the rider—he forced me off the road."

The woman looked uncertain. Gin could tell she wasn't convinced that Gin had her wits about her, but she placed the call, reporting their location and only saying that there had been an accident.

"They're on their way," she said after she hung up. "Are you cold? I have a blanket in the car. Maybe for your legs . . ."

"I'm truly all right." Gin knew the paramedics would insist on checking her over. Before that happened, and she lost the opportunity to see for herself firsthand what had happened to her car, she needed to get up and go see.

She got to her feet, ignoring her Good Samaritan's protests, and carefully shuffled across the slick pavement to the edge of the road. The construction barriers were smashed and lay in pieces on the road. Her tire tracks were quickly being obscured by the white, fluffy flakes that had begun to fall. Soon, any evidence of the incident, any proof that the other driver had ridden much too close to her, would be gone.

She held onto one of the construction barriers that was still standing and peered down into the gully far below. There—slanted obscenely and marked by long creases in the metal—was her car, just short of the creek that meandered through the bottom. One headlight still burned, facing askew into a tall pine.

The night was as silent as a grave.

A wave of nausea passed through Gin, and her breath grew ragged. Someone had tried to injure her—maybe even kill her. But why? She had a nagging feeling that it had something to do with the discovery of the body on Jake's construction site or the fire or both. But how was that possible? Gin hadn't discovered anything that could help solve either mystery.

Unless she had missed something in the autopsy.

Gin shook her head. That was ridiculous—she and two qualified colleagues had examined the body, and none of them had noted anything extraordinary besides the clothing.

And yet, the motorcyclist had acted deliberately, she was sure of it. It *hadn't* been an accident. The tire iron proved it. Gin had stared into the visor of the helmet, behind which the eyes of a would-be killer had been hidden. She was sure that her confusion and fear were written all over her face, but all she had seen was the black void that covered the rider's face.

Maybe her attacker had made a mistake, a case of mixed-up identity. Maybe the motorcyclist had been after someone else—someone who drove a similar car, or someone else who was meant to be in the darkened school parking lot that night. Gin scanned her memory for the parents who'd come to pick up their daughters after the practice but came up with ordinary men and women, tired from their workdays, eager to get home to dinner.

She heard the sound of approaching sirens as the woman followed her to the side of the road and gently took her arm. "Come away from the edge," she implored. "You might be in shock and not even know it. It isn't safe, you could fall."

Then she stared down past Gin at the ruined car below, and her face went pale. "Oh, my lord," she whispered.

Two vehicles rolled to a stop with their lights flashing. In addition to an ambulance, there was the familiar Trumbull Police Explorer. Chief Baxter had come himself. He'd told Gin he was headed home for the evening when he dropped Cherie off; he had responded to the call anyway. He was out of the car in seconds, slamming the door forcefully behind him and striding her way in heavy, lug-soled boots far more suited to ice than the athletic shoes she'd worn to practice. He barely glanced at the overturned motorcycle before addressing the two women.

"What the hell," he muttered. "I heard the call go out, and I couldn't imagine why anyone would be up here at this time of night, except for the basketball practice. What happened, Gin?"

"She says a man on that motorcycle ran her off the road," the other woman explained. "I thought—I'm sorry, honey, I thought you must have been drinking—but she was right. Her car's down there smashed flat."

Gin let the comment pass. "The rider ran into those woods," she said. "He's on foot, and it's snowing. Do you think there's any chance you could catch him?"

Her attacker's footprints were barely visible anymore under the blanket of fresh snow, and it was impossible to tell where the tracks led once they disappeared into the knee-high reeds and shrubs on the other side of the road.

But it was unthinkable that he would get away before they could question him and find out why he had come after her.

"He was wearing a black—a black jacket. Leather, or heavy wool, but definitely black. Black helmet, black pants. Boots . . ."

"Slow down," Baxter said. "What makes you so sure he was deliberately trying to hurt you?"

The paramedics were hurrying over with their equipment bags.

"Ma'am, can you come with us?" one of them asked. "Can you walk?"

"Of course I can walk." Gin felt impatient. She didn't want to waste time in the ambulance—she wanted to make Baxter understand the urgency of tracking down her attacker. "Please, I'm a physician; I can assure you I'm fine. Just a few contusions that I can treat them at home, I—"

"Ma'am," the paramedic said firmly. "This won't take long, but you know we have to check you out."

They were right, and arguing wouldn't change anything. Gin sighed and resigned herself to the examination. A second police cruiser arrived and two more officers got out; Baxter went to confer with them as they shone a flashlight across the road.

As the paramedics examined her and treated her cuts, Gin watched the officers take a statement from the woman. A tow truck arrived, but after Baxter had a word with the driver, he climbed back in the cab and rolled up the windows, running the engine to stay warm.

Finally the paramedics finished with her and started packing up their equipment. She walked over to talk to Baxter.

"Your friend wanted me to give you this," he said, handing her a piece of pale-blue notepaper with a phone number on it.

"What friend?"

"Your witness. She said she thought she remembered you, but she wasn't sure until I told her who you are. Does the name Rosa Barnes ring a bell?"

A memory came to Gin's mind of a shy, quiet girl who had struggled to keep up in school; she'd disappeared the summer before high school. Gin tried to remember if she'd ever known what became of Rosa and her family and came up blank.

"I went to school with her a long time ago," Gin said. "Her last name was Escamilla then. She must have gotten married."

"Well, she was pretty concerned about you. Asked me to have you call her and let her know you're okay." Baxter shrugged. "So call her tomorrow. Now, you want to tell me what the hell happened here?"

The heater inside the ambulance had warmed her, but the cold seeped relentlessly under her thin jacket, and her teeth chattered as she went over the incident again. As she described the rider's pursuit and inexplicable actions, a few more details came back to her.

"His gloves had a strip along the cuff—neon yellow or green reflective material. And his boots were old-fashioned, like—industrial, you know, with a thick sole?"

"We can have you look at some images," Baxter suggested dubiously. "Best chance is going to be tracing the bike, obviously. They're just about finished up here, and we'll get it towed to the yard. Even if it's stolen, we'll check it over for prints and other evidence."

Gin's heart sank. She hadn't considered the possibility the bike was stolen; if her attacker had been wearing gloves when he took it, there would be no prints. Nothing to connect him to the incident at all, now that his trail had been covered by the snowstorm.

"Look, there's no sense in having you freeze to death here," Baxter said. "If the paramedics are finished with you, I'll have

Sanders take you home. I may want you to come in tomorrow, though. The tire iron makes this a little more complicated." His jaw hardened. "I assume Crosby can bring you."

"I'll call my insurance company," Gin said. "I'm sure I can get a loaner."

"Safe to say, no one's going to be driving that car of yours."

"Listen, Chief Baxter—"

"Tuck. Rhymes with duck. Remember? We're on a first name basis."

"Okay. Tuck. There's something that I need—that I should probably tell you."

She explained briefly about going to see Griffin Rudkin while Tuck's expression grew stony.

"You're telling me you pretended to be a journalist so you could go and ask Griffin Rudkin if he wanted vengeance on his estranged family?"

"It wasn't like that," Gin protested.

"It sounds like it was exactly like that. Look, Gin, if the man is as unhinged as you're implying, that was stupid and dangerous. You also could compromise the investigation."

"I don't see how," Gin said hotly. "No one else was going to talk to him."

"You don't know that." Tuck paused, then sighed. "Although, you're probably right. But you could have come to me with your concerns."

"*You're* not on the case either." Before Tuck could scold her further, Gin had another thought. "You got to see the autopsy report, right?"

"Yeah, they shot me a copy as a courtesy."

"Then you know that we weren't able to determine how long the body's been there."

"I know that your report suggested that. I also know that quite a few pieces of evidence have been sent out for analysis, so basically we don't know shit until the results come back."

He shifted from one foot to another, his breath making clouds in the frigid air.

"How do you know that? Since they took the case away?"

"I checked with a friend. And before you ask, yes, it's someone in the ME's office, and no, I'm not telling you who."

"We're on the same side here," Gin said in frustration.

"You're not on any side. You're a civilian with no connection to the case other than a dubious consulting relationship that my contact says probably wouldn't hold up in court. And besides, I'm the chief of the fucking police, and I barely know what the hell's going on with this one."

And yet he'd taken the risk of going behind the backs of the detectives to learn what had been discovered in the autopsy, Gin thought. He wasn't going to let go of the case easily.

"We both have our own reasons for wanting to know what's going on," she amended. "I don't want to see Jake caught in the crossfire when he didn't do anything wrong."

"If he didn't do anything wrong, he doesn't have anything to worry about."

"I just want to know if you've looked at missing persons for the last, say, five years."

Tuck raised an eyebrow and considered her. "In the first place, while I will certainly take a look at any and all potential suspects if this does turn out to have happened in the last decade or two, I wouldn't be doing my job if I didn't start with those with the most to gain—or lose. And second—are you seriously telling me how to do my job?"

"No, I'm—"

"Because I'm really grateful for the attention you've shown my daughter. More than you could know, to be honest. But there's a firm line I draw whenever I put on my badge, and I'm not going to cross it just because you've done me a few favors. Look, I know Lawrence Crosby used to have his own way of running the show around here. I know a lot of folks were fond of him. But the days of good ol' boy justice are over. We're well into the twenty-first century, and it's time for the Trumbull police department to begin acting like it."

Gin bristled. Her mother had dedicated the last two decades of her life to improving the town—failing downtown and shuttered factories and vanished economy and all. "What Trumbull's had to deal with is the collapse of an industry and the problems that come along with poverty and lack of opportunity," she said. "That doesn't make its citizens incompetent."

"Oh, I'm not suggesting that they are. Believe me. And that's a goddamn good reason to clean up the way we operate around here. We can't expect the county to take our budget requests seriously if we can't prove we've got our own house in order. You know why I'm out here tonight?"

Gin stared into his flinty green eyes. "Because you care," she said flatly. "Because you're going to make a difference. At least, that's probably what you said during your interviews. But also because, somewhere along the line, you screwed up badly enough to get yourself banished. You lost your temper or got caught up in an Internal Affairs investigation or slept with the wrong person—or didn't sleep with the right one—and got yourself sent here as a punishment."

The corner of Baxter's mouth twitched—whether in anger or amusement, Gin couldn't tell.

"That's a little beyond the scope of what I was asking," he said. "I'm here *tonight* because I've put my whole department on notice. I told them to expect me on their ass anytime, anywhere. That I might show up at any call, and I expect departmental procedures to be followed to a *t*. There's no room for sloppiness or shortcuts or half measures in my shop—just solid police work. So yeah, I heard the call go out, and I talked to Brandon Hart and made sure the girls got home okay, and then I came straight over to make sure that everything was done right. Now you're asking me if I've considered that a body buried in my patch might be someone who was reported missing, like it never occurred to me? Like we're just a bunch of Keystone Kops?"

"Look." Gin took a deep breath and tried to keep her voice steady. "I apologize if I insulted you. I'm sure you're a very good cop. I'm sure you've already got a list of everyone gone missing in the area. I'm just asking . . . if there's any way, while following those policies you've been talking about, that you could expedite releasing the site. Jake could really, really stand to get back to work."

She stared at the ground, her heart thudding. *Don't make me beg*, she thought.

"I'd . . . be really grateful."

For a moment, he didn't answer. The ambulance began making a slow turn, the driver giving them a wave. The tow truck operator was loading the mangled motorcycle onto the lift.

"I'm not promising anything," Tuck finally said. "But I guess I may owe you. I've seen how you go above and beyond with the girls. Cherie can't stop talking about how much she loves practice. So . . . I'm going to tell you something that I have no business making known. It's true that I resent being sent here, but I resent even more being excluded from a case that's happening right under my nose. So I'm not sitting on the sidelines. The county boys don't need to know all the details, but I'm looking into a few things. And that's all I have to say."

"Thank you," Gin said quietly.

"Oh, I'm not doing it for you. I'm probably doing it for my own stupid pride, which is a lesson I evidently have yet to learn."

Gin thought of her earlier conversation with Brandon, about Jake's pride and the gulf it had created between them.

"Isn't pride the thing that comes before a fall?" she asked.

"So they say," Baxter said. "I guess we'll have to wait and see. Now, I need to talk to the tow guy, so if you don't mind doing just one small thing I've asked you tonight, please pretend to be a reasonable woman and let Sanders drive you home."

13

By the time Officer Sanders dropped her off in front of the house, lights burned in every window. She glanced at the dashboard clock and was astonished to see that nearly two hours had passed since she left the school. She should have asked to borrow a phone to let Jake know she'd be late.

He came out of the front door, his face set in fear that gave way to relief. "What the hell happened to you?" he thundered as Gin walked slowly to the door. Her body was starting to ache now, her various injuries throbbing. "Are you all right?"

"I'm fine," she said, giving him a weak smile. She turned and waved at the retreating cruiser. "I, um, got a ride home."

Jake folded his arms over his chest and glared at her. "You're fine? You don't come home for two hours in what they're saying is going to be a severe winter storm, and you don't bother to call or let me know you're all right—and then the *police* drop you off, and you've got a huge bandage on your face, and you're *fine*?"

"You're angry," Gin said. "I understand. I'm sorry. It was thoughtless of me."

"It was—" Abruptly, Jake bit back his words and shook his head. When he spoke again, he'd managed to reel in his fury. "No, Gin, it wasn't thoughtless. It was terrifying. In the last year, I lost my father and I almost lost you, not to mention my own life. So you'll forgive me if it's just a little more important to me to know that you're all right."

"I'll try to do better," Gin said quietly. "Can we please go inside? It's cold out here."

Jake took her arm without comment, his touch much gentler than his voice. Gin leaned into him as they made their way inside. He helped her remove her boots, coat, and hat and guided her over to the sofa. Then he went to the fire and gave it a stir.

"All right. I owe you an apology," he said quietly. "You were right; I overreacted. Can we start over now?"

Gin nodded. "You're forgiven. It's actually . . . kind of nice to have someone worry about me."

"Okay. You were in an accident?" His was standing over her, his arms crossed over his chest, and Gin still felt like she was being interrogated.

"Yes. I was leaving practice after all the girls got picked up. I wasn't paying attention, not like I should have been, given the weather. A motorcycle pulled up beside me, much too close. I swerved and ran through the construction barriers, but I was able to get out of the car." She avoided his gaze, knowing she wasn't telling the whole story.

"And I assume your car was damaged."

Gin swallowed. "You could say that. It's sitting at the bottom of Kitts Creek."

Jake blanched. "Back up and tell me the rest."

She sighed, realizing there was no way to get out of it. So she described the incident, keeping her description as brief as possible and focusing on Rosa's arrival and the paramedics' examination, deemphasizing the fear she'd felt.

"Wait just a goddamn minute," Jake said.

"Could you at least sit down if you're going to yell at me?" Gin asked.

"I'm not—I don't mean to . . . Christ, Gin, are you absolutely sure?"

"Am I sure about what? That he ran me off the road? Or that he did it on purpose?" Gin was suddenly exhausted. "Look, I can tell it to you as many times as you want, but it's not going to change the basic facts. I don't know who, and I don't know why, but I do know that someone wanted to hurt or frighten me."

"And Baxter didn't even order a search!"

"No, that's not true. There were other officers there at the scene. At least one of them was in the woods, but the tracks were already obscured. They're taking the motorcycle in as evidence." Something else occurred to her. "Do you remember a girl named Rosa Escamilla from middle school?"

Jake's forehead creased with concentration. "Barely . . . quiet kid, kind of pretty, had an older brother who was a year ahead of me?"

"I didn't know her brother. I don't really know much about her at all, except her name's Rosa Barnes now. Anyway, she was the one who stopped and helped."

"No kidding. That's a coincidence. Although I'm surprised she's back here."

"Surprised why?"

"Don't you remember? The reason they moved was that her father was in prison, so they went to stay with their mother's family."

"Oh. I guess I never knew that." Gin remembered the neat braids Rosa used to wear to school, the too-small clothes, the battered and worn khaki backpack that must have been a hand-me-down from her brother.

"Look, Gin, are you hungry?"

"I . . . think so?" Gin tried to remember the last time she'd eaten. "Yes, actually."

"Stay right here," Jake said gruffly. "I'll be back with some grub. You can eat it on the couch, and I won't even mind the crumbs."

He caressed her cheek gently with his fingertips before going into the kitchen.

They were both trying so hard, both searching for the right thing to say. Too late, Gin remembered her plan to talk to him about what she'd learned from Brandon. But that could wait; tonight she longed to simply fall asleep in Jake's arms.

*   *   *

The next morning, Gin woke early, well before dawn. The aches of the night before had subsided, and she felt refreshed. She grabbed her phone off the nightstand and burrowed deeper under the covers so the screen's glow wouldn't wake Jake. He was lying exactly as he'd gone to bed the night before, one forearm slung over his face, turned slightly away from her.

She checked her e-mail. There were messages from an old colleague from Chicago, just checking in, and a link to an article from her mother.

And one from Rosa Barnes.

"How are you?" was the subject line. Gin stared at it for a few moments, thinking of the woman who'd come to her rescue yesterday. Her emotions wavered between gratitude for Rosa's kindness and shame over the way she'd treated her when they were children. She'd barely acknowledged the shy girl at school, never even had a single conversation that she could remember. Gin hadn't realized then that the advantages of wealth and attentive parents had made her path easy, nor had it occurred to her that she might try to reach out to those who had far less.

She tapped the message and scanned it quickly. It was short and to the point, but warmth showed through the words.

Dear Gin,

I hope you're not feeling too bad after yesterday! That must have really shaken you up. I was wondering if you would like to come to dinner. Nothing fancy, pretty much any day this week, tonight is good because I have the afternoon off and Mom and I are making tamales.

She added her address; it was on a street in the part of town that featured as many boarded-up shops as active businesses, on the edge where Gin's mother's redevelopment efforts had yet to reach.

Gin wavered, glancing over at Jake's sleeping form. Last night, just before turning out the light, he'd yawned and said he was going to see his lawyer in Pittsburgh today and that he'd probably have dinner with an old friend and stay in the city overnight. Gin hadn't even known he had a lawyer; when he'd been under investigation for Lily's death the first time, his father couldn't afford one, and the second time, he had never mentioned consulting one.

Of course, Jake must have a lawyer for his business, someone who helped him with the financial side of things, like setting up the company and helping him with real estate transactions.

He didn't offer any further explanation. She had offered to go with him, and he'd turned her down so fast it had stung.

"There's no need," he'd said shortly, taking off his reading glasses and setting them on the nightstand. "It'll be boring, and I'm sure there's nothing he can do, anyway."

And then he'd turned over and said nothing more, while Gin lay awake, brooding.

Again she wondered if that wasn't the point of a relationship, in part—to ease the dull and the difficult, to stand by someone when life's hard moments weighed them down.

Gin hit reply and tapped out a message before she could change her mind.

"I'd love to come," she wrote. "I'll bring beer."

*   *   *

After she showered and carefully applied concealer to disguise the bruising on her face, she called her father. "Hi, Dad . . . Any chance you could spare the Land Rover for a few days?"

Her parents had bought a used Land Rover a decade earlier for taking up to the Catskills, where they often rented a cabin for ski vacations. For most of the year, it sat in the unused garage stall, collecting dust. It was a rusted, cumbersome vehicle, but it ran well enough to get them reliably to the mountains.

"Why on earth would you want to borrow that old thing? It's got almost two hundred thousand miles on it."

She explained briefly that she had been in a fender bender, not wanting to worry him with the truth. "I've been thinking of getting a new car anyway," she said. "I'll see what the dealer will give me in trade once mine's fixed."

"Well, if you're sure. I'll come pick you up, and you can bring me home."

He arrived half an hour later. The Land Rover looked even more decrepit than Gin remembered, but the inside was clean and smelled pleasantly of leather and motor oil and her father's cologne.

"I had it tuned up in September," her father said after moving to the passenger seat. "It should be okay for a few days. Hey," he added, "did you do something to your face?"

Gin tried to smile, keeping her eyes on the road as she eased the old hulk out of the driveway. "Just a little collision with the medicine cabinet. I'm fine."

"All right. Listen, honey . . . your mother tells me that Jake's taking the fire pretty hard. And that nonsense about a body being found on the property—I hope this doesn't make me sound insensitive, but I would think this whole family deserves a break from that sort of thing."

"I couldn't agree with you more, Dad."

"Still, Mom says the new chief is pretty good. He's got some big shoes to fill, I guess, but he ought to keep the county detectives in line and let Jake focus on getting back to work."

"I'll tell him you said so, Dad." She told Richard about the chief's daughter playing on the team.

"I hope you'll save first-row seats for your parents," Richard said. "I'm counting on this being a good year for basketball. But listen, honey, back to Jake for a minute."

They were almost all the way back to her parents' house, and Gin wished she'd driven just a little faster. She didn't relish the thought of discussing her love life with her father.

"Yes . . ."

"I've just been wondering . . . see, your mom and I, well, we worry about you kids."

"Dad! Jake and I are in our thirties. We aren't kids."

"Well . . ." he laughed awkwardly. "To your parents, you still are. It's just, we hate to see you struggle."

For a moment, Gin worried he had somehow intuited the strife between them, and then she realized that her father was talking about money.

"We're not struggling," she said. "I've got tons of savings."

"But you haven't found a new job yet, and—"

"Dad, I'm not working for the ME for free, you know. I have some income coming in. And this thing with Jake's job is just temporary." She tried to sound more confident than she felt. "He'll be able to sell those other two houses while he rebuilds the first one."

"Well, honey, I certainly hope that's true. But—now don't get mad—your mom and I talked about this project when he first started it. We both felt like he'd bitten off more than he could chew."

"Dad!" Gin felt fourteen again, trying to sneak out the door in shorts that her father deemed too short. "It's really none of your business. And Jake is doing *fine*."

The lie tripped awkwardly off her tongue, but it was galling to have her father opining on matters that were none of his business. Perhaps the earlier retirement he'd taken had been a poor idea if it left him time to meddle like this.

Richard was silent until they pulled up in the circular drive in front of the house. "Look, honey, Jake is a fine craftsman. Really, an artist, I would think we would both agree. But he isn't a businessman. And your mother and I—well, just me, I suppose—aren't willing to see our dreams for you just . . . just jeopardized like this when there are simple means to give you and Jake both some security."

"So wait just one minute. What are these *dreams* you have for me, anyway?"

"Your mother was able to be home with you when you and your sister were young," Richard continued doggedly. "If you and Jake have children, wouldn't you want that?"

Gin goggled at her father. "My mother is the *mayor* of one of the best-managed cities in the county," she said. "Maybe in the *state*. I'm pretty sure she isn't on board with your plan to get me in an apron in front of the stove. I do have a job, Dad, and while I'm not working full time at the moment, I'm sure I will again. And even if I don't, those decisions are mine—and Jake's—alone."

Richard ducked his chin. "I'm sorry, honey," he said quietly. "I guess I overstepped. I didn't mean—I didn't mean to offend you."

He reached for the door handle and got out of the car, moving slowly. Gin wanted to call after him, but she couldn't find the words to tell him how important it was to her that he allow her the independence she craved while still appreciating all the love and support her parents tried to give her.

Instead, she watched him trudge up to the house. At the door, he glanced back and gave her a small wave, his mouth twisted in a smile that disappeared even before he turned away.

*   *   *

Stephen Harper called her while she was standing in front of the imported beers in the liquor store, trying to figure out which to buy.

"I thought you'd want to know," he said. "Ellerth Morton recommended someone to examine the uniform samples. We sent them over to the university—they've got someone in the history department who said she'd take a look. All we were able to do was confirm that the fibers and dyes seem to be authentic."

Ellerth Morton was the consulting anthropologist the department had used in the past. Gin respected his work and trusted that his recommendation would be sound.

"That's great, Stephen," she said. "Listen, did you send the soil mass from underneath?"

"The . . . mass?"

"I know there wasn't any obvious evidence, but remember how impacted it was?"

"Yeah . . . it was like a giant mud pie. We sent a section of it with the other soil samples, but we've got the rest of it just sitting in a tray. But now that you mention it, why weren't there any fragments of the uniform underneath? We found pieces of it all over the top of the remains."

"As the body fluids leaked out, they would have soaked the fibers, making them attractive to organisms to feed on. The area around a decaying body is especially organically rich, and it's not uncommon for it to be a virtual feeding ground."

"Yeah, there were definitely a lot of bug parts and other stuff in that section."

"They'll be able to tell a lot from the sample. But I'd send the rest down to the university and let her go through it. She'll know what to look for if there's any part of his uniform left intact in the soil."

"Okay, you got it. Listen, Chozick asked me to see if you could talk to her once she's had a chance to review everything. Her name's Pia Farrar. I sent her your information, but I'll text you her contact info too."

"Of course, Stephen. I'll be glad to talk to her." After the conversation with her father, Gin was grateful to have a professional challenge to focus on. "Listen . . . do you know anything about beer?"

"Uh, yeah, I guess, if you count knowing that Budweiser's on sale at Star Market."

Gin laughed. "Okay, thanks anyway. I'll just pick the prettiest label."

"Geez, Gin, every once in a while you say something that threatens to knock you off the pedestal I've put you on."

"The sooner, the better," Gin said, with feeling. She doubted that Stephen Harper—or any of her other male colleagues, for that matter—had to endure their own families' attempts to meddle in their professional lives. "It gets awfully lonely up there."

*   *   *

She was loading the six-pack of a local IPA into her car when her phone chimed a text.

> So sorry to have to ask but is there any chance you can take Olive tonight after practice, forgot Austen has cub scouts

A few seconds later, another text came in.

No worries if not she can stay home alone

Gin knew that Brandon had been reluctant to leave Olive home by herself. Though she'd been independent and confident before her mother's death, she'd experienced nightmares and anxiety, particularly in the early weeks following the funeral. Brandon had confided that she was doing better now, but Gin hated to see her fragile recovery threatened by moving too fast.

She texted back.

I'd love to take her. I'll see if Cherie wants to come over too.

That would be great IOU big time

Gin stared at her phone thoughtfully. She would take the girls so that Brandon could spend time with his son and Tuck could focus on the case. Maybe her father would see her contributions as women's work, the way her mother had watched not only her own children but those of her husband's best friend, a widower, so that he could work without distraction.

But Gin didn't see it that way. The favors she was doing now would be repaid in kind when and if she had children of her own. At least, that was true of Brandon. Her motives were murkier when it came to Tuck. She liked his young daughter, and she was happy to see the girls' blossoming friendship, but it was also true that she hoped he would be able to help wrap up the case, for Jake's sake.

Before she could examine her motives too closely, she texted Tuck that she would keep the girls after practice.

She'd have to cancel with Rosa. Disappointed, she sent a text expressing her regrets and explaining the situation. It had been a long day, one marred by the conversation with her father and her unease at the way she had left things with Jake.

Almost instantly a text chimed back.

Bring the girls! It will be fun. Mom loves kids, and we have plenty of food.

Gin texted a quick thank you and started the car, pleased that she wouldn't have to cancel the evening after all. Jake was in the city—she might as well enjoy her evening too.

It wasn't going to be a typical Girls' Night Out—not with one elderly parent and two thirteen-year-olds in the group, not to mention a reunion with someone she hadn't seen in over twenty years. But, Gin reflected as she drove home, it was sure to be memorable—and it beat sitting home and worrying about things that she couldn't control.

14

During practice, Gin watched Olive running around the court, her long legs pumping, her ponytail flying. In a painful contrast, Cherie spent much of the practice shuffling out of the way, reaching for balls that she never quite seemed to catch and several times running into other girls. Gin had heard some of the other girls teasing her about being "a retard" and was grateful that Olive wasn't among them; but Olive steadfastly ignored both Cherie and Gin as though avoiding the possibility that Gin might try to pair them during drills.

Announcing to Olive that both girls would be going with her to a dinner party would be a challenge, but Gin was hoping that Olive would get through it with her usual cheer and good nature. As the practice wound down, she took Olive aside and explained briefly.

"I know this probably wouldn't be your first choice," she said, "but your Dad has his hands full and . . . well, I was hoping it might be an opportunity for you to get to know Cherie a little better."

"I don't *want* to know her better," Olive hissed back. "Why can't you understand that?"

Gin suppressed a sigh of frustration. She remembered being that age—appeals to Olive's better nature were unlikely to do anything but further frustrate her. "I *do* understand. And I know I can't tell you what to think or feel. All I expect is that you'll be polite to both Cherie and my friend and her family tonight." When Olive rolled her eyes, Gin bit back the urge to snap at her. "Can I count on you to do that?"

Olive refused to look at her, her mouth compressed in a stubborn frown. Finally she glanced up, eyes flashing with anger, and muttered, "You're not my mom!" before dashing away.

Gin shut her eyes and counted to ten, wondering if she was helping Olive or making things worse. Either way, they were committed at least for this one evening. She forced a smile on her face and found Cherie, explaining that she'd been invited to a special dinner with new friends. As they walked to the car, Olive held back, calling out good-byes to her friends, while Cherie chattered with Gin in excitement.

"I love tamales! They're my favorite." She handed Gin her bag, and as Gin set it into the back of the Range Rover, Olive caught up, silently glowering.

"Do you like tamales too?" Cherie said.

For a moment, Gin held her breath, hoping that Olive wouldn't take out her frustration on Cherie. At last, she muttered, "Sure, I guess," and got into the car. As both girls buckled up in the back seat, Gin silently prayed for a further thawing in their relationship.

She found a parking space halfway down the block of Rosa's street. She remembered visiting the neighborhood with her mother as a child before the worst of the economic downturn had taken hold of Trumbull. There had been an Italian bakery nearby, where her mother sometimes bought pink and green sugar cookies. Not far away had been a tobacconist where her father bought pipe tobacco before giving up smoking for good.

And nearly every other block featured a corner tavern, a place where the steelworkers stopped for a drink on their way home from the factories below.

As the factories closed and fortunes plunged, many of the former single-family homes had been converted to apartments, and later to rooming houses, places of last resort for people who were barely getting by. The neighborhood descended into an attitude of despair, and crime worsened as more and more jobs disappeared.

At its worst, entire blocks had been vacant, shop windows smashed and boarded up, and abandoned property piled on porches. Before Gin left for college, she'd vowed never to return to Trumbull voluntarily, and on her few visits home in the intervening years, she'd renewed her promise to herself.

Now, however, there were signs of renewal sprouting even on the worst streets, like crocuses poking their tender shoots through the snow in an early thaw. As they walked down the street to Rosa's, they passed a little bungalow, painted yellow and decorated with greens tied with a cheery red plaid ribbon, defiantly celebrating the season. A gas station across the street that once sold liquor now advertised organic milk and honey. And a man in a parka pulled two toddlers along the snowy sidewalk on a saucer-shaped sled, the children shrieking with laughter.

Rosa lived in a battered-looking gray house on a corner. It desperately needed a coat of paint and a new roof, but someone—Rosa?—had shoveled the porch and walkway and sprinkled salt on the steps. A little red wagon, filled with toys, was stowed in the corner of the porch.

Before Gin could ring the doorbell, the door burst open and Rosa greeted them with a warm smile. She had a squirming little boy in her arms and a smudge of sauce on her cheek, and her hair was escaping its ponytail, but she looked vivacious and pretty. When she'd come to Gin's aid the other night, she'd been covered up in a scarf and hat and coat; now Gin saw that she'd stayed trim and taken good care of herself. Her hair was glossy and a rich shade of brown, and her skin was unlined and lightly accented with makeup.

"Welcome, welcome!" she said. "This is Antonio. He's been talking about you for the last hour, but all of a sudden the cat's got his tongue."

"I like Legos," he said shyly, peeking out from under his impossibly long lashes. "Want to see?"

Olive, who'd silently focused on her phone on the whole drive over, slipped it into her pocket. "Sure," she said. "I like them a lot."

"Me too!" Cherie exclaimed.

Olive glanced at Gin with a guilty look on her face. "Maybe we could all three play Legos," she said quietly, and Gin realized that was her apology.

Antonio wriggled out of his mother's arms and ran up the stairs, and the girls trailed behind, Cherie chattering enthusiastically. Gin followed Rosa into the kitchen, where a tiny woman with a lined brown face and a long white braid was deftly folding a mound of masa dough and savory meat into a cornhusk.

"Mom, this is my friend Gin," she said. "Mom's famous for her tamales. People all around the neighborhood ask her to make them."

"I don't remember so good, but this I remember," the old woman said, adding the finished tamale to a tray and reaching in a bowl of water for another husk.

"Mom's already made enough for dinner and the freezer," Rosa said, wiping her hands on her apron. "These are for the family next door—they just brought a new baby home from the hospital."

Gin closed her eyes and inhaled the intoxicating aromas while Rosa opened two beers. She handed one to Gin, and they clinked their bottles together.

"To friendship," Rosa said.

*   *   *

A couple of hours later, stuffed with tamales and homemade orange pound cake, and pleasantly relaxed from the beer, Gin and Rosa finished the dishes and then moved to the living room to enjoy a cup of coffee. Mrs. Escamilla had gone to bed upstairs, tired from a full day of cooking. The girls were in the kitchen helping Antonio with a craft project that Rosa had planned for them, and to Gin's relief, everyone seemed to be getting along well. There were frequent bursts of laughter as they glued tiny beads to patterned frames to make Christmas ornaments.

"You've got your hands full," Gin observed, noticing a basket of clean clothes waiting to be folded and a stack of papers that Rosa had brought home from her job as an elementary school teacher. "When do you ever get to relax?"

Rosa laughed. "Trust me, every day is a vacation since I got rid of my ex-husband." She clapped her hand over her mouth in mock dismay. "Sorry. It's just that I'm so careful to stay positive around Antonio, and I hardly ever have a chance to let loose and say what I really think."

"Does he have a good relationship with his father?" Gin asked diplomatically.

"For the most part, yes. He doesn't need to know that Sam's usually late with his support payment, if he sends it at all, or that if I didn't remind him, he would forget to come to Antonio's choir concerts." She reflected for a moment. "Sam's lazy and irresponsible, but at least he's a lot better than my father. My mom had to raise me and my brother with no help at all after he went to prison. Most of the time, she worked two jobs.

So now that she has dementia, I'm going to keep her at home for as long as I can. She deserves the best."

Gin was searching for words to express her admiration when there was a knock at the door.

"That's probably Cherie's dad," Gin said. "He's picking her up here on his way home from work—I hope that's okay."

"Sure, the more, the merrier," Rosa said cheerfully.

She opened the door, and there was Tuck standing with his hat in his hands, snow dusting the shoulders of his coat. "Ma'am," he said politely.

Gin noticed a change come over Rosa—a stiffening, a sense of apprehension—and she wondered if she should have mentioned in advance that he was a police officer. The relationship between the residents of this neighborhood and the police had been a rocky one and had worsened in recent years as policing practices came under scrutiny all over the country.

Nevertheless, Rosa was perfectly polite, if slightly formal. "Please come in," she said. "We've enjoyed having Cherie visit. Would you have some cake?"

"Dad!" Cherie screeched, running into the room, holding her ornament carefully with both hands. She threw her arms around her father and hugged him hard. "I had the best day! Look what I made!"

The light in Tuck's tired eyes broke the tension. "Hiya, Princess," he said.

Cherie rolled her eyes. "Dad, I'm *not* a princess. He only calls me that 'cause we read books about princesses sometimes," she explained to Rosa. "It's dumb." Then she dashed back into the kitchen.

Tuck stayed for cake and coffee, but after praising Rosa's cooking and thanking her repeatedly for inviting Cherie, he stood and called for his daughter. "Time to go. School tomorrow."

"Five more minutes!" Cherie pleaded. "Please, please, *please!*"

"No, you said that five minutes ago. It's time to go home now. Let's get your things." He followed Cherie into the kitchen so that she could get the rest of the ornaments she'd made.

"I'd better get going too," Gin said, standing and stretching. "I had such a wonderful time. Let's get together again soon."

"I'd like that," Rosa said. She pressed a sack of tamales into Gin's hands, then whispered confidentially, "He's a nice man, and handsome—anything going on between you two?"

Gin laughed, caught by surprise and embarrassment. She hadn't mentioned Jake this evening, and she tried to tell herself that it was only because the children and Rosa's mother were present and so conversation hadn't gotten around to personal matters.

"Absolutely not," she said. "I'm . . . well, it's complicated. When we get together again, I'll tell you all about it."

"You have a deal," Rosa smiled. "One of these days, I hope to start dating again, but between Antonio and Mom, I haven't made the time. So I guess my life is complicated too."

The girls trooped into the room after Tuck, and they all said their good-byes, Antonio begging them to come back again soon.

Outside, the snow had begun again.

"You girls go get in my car," Tuck said. "I'll get your things out of Gin's car."

As they walked down the street, Tuck put his hand under her elbow to help her keep her balance on the slick sidewalks. Gin wondered if she should say something about Cherie, perhaps apologize for the behavior of some of the girls on the team. But then she decided that Tuck was probably well aware of his daughter's social challenges.

"Rosa seems nice," Tuck said. "It took her a minute to warm up to me, though."

"I imagine it can be difficult to be a police officer these days," Gin said diplomatically. "The press isn't particularly fair, in my opinion."

"It's all just part of the—hey, I thought you were going to get a rental. Where did you get this heap of junk?"

Gin laughed. "Better not let my dad hear you say that. He loves this old thing. They keep it around for trips to the mountains."

"Doesn't look especially safe to me," Tuck said. "You need new tires, at the very least—these are half bald. I'm surprised Crosby lets you drive around in this thing."

Gin bristled at his words and tried to pretend it was only indignation. But there was something undeniably appealing about his concern for her—and about his firm grip on her hand as he helped her over an icy patch.

"I'm perfectly capable of buying a new set of tires without anyone's help, Tuck," she said crisply.

He put his hand on her shoulder and gazed directly into her eyes. "Then do it. I'd prefer to know that you *and* my daughter are safe on the road. Which . . . by the way, thank you again."

"You're welcome, again," Gin said. "It's not . . ."

Her words trailed off as awareness of how close Tuck was standing somehow interfered with her ability to speak.

"Looks like you're mending," he said, his voice going low and hoarse as he finally released her arm. "I talked to Griffin Rudkin today. He swears he wasn't anywhere near Trumbull last night. But I'm going to follow up with his brothers."

"I—I suppose that's a good idea," Gin said, trying to focus on Tuck's words and coming up short. She could feel his breath, warm on her face. He was standing too close—she could practically count the teeth in the zipper of his parka, see the flakes of snow caught in his eyelashes before they melted.

What was she doing here, lingering under a star-studded sky in the twinkling light of the holiday decorations lining the street, like a scene in a romantic comedy? Gin's flash of guilt was tempered by the knowledge that Jake was in another city tonight, meeting with an attorney he'd never mentioned to her, discussing problems he wouldn't share with her. It wasn't fair to compare him with the man in front of her, but she had a brief and unwelcome flash of wondering what Tuck's lips might feel like on hers, his shadow of beard scraping along the hollow of her neck, his hands . . .

Gin shook her head, banishing that train of thought. "I need to go," she blurted. "I've—it's late and—"

Tuck cleared his throat and stepped backward. "And I got the fire investigators' preliminary report back," he said in a gravelly voice laced with regret. "They found traces of the accelerant around the perimeter of the house. It's going to be ruled deliberate, Gin. You should let Jake know that it's going to be a while before the investigation is over."

Gin's heart sank. The moment was broken—and it was a good thing too, because she'd been in danger of forgetting that Jake's fate rested at least partly in this man's hands.

"I'm sorry to hear that," she murmured. "Especially because I know that he's innocent of anything except trying to make an honest living."

Tuck gave a stiff nod, then hesitated. "Look, I'm probably out of line," he said, "but this isn't the first time you've gotten dragged down by Crosby. I'm the last person to accuse anyone before they've been proven guilty—but I can't help noticing that you don't seem happy." He searched her eyes with his own, unspoken emotions plain on his face. "You deserve better, frankly. You deserve a man who has the desire and the means to give you what you need."

Abruptly he turned away, walking around to the back of the Land Rover to get the girls' gym bags out of the back. "All right. Thanks again," he called, not turning back. "I'm sure we'll talk soon."

Gin watched him walk back down the street, his back ram-rod straight, carrying the two bright-pink bags.

The evening was over. She was headed home to an empty house, feeling no more settled about any aspect of her life than she had when the day began.

*   *   *

Jake was back from the city the next morning by a little before ten.

"You got your Dad's car?" he asked when he came through the door. "Don't you think you'd be better off with a rental?"

That made two men who wanted to tell her what to drive. "It's fine," she said through gritted teeth. "I like it."

"Okay, sorry. I didn't mean anything by it. I just want you to be safe."

Gin regretted speaking so sharply. "I picked up muffins in town. Would you like me to heat one up?"

"No thanks. I need a shower," he said. "I'll be back down in a few minutes."

"How was your meeting with the attorney?" she asked when he returned, dressed in work clothes, his face shadowed by several days' growth of beard.

"Fine. All good. Look, I'm sorry, but I need to get over to the site. Can we talk more later?"

Gin kept her hurt to herself. She watched him drive back down the hill, his truck making fresh tracks in the snow, and decided to bury herself in work. She needed to catch up on e-mail and arrange a time to speak with the professor who was studying the uniform.

The hours ticked by slowly, Gin's mood improving as she delved further into the e-mails that had accumulated in her in-box. Work had always been a reliable salve when she was feeling down, and it was no different now that she was work-ing as a consultant. She was reviewing the soil analysis that

Stephen had forwarded when her phone rang. She glanced at the time and was surprised to see it was already midafternoon.

She checked her phone's screen: Jake. Maybe he'd be ready to knock off early, and they could catch dinner in town. Maybe they could even see if there were any movies playing that were worth seeing.

"Hello?"

"Gin . . . something's happened." He sounded tense, his voice clipped.

"What?"

"They're protesting. A dozen of them at least, at the site. They showed up on a bus half an hour ago."

"At the construction site?" Gin repeated. "Why?"

"They want the whole thing shut down for good." Jake sounded like he was struggling to stay calm. "They're claiming it's historically significant. They've called in the Civil War Sites Advisory Commission—I didn't even know there was such a thing. Apparently if they can prove beyond a reasonable doubt that events of historical significance took place on that land, the National Park Service can get it a protected designation."

"But—how would they ever be able to prove that?" Gin asked. "The ME's office isn't anywhere near ready to confirm that the body's Civil War era. And even if they did—one dead soldier doesn't mean anything."

"They want the whole area excavated," Jake said wearily. "They say that riverine transport patterns support the possibility that this was a burial ground—that boats transporting the dead might have gotten stuck here during bad weather and decided to bury the dead rather than attempting to transport them any farther."

"But that's—that's pure speculation," Gin said. "They've found relics from the war all over the county. What with Pittsburgh being a major hub for rail and river transport, there were troops through here on a regular basis. If they set aside every acre where something happened during the war, this whole town would be a historic site."

"Well, according to the very brief conversation I had with the protestors, they might like to see that happen," Jake said. "I don't think they give a shit that I'm trying to make a living here. I tried to talk to them, but they're already trying to get an emergency injunction to stop me from building. Maybe forever."

Gin could hear them now—the indistinct sounds of shouting and chanting. She turned over what Jake was telling her in her mind. Was it possible that the protestors could move the investigation in the direction they apparently wanted—even without confirmation that the evidence backed them up? "I can't believe they can do that. Can't your attorney help?"

"I've already called him, but it's not his area."

"Not his—"

"Look, Gin, he's a bankruptcy attorney, okay?" Jake burst out. "I didn't want to talk about—I *don't* want to talk about it, at least not until I know I'm going to have to—look, he's trying to get me a referral, but meantime, I need a favor. I thought your mom . . . maybe she can do something. Make some calls. Talk to the city council. Something."

Gin tried to come up with a response, but she was stuck on what Jake had admitted. She'd had no idea that his finances were so precarious. It explained his moodiness, but there wasn't time for her to try to adjust to this new information—and he'd made it clear that she was to mind her own business on the subject.

"What about the police?" she finally ventured. "Did you call them?"

Jake cursed. "They're useless. They're just standing around, doing nothing. They're almost as bad as the protestors. I asked them to keep the media out, and they can't even seem to do that. In fact, just while I've been talking to you, another news van just drove up."

"Okay," Gin said, thinking fast. "I'll call Mom, but I may not be able to get a hold of her right away if she's in meetings. And then I'll come over."

"You don't need to."

"It's fine, I don't have anything going on this afternoon."

"Seriously Gin, there's no need. Look, thanks for calling your mom—I've got to go." He hesitated, and the silence stretched between them. "I'm sorry about all of this," he said in a rush. "Talk to you later."

He hung up before Gin could respond, and she was left staring at her phone.

She walked to the tall windows at the front of the house and stared out at the valley spread out below, the river winding lazily through town, the sun glinting off the bridges visible both up and down the river. The snow from earlier in the week had given way to a bright, bitterly cold afternoon. Snow sparkled, crystalline and brittle, in the branches of the trees. Ice skimmed the windshield of her father's car.

One hundred and fifty years earlier, the river had teemed with soldiers heading south to fight, as well as the cargo provided by the northern cities. Pittsburgh's armories and foundries had provided weapons and ammunition, and her passenger tugboats were converted to cargo transport craft. When the war department grew concerned that the South might target Pittsburgh for invasion, forts were constructed around the city to protect it.

What were the odds that the remains discovered on Jake's jobsite had lain there for so long? Gin was trained to remain objective, and she'd certainly seen her share of cases that defied the conclusions one might draw at first glance. As a medical examiner, she had to resist the temptation to believe she knew what had caused a person's death, no matter the condition of the body before her.

Her instincts were telling her that the man had died much more recently than the protestors believed. Now her task was to separate that conclusion into what was based on empirical evidence and what was owed to her personal bias. It was a challenge for even the most careful pathologists, one that her mentor had trained her to take seriously.

In addition to the deliberate removal of the teeth and the shallowness of the burial, something else was nagging at the back of her mind, some detail of the body's condition that didn't quite fit, but she'd been unable to identify it in the days since she attended the autopsy. Now as she stared out at the wintry scene, the details stored in her subconscious mind shifted and settled . . . and something came to the fore.

Gin ran to the computer to check the autopsy files. She reviewed the photographs, finding the one she was looking for, and grabbed her phone.

She still had Stillman's number stored in her contacts from when he was investigating her sister's death. He picked up on the first ring.

"Detective Stillman here."

"Detective, this is Gin Sullivan. I'm calling because I think there's evidence that the body on Jake's land isn't from the Civil War after all. I think he died sometime in the last century."

"And what makes you say that?"

"The old injury to his wrist. The Colles fracture—do you remember it?"

"I remember something about a broken wrist, yeah."

"It was actually a very specific subtype of fracture commonly called a chauffeur's break. It happens when the scaphoid bone of the hand is compressed against the styloid process of the distal radius. The first time doctors started seeing it in patients was during the early twentieth century when automobiles had hand cranks to start the engine. When the engine backfired, the crank would spin along with the crankshaft and strike the operator with sufficient force to break bone."

"So? You're telling me that the body's a hundred years old? That seems like pretty thin evidence. There's no other way to break a bone that way?"

"Well . . . it's possible, I suppose, if a person fell on their outstretched hand at just the right angle. But extremely unlikely. In all my years of practice, I've never seen one happen like that. In fact, I've only seen it once before, and it turned out to be in an antique car enthusiast who had tried to crank his vintage Model T."

"But it *is* possible."

"Yes, but there's more. The fact that the initial break is still visible in the bone without any attendant deformity suggests that it was manipulated surgically—that a doctor went in and realigned the fragments to restore normal anatomy."

"But if there was a plate or screws or something, you would have seen it, right?"

"Yes, but it's possible it could have been done completely with casting. There would be no evidence given the condition of the remains."

"And you're telling me they hadn't invented casts yet during the Civil War?"

"Well . . . no, actually. Plaster of Paris casts were first used in Europe in the 1850s, but it took a while for them to gain widespread use here. The odds of the technique being used in a battlefield setting at that time are—well, extremely unlikely."

"There's that word again, Dr. Sullivan," Stillman said. "*Unlikely.* Which, as you know, doesn't amount to a hill of beans in court. Let me ask you something. Could you be bringing this up because it would be convenient for your boyfriend to be able to send those protestors home? If it didn't come so close to home, would you have even brought up this so-called evidence?"

"But they don't have any evidence either," Gin protested. "The results of the autopsy were inconclusive. There's simply no way to know the age of the remains."

"I don't know about that. The uniform's real, according to your colleague Stephen Harper."

"Not necessarily. It's still being studied, and—"

"Then let's put off talking about this until you've got more proof. Listen, Doc, I don't know if you've seen the news yet, but the media's loving this story. It's been picked up nationwide. And Wheeler's all over the press coverage."

"Why does she care? If the protestors are right, there isn't a crime here, other than the arson, and all that press attention is going to dry up fast. And if the protesters are wrong, and it ends up being a murder, that will be the wrong kind of press attention—she'll want to minimize the coverage of the county's handling of it, because they'll look incompetent."

"We're on site monitoring the protest," Stillman said. "Every image going out to the media has county police officers in the picture. Wheeler knows that protestors don't help when you're running for office. And even if this is just a bunch of history nuts, she still stands to score a few points if she can make them happy. If she plays it right and gets the Park Service to designate it a historic site, she can ride that publicity for months."

Gin had a sick feeling in her gut. If the police captain was determined to satisfy the protestors, then she'd have little motivation to press for further investigation.

"When are they going to make a ruling?" she asked.

"They're asking a judge for an injunction this week," Stillman said. "Then they'll try to tie it up in court until they get the official designation. Listen, Doc, you're just going to have to face the fact that Jake's project isn't going anywhere. He needs to accept his losses and move on."

Gin hung up and resisted the temptation to throw the phone across the room. There had to be something else she could do. She dressed in boots, thick leggings, and layers and wound a warm scarf around her neck.

After scraping the ice from the Land Rover's windshield, she was warm everywhere but her fingers, which felt numb in her thin leather gloves. As she sat in the car waiting for the old engine to warm up, she called her mother, but the call went into voice mail.

"I'll call you back as soon as I can," her mother's recorded voice promised briskly.

"Mom . . . it's Gin. Um, listen, Jake needs—we need—a little help." She deliberated about giving more information. She wasn't sure what Madeleine could do to help. And besides, there was the possibility that the protestors were right. "Look, just call me when you can, okay?"

She hesitated a moment before adding "Love you" and hanging up.

They weren't a "love you" kind of family. Richard had been preoccupied with work, and Madeleine had been a caring but coolly efficient mother. She showed her love by being present in her daughters' lives, volunteering in their schools and helping them with their homework and making their after-school snacks. But no one could ever have called her affectionate.

Since returning to Trumbull, Gin had found herself wanting to strengthen the bond between her and her parents. Two decades of a fairly distant familial relationship no longer felt like enough.

And, she thought as she maneuvered the Land Rover carefully into town, there was also nothing like a harrowing brush with death to make a person's emotions go into overdrive. Though she'd deliberately underplayed the danger when she described her accident to her parents, the small-town grapevine was bound to alert them to the truth.

And when that happened, Gin was going to have some explaining to do.

15

She heard them before she saw them, even through her car's closed windows. When she rounded the bend at the top of the ridge, the first thing she saw was a bus bearing a hand-painted banner draped from the windows reading, "Respect Living History—Post 133!"

Two dozen men and women—and a handful of children—marched back and forth in front of the burnt skeleton of the house. Some of them were dressed in Civil War costumes, with both confederate and union soldiers represented among their ranks. A few held signs saying, "Don't Bury Our Past" and "This Is Sacred Ground."

Next to the bus, two county police cruisers were parked end to end, effectively sealing off the approach to the site. Behind them were two news vans and half a dozen other vehicles, including Jake's truck parked next to one of the unfinished houses in what would have been the driveway. Reporters appeared to be trying to interview the protestors as several cameramen filmed the action.

The county officers didn't appear to be doing anything other than watching. There were no Trumbull police present that Gin could see.

She spotted Jake, on the opposite side of the site, standing on what would be the porch of one of the unfinished homes. Even from a distance, Gin could read the fury in his body language. He stood ramrod straight, his fists clenched at his sides. He was glaring at the reporter interviewing a paunchy middle-aged man in an ill-fitting officer's uniform, complete with shiny brass buttons and an ornamental sword. The call letters on the equipment the cameraman was using identified a Pittsburgh station, and the female reporter looked familiar. Gin edged forward to hear what she was saying.

". . . embattled local building contractor Jake Crosby, who was a person of interest in the Lily Sullivan case that plagued this town last year. Though cleared of murder charges in that case, Crosby is once again finding himself under scrutiny of law enforcement in this bizarre case of arson and murder. Rumored to be facing financial devastation, Crosby is sus-pected of setting the blaze to his half-finished project himself.

"And in a truly shocking twist, a body discovered on this property is rumored to belong to a soldier who fought for the Union during the Civil War. Joining me now is Tim Pagano, a reenactor and amateur Civil War historian from Cham-bersburg, who made the three-hour trip here today to, in his words, make sure that history isn't sacrificed to greed. Wel-come, Mr. Pagano."

The protestor nodded stiffly. "Thanks, Melanie."

"You've written a book on the Battle of Hanover, which you published yourself, about a chapter of the war that you believe has been unfairly overlooked by historians, is that correct?"

"Well, first, Melanie, let me start by saying that we prefer the term 'living historian' to reenactor. We feel that by recreat-ing historically accurate—"

"But now the body of a soldier may have been discovered just a few yards from where we're standing," the reporter interrupted smoothly. "Some experts believe that this site overlooking the Monongahela River may in fact have been a burial ground for soldiers who were too gravely injured to make it home. How likely is that, in your opinion?"

"What you have to understand is that there's a lot that never got recorded back then," Pagano said. "Communications in general just didn't happen. It's not like there was CNN or Facebook or what have you. In the Battle of Hanover, for instance, and you can read all about this in my book *Hell in Hanover*, which you can get on Amazon, Confederate Major General Heth's infantry division literally ran smack into Buford's Union cavalry. It wasn't planned, it wasn't—"

"Right, but in terms of the body discovered here. It was dressed in what is reported to be a Union infantry uniform. Would it have resembled the costume you're wearing today?"

Pagano goggled at the reporter, seemingly astonished at her question. "This isn't a *costume*; it's a historically accurate *replica*. And it's an officer's uniform. The braid and insignia here mean that I'm a first sergeant."

"I see. And just one more question for you." She attempted to arrange her smooth, Botoxed features into an attitude of concern. "If protected status is conferred every time a historic artifact is discovered, a great many homes and businesses could be threatened. What would you say to those who stand to lose a great deal of money if that comes to pass?"

"It's for the greater good," Pagano said witheringly. "I'm not talking about slapping a 'Lincoln Slept Here' sign on some motel. This is a sacred resting place for a soldier who lost his life in one of our nation's great conflicts. And he might not be the only one. This area should be examined carefully and respectfully, not paved over so that a millionaire can put in a tennis court."

"Mmm. How long do you and your group plan to protest?"

"Until the decision is made to respect history. As long as it takes."

"All right, well, thanks for speaking with us, and stay warm out here."

She stayed motionless, grinning at the camera, for several seconds and then abruptly switched off her mic and handed it to the cameraman, dropping the smile. She headed back to the news van, while Pagano wandered back to join the other protestors and picked up a sign reading, "What Is the Price of History?"

Jake had made his way over to Gin while the interview was going on. "Did you talk to your mom?"

"I left a message," Gin said. "She'll probably call me back this afternoon. She's got—"

"If people pay attention to this, it's not even going to matter if it's true or not." He raked his hand through his hair in frustration. "And that's assuming I can convince them that this emergency injunction is bullshit. If they get *that* past a judge, I'm sunk."

"Jake . . ." Gin hadn't been planning to bring it up, but Jake seemed to be starting to panic. "I was just wondering, I talked to Brandon Hart the other night. He happened to mention that he knows a banker you worked with and—"

The flash of anger in his eyes stopped her. "What were you talking about?"

"I'm sorry. Never mind."

"No, tell me. What does a guy who barely knows me, who I've talked to a total of maybe four times in my life for more than a hello, have to tell my girlfriend about me that she doesn't already know?"

The word *girlfriend* caught Gin's attention. They'd never put their relationship into words, not since they were teens. Though they'd once said *I love you* every single day, neither of them had since reuniting. It was as though she had become so leery of commitment that even the words were off limits.

"Look, Jake, I'm just worried about you, okay."

"Worried enough to ask someone besides me about my finances? That's what you were doing, right?"

It was pointless to correct him when he was so angry, so Gin didn't bother to explain that Brandon had volunteered the information. "Listen, Jake—I know none of this is your fault. I know you couldn't have predicted any of it. I want to help. Just for now, just until you get this all straightened out. We could put it in writing if you want, you could decide on the terms—"

"*No*. Gin . . . I'm sorry, and I know you're trying to help, but I just can't."

Jake turned and walked away, his words hanging in the air against a backdrop of chanting voices.

*   *   *

An hour later, Gin was waiting quietly outside her mother's office, listening to her talking on the phone. She'd beaten a hasty retreat from the jobsite when several reporters recognized her from news coverage of previous cases and badgered her for an interview. Gin knew that her connection to the case would be speculated on in the media, but she had no intention of making the reporters' jobs any easier.

It was strange to hear her mother—who had once tested Gin on her Spanish vocabulary words, who had sung soprano in the church choir for over a decade—speaking with such authority to a caller whose hopes were clearly being dashed.

Finally, she finished the conversation with "I'll remind you that you said that when the new reserve expenditure report comes in."

Gin poked her head in the door. "Got a few minutes?"

Madeleine gave her a tired smile. "For you? Absolutely. I've made eleven calls this morning already, I've got fourteen more to go, and none of the committees are meeting their budgetary targets. If I'd known I'd have to wear so many hats, I might never have gotten into this."

"Aw, you love it, Mom," Gin said. "You're a natural. Listen, I was wondering . . ."

She described the situation at the jobsite, leaving out Jake's reaction and the perilous state of his finances. "I just wondered if you'd be able to, I don't know . . ."

"Suppress free speech?" her mother asked, lifting an eyebrow. "That's generally frowned on, I find."

Gin sighed. "I know. I'm not even sure how you could help. I'm just . . . well, I'm worried about Jake. He isn't handling the stress well."

Both women were silent for a moment.

"I'm worried about your dad too," Madeleine finally admitted. "Retirement isn't exactly agreeing with him. What is it with these guys?"

At the time of Richard's abrupt retirement, he claimed he wanted to spend more time gardening, playing golf with the retired judge who lived across the street, and writing some articles for professional journals. But with the onset of winter, he'd put the gardening tools and golf clubs away in the garage and had yet to even begin doing the background research for the writing he claimed to want to do. Instead, he spent most of the day reading in his office, sometimes napping before dinner.

"I don't know, Mom. It's been a hard time for both of them."

"You know what I think? Men are ill equipped for the challenges that we women are forced to take in stride."

"Maybe. But you know that if you ever retired, you wouldn't be able to stay away. You'd be right back here the next week, offering to do the same job for free."

Madeleine grimaced. "I practically do it for free already."

"And if a bunch of protesters tried to stop you from getting your work done?"

Madeleine set her jaw. "I guess I'd just keep doing it—right up until they hauled me off to jail. Is that what you're worried will happen to Jake?"

"I don't know," Gin said. "I've never seen him like this."

"Gin. Right now you're focusing on things you can't do anything about. Jake will let you help or not. The protesters will get their way or not. Meanwhile, you're wasting time sitting here talking to me. If you really want to help, what else can you do?"

Gin blew out a breath in frustration. "I already talked my way into the autopsy by claiming to have skills no one else in the ME's office had. This time, though, I just sat there with everyone else going yeah, I have no idea how he died, but he suffered blunt force trauma to the skull, which was totally obvious because he's missing all his teeth. And the one thing I noticed that other people missed turned out to be unhelpful." She briefly described the evidence of a fracture.

"So maybe it's not the autopsy that you need to concentrate on. What else is going on in the investigation?"

Gin thought. "Well, they sent the uniform to a professor up at the University of Pittsburgh. I'm supposed to meet with her when she's had a chance to examine it."

"Don't wait," Madeleine said. "Put some pressure on her. Besides, academics love it whenever anyone asks for their opinions."

"Good point. And we got some of the soil analysis back, but there's nothing unusual about it. High acidity, as we expected, and the usual gamut of mineral and organic features."

"Okay, well, I guess you better do what I do, then," Madeleine said, picking up her phone. "Pound the pavement and kick some ass. Now excuse me while I raise my quota of hell for the day."

*   *   *

Dr. Pia Farrar was as pleased to hear from Gin as Madeleine had predicted. Her office was located in the basement of a beautiful old brown-brick building in the original campus. "They offered me an office in the new liberal arts building," she said as they walked down the stairs. "State of the art everything. But I'd miss this place. It's usually quiet as a tomb down here, and this is where we store a lot of the oldest materials after they're digitized. Any time I want to experience that library smell that you can't get in libraries anymore, I just step next door."

"Reminds me of my med school days," Gin said. "I used to study in the old Harper Memorial Library at the University of Chicago. I could get lost in the history of that place."

"Well, I can't promise you anything like that, but I took over an unused office for this project. Come this way."

Pia grabbed her laptop, led Gin down the hall, and unlocked a heavy wooden door. She stepped inside, snapping on a bank of fluorescent lights that sputtered to life. On a long wooden library table marred with a century's worth of graffiti, the remains of the uniform belonging the dead man were arranged on a white fabric surface, sections marked with fine pins and brightly colored tabs. Pia opened her laptop and turned it so Gin could see, scrolling through a long, dense document's text that was interspersed with photographs of the evidence.

"Radiocarbon dating has been around since the forties, as you probably already know."

"Care to give me a recap as it relates to this?"

"Well, it's actually pretty simple. The parts of the uniform that survived were made primarily of wool, which is an organic material. The minute the sheep was relieved of its wool, it stopped exchanging carbon with its environment, and from that moment on, the amount of carbon it contains began to decrease in a process called radioactive decay. The older the sample, the smaller the amount of carbon remaining."

"Yes, of course. I should have explained my background." Gin gave Pia a brief summary of her work. "But I don't know much about textiles."

"Oh, okay. Well, I put a tiny fiber sample under the microscope. Wool's morphological features are pretty distinctive." She scrolled to a magnified image of dull gray fiber. "You see the scalelike areas here. And this—the slightly darker column here—this is the medulla, or the central air space that runs along the length of the fiber shaft.

"Once I established that it was wool, I used fluorescence to determine what the original dyes might have looked like. You're familiar with the technique?"

"To some extent—the analysts I've worked with have used it to track blood stains on clothing, for instance."

"Right. Well, I simulated daylight, ultraviolet light, and infrared, and photographed the fragments with special film and light-filtering equipment. You can see the result here." She scrolled down to a photograph of a fragment—in a beautiful cornflower blue, the same shade as the reenactors' uniforms.

"Federal blue, I believe it's called," Pia said with satisfaction. "A term that dates to the Civil War."

"So you're certain," Gin said. "There's no way someone could have faked the age of the fibers?"

"No, there really isn't."

"What about if they'd come across a vintage uniform? I spent a little time online, and I saw that you can buy all kinds of Civil War memorabilia on eBay."

"Sure. Buttons, maybe. Anything made of metal . . . including some of the metallic embroidery threads and braids. But to find an entire uniform . . . it would be difficult."

"But people stumble on old uniforms in trunks up in their attics all the time."

Pia smiled. "Not all the time, but you're right; they do turn up now and then. But they're usually pretty fragile. I'm not sure anyone would deliberately expose them to the stress of everyday wear. Listen, if you don't mind me asking, is there really any question that the remains are authentic? Judging from what's been on the news, I thought it was pretty open and shut."

"I suppose," Gin said. She didn't want to explain her special interest in the case, so she settled for saying, "As a consultant on the case, my job is to investigate every loose thread."

"So to speak," Pia said, giggling. "Sorry, can't help it—anthropology humor. Listen, there is one more thing . . ."

She picked up a tray from the counter. "They sent over a soil sample that I understand was taken from the burial site."

"Yes, that's correct."

"Well, it didn't really shed any new light on the textile analysis. But I discovered something you'll probably find interesting."

She set the tray down on the table. In the center, nested against the white fabric, was a small rounded lump of bronze-colored metal.

"I believe that's a musket ball," Pia said. "Not my area of expertise, but I had a colleague take a look at it. It's definitely consistent with munitions of the era, apparently. It was lodged in that sample you sent over, completely covered in dirt, but it could easily have traveled from the body to the soil as decomposition progressed. So maybe you found your cause of death after all."

Gin examined the ball, which looked like a misshapen iron marble. "May I take this?" she asked.

"Sure, I guess. They said they'd send someone to pick this all up, but they didn't say when."

"I'll make sure to let them know," Gin promised, not meeting Pia's eyes.

They walked back to Pia's office and said their good-byes. "I really appreciate everything you've shared with me," Gin said.

"It's been my pleasure. Come back anytime."

As Gin walked up the old marble steps, their surface polished and worn from thousands of footfalls, she fingered the lump of metal in her pocket.

What was it her mother had said? "Pound the pavement and kick some ass."

Maybe Madeleine had a point.

*   *   *

When she got to her car, she called Baxter.

"Hi, Gin," he said guardedly. "Look, this isn't really a good time, so unless this is something important—"

"It is. Look, I called you because I don't trust the county cops to follow up. I've got the bullet that may have killed our unidentified soldier. Or I guess I should say, the musket ball."

There was a silence, and then Baxter said, in an entirely different tone, "Where?"

Gin quickly explained her visit to the university. "I'm afraid if I turn this over to them, they won't even follow up, given how eager they are to wrap this all up. I was wondering . . . do you know anyone who could tell us if it's real?"

"I do—I've got a friend who does some consulting on this type of thing. But what exactly are you hoping for?"

Gin drew a breath. "The truth, I suppose. This thing was found in the soil underneath the body. Not *in* the body. I'm not sure how much a ballistics expert can tell from an artifact this old, but maybe they can at least tell if it was fired."

"Even if this gives more credibility to the case for shutting down the site."

"If you're suggesting I'd hold this back to cover it up—"

"I've seen people do a lot worse and justify it to themselves."

"No. Absolutely not." Maybe it was a product of the job Gin had done for so long, but not pursuing the truth was unthinkable. "Look, it doesn't prove anything. There was no damage to the skeleton that would indicate a gunshot wound, but the ball could have missed the bones entirely. Or it could have been fired many years ago, then someone could have dropped it in the hole with the body for reasons of their own."

"Then why are we even bothering?"

"Because I don't know what else to do," Gin said. "Because Jake's barely speaking to me, and I don't know how else to help."

Gin could practically sense Tuck deliberating. "Look, Gin. If we do this, it's completely off the record. You can't reveal I helped you."

"Understood."

"Where are you now?"

"Still at the university, why?"

"There's a bar in Squirrel Hill, not too far from where you are. I can be there in an hour." He gave her the address.

"And you're sure your friend can meet us?"

"Oh, yeah, I'm pretty sure. If you don't hear from me, assume I'll be there. I'll let my friend know to expect you—his name's Dusty, and he's pretty hard to miss."

"Okay. Look, I'm not expecting much. This probably is just going to make their case for them. But I guess . . . well, I guess I need to know the truth. There's a lot riding on this, and . . . well, I don't want to look back and think I didn't do everything I could."

She could hear him breathing. After another long pause, he finally said, "I can clear out of here in a few minutes. I'll be there as fast as I can."

"Okay. See you soon. And . . . Tuck?"

"Yeah?"

"Thanks."

16

The Squirrel Hill neighborhood of the East End of Pittsburgh was a lively mix of shops and restaurants and old houses and apartment buildings where hip, young students rubbed elbows with longtime residents, recent immigrants, and artists. The bar Tuck had directed her to, however, was in a seedy pocket catercorner from an abandoned gas station and wedged between a decrepit apartment building and a body shop. There was no sign out front, and Gin knew she was in the right place only because, as she drove by the address dubiously, two men stumbled out of the door looking like they'd spent the entire day hunched at the bar.

She found a parking spot around the corner and walked back with a sense of trepidation. Tuck wouldn't be here for a while, and she could have waited in the car except that it was too cold.

A cup of coffee would be nice. But she doubted that this place brewed fresh coffee very often.

It took a moment for her eyes to adjust to the dim lighting. There was the gentle knock of pool balls against each other and the murmur of conversation from a couple of women in their sixties who'd taken a booth in the corner and were smoking cigarettes, exhaling toward the window, which they'd opened slightly. Gin could feel the draft from where she stood and headed toward the back of the long, narrow room. She found a seat at the end of the bar and was eying the long rows of bottles when a man rose from a table and lumbered over to join her.

He was not a tall man, but he was thick and powerfully built, every inch of exposed skin up to his jaw covered in elaborate, scrolling tattoos. His muscular arms bulged in his tight-fitting T-shirt, and when he sat down on the stool next to her, his presence panicked her for a moment.

"You Gin?"

She gave him a weak smile, relief washing through her. "I am. And you must be Dusty."

He laughed. "Only to Baxter, and a few other donuts. To everyone else, I'm William."

"Donuts?"

The bartender materialized with a bottle and a glass and poured an inch of amber liquid, pushing it across the bar without a word. Then he pointed at the bar in front of Gin.

"He don't say much," William said. "What are you having?"

"A Coke?"

The bartender nodded impassively and moved away.

"Okay, so 'donuts' was a nickname our class of recruits earned. Tuck and I went through academy together. He didn't tell you that?"

"No, actually."

"Yeah, we had some real clowns in that bunch. A few of us got into the habit of meeting in this little donut shop before class. Not many of 'em around anymore. Hell, I went out on disability almost fifteen years ago." He patted his knee. "Went over a fence I should have left alone, spent three months in a cast and came back hooked on painkillers. Took another couple of years to sort *that* mess out. Anyway, now I set my own hours, pick my clients . . . it's all good."

"Tuck says you have your own consulting business."

"Yeah, mostly testing new product. I work with weapons man-ufacturers in the design phase, run their testing prior to qualify-ing. And I've done some work with body armor, especially when they come out with new armor-piercing rounds. But I do a little private client work on the side." He paused, searching her face. "Very private, which I understand is what you're looking for."

Gin dug the sample bag from her purse. "So I need to know if this is authentic," she said. "Do you know anything about Civil War–era armaments?"

"Oh, hell yeah," William said, his eyes lighting up. "Kind of a specialty of mine. I work with some reenactors—those dudes are freaks about the details, you know? I've worked with muskets, breech loaders, all kinds of shit. This is pretty stan-dard, though. Called a minié ball. They cast these things with whatever they could get their hands on—lead, obviously, but there's often an iron plug in the core. It's made to expand when fired, see, so it didn't have to be the same diameter of the bar-rel. Made it a lot easier to load—which was kind of the point if you had someone running at you with a bayonet."

"Looks like you two started the party without me." Tuck came walking toward them and clapped William on the shoul-der. "I see you've already made each other's acquaintance."

"Dude, you said she was hot," William said. "You didn't say *how* hot."

Tuck raised his eyebrows and scowled. "I said no such thing. Please excuse him, Gin."

"Sorry. Okay, prissy pants, you said she was an 'attractive brunette.' I mean, who even talks that way? Still spending your evenings playing Madden NFL? Tell Cherie her Uncle Dusty says hi, by the way."

Tuck laughed. "Tell you what, I'll buy a round—why don't you guys get a table?"

"Take my seat," William said, finishing off his beer. "This won't take long. I'll be back before you finish your wine cooler."

"You're—testing it *now*?" Gin asked.

"I may have forgotten to mention he lives upstairs," Tuck says. "You can't think I picked this place for the atmosphere."

"Ta," William said, heading for the doors.

"You need another?" Tuck said, pointing at her half-empty Coke. Without waiting for an answer, he signaled the bartender. "Straub IPL and another for the lady."

Gin laughed. "You really are kind of old fashioned, aren't you? I wouldn't say prissy, exactly . . ."

"Your mood seems to have improved."

"I don't know, maybe I just needed to get away for a while. And I like your friend."

"Dusty? Yeah, he's a good guy. And a hell of a lucky one. Doctors didn't think he'd survive, back when he got shot."

"I thought—he said he went out on disability for his knee."

"Yeah, his knee and the two bullets in his chest," Tuck said. "He didn't just fall over that fence on his own."

"Oh." Gin sipped at her fresh Coke. "Sometimes . . . sometimes I wonder why anyone would choose to do the job you guys do."

"Well, in my case, it's because I couldn't make ends meet playing pool. What do you say, Gin, want to wager a buck or two?"

Gin slid off her barstool and grabbed a cue from the rack. "Those are fighting words. We had a pool table in the basement when I was growing up."

For the next hour they played, neither of them making as many shots as they missed. Someone put old Springsteen on the jukebox, and Gin let Tuck talk her into trying the local beer. By the time William returned, she'd almost forgotten the gravity of her errand. It seemed like such a long time since she'd had this much fun.

"It's a fake," William said without ceremony, sliding back on his stool. The bartender was already reaching for his whiskey.

"You're kidding," Gin said. "How do you know?"

William pulled a folded sheet of paper from his pocket. It was covered with numbers and acronyms and technicalese. "I ran a few different tests on this—pretty standard stuff, started with ultrasonic diagnostics and then radiography and particle inspection. And for the most part, the composition is indistinguishable from the real thing. But I found traces of zinc and calcium, which you would not expect to find in a nineteenth-century sample. Nowadays, amateur casters get their lead mostly from wheel weights. So the calcium could be from battery plates, and the zinc from zinc weights. But I still couldn't be sure."

He took the small lump of metal out of the bag and held it up. "There's one more thing all casters use, and that's some sort of flux."

"Flux?"

"Some substance to improve flow. Early examples of things people used include beeswax, rosin, even sawdust and salt. But whoever made this little guy used Marvelux."

"No kidding," Tuck said, shaking his head. "Hell, that blows this whole thing out of the water."

"Wait, why? What's Marvelux?"

"It's a fluxing agent—people like it for lead because it's nonsmoking and nonfuming. But more importantly, it's only been around since the seventies." He tossed her the ball. "No way this is more than forty years old."

"I don't know how to thank you," Gin said.

"I take it that's the answer you were looking for?" When Gin exchanged a glance with Tuck, William shook his head. "No, don't tell me anything about your case. It's better for me not to know. But I'm always glad to have a satisfied customer."

"Listen, William, one more thing. You said you knew some reenactors?"

"Yeah."

"Do you think you could make an introduction?"

"Sure, but you don't need an introduction. They're way short of chicks. Show up at one of their meetings and they'll be lining up to talk to you. Here, I'll write down the name." He scrawled something on a cocktail napkin and handed it to her. "Just Google that. They meet in the basement of the Veterans Hall in Munhall."

Gin glanced at what he'd written. "Pennsylvania Volunteer Infantry."

William shrugged. "Not very catchy, but it gets the point across, I guess."

"So what do I owe you for today?" Gin asked, tucking the napkin and the sample bag containing the ball carefully into her purse.

"Tell you what—Tuck picks up this round, we'll call it even."

"No, I couldn't," Gin protested. "I want to compensate you for your time and expertise."

"How about you just keep an eye on my buddy here," William said. "Since he took off for the sticks, I've been a little worried about him."

Tuck pulled some bills out of his wallet and tossed them on the bar. "I got a call from impound. They've got an ID on the motorcycle's owner. Can you come to the station and take a look?"

"Is that what the kids are calling it these days?" William said with a wink. "You two have fun at the *impound*."

* * *

Gin and Tuck headed back for Trumbull in their own cars. Gin dialed Stillman on the way. He picked up on the first ring.

"Stillman here," he barked.

"Detective, this is Gin Sullivan. I wonder if you could meet to talk? I have some new evidence that I think you'll be interested in."

"Is that right." She could hear him sigh over the phone. "I really don't have time for this. We're handing the case off to the Park Service. They're sending in experts with the Battlefield Protection Program. They've got their own attorneys, their own PR machine."

"That's—that's really premature. I'm in no way convinced that the body found on the Rudkin estate dates back to the Civil War."

"Dr. Sullivan, I was in that autopsy room. There was not one goddamn shred of proof that the body *wasn't* lying there for the last hundred and fifty years, and now we've got confirmation that the uniform is authentic. There's this thing us cops have called circumstantial evidence—you may have heard of it?"

"I'm not saying that it's impossible; I—"

"What I'm wondering is, could your position have anything to do with the fact that you're shacking up with Jake Crosby? I did a little digging myself. I'm sure you already know all this, but he stood to make a lot of money on that deal. Which must have looked pretty good to both of you."

Gin felt her face burn with anger. "It's none of your business, but it's true that Jake Crosby is very important to me. But I think a lot of other people would want to know the truth about this. The media's certainly interested."

"They're interested as long as the story's relevant," Stillman said. "People want to believe that body belonged to a soldier, not some bum who got himself rolled and stuck in a hole. Listen, Captain Wheeler's sister serves on the Historic Review Commission. She's practically peeing her pants with excitement over this discovery."

"That's not—"

"Your mother's in her first term of office, isn't she? Seems like she could turn this into a real boon for business if she plays this right."

"But it isn't true! That man was probably not a Civil War soldier, and pretending otherwise won't make it so."

"Let me give you a little advice, Gin, and then I've got to go. Trumbull's been nothing but a mosquito bite on the county map for quite a few years now. But times are changing, and your mom has managed to breathe some life into it. Just like Wheeler, she knows how to keep the wheels greased—and those of us who follow her example are doing okay. You ever wonder why your new chief of police ended up down there?"

"I—no."

"Well, you might let him be your cautionary tale," Stillman said. "Just like you, he didn't know how to let well enough alone. All right, this has been a laugh riot as usual, but I've got work to do."

He hung up, leaving Gin staring at a line of traffic stretching as far as she could see. The rush-hour backup was already beginning, and she had lost sight of Tuck's car up ahead.

When she arrived at the police station half an hour later, the receptionist directed her around the back of the building. Tuck Baxter was standing in the drafty garage that served as the county motor pool, talking to a man sporting coveralls and a full gray beard. Nearby, the mangled motorcycle was lying on its side on the floor.

"Took you long enough," Baxter said by way of a greeting, but the smile he gave her was warm.

Gin rolled her eyes. "Maybe if I was driving a cop car, I could have exceeded the speed limit all the way back too."

Tuck chuckled, then turned serious. "Gin, this is Darby McKenna. He's the one who found the VIN."

Darby wiped his hands on a rag. "It wasn't easy. They filed it clean off the steering neck. It took me a while, but I was able to raise all but two digits. Then I ran it against the database and came up with all possible matches, then narrowed it down based on DMV records."

"Wait—if the number was filed off, how did you read it?"

"Here, come take a look." Darby took a small flashlight from his pocket and shone it on the bike. Gin leaned closer, and sure enough, she could make out the faint impression of numerals on a section of metal that had been polished to a shine. "When the number is stamped on the metal, the material underneath gets compressed and hardened. What we do is put acid on the area, and it eats away the metal at different rates depending on the density. Then we photograph it and refine the image until we can make out the numbers. That's if we're lucky."

"So today was lucky?"

"I don't know if I'd say that," Tuck said. "Come on in my office."

They went back into the building through the garage. Gin was grateful to be inside, where it was warm. She removed her coat and hung it over the extra chair in Tuck's office. He pulled his own chair around to her side of the desk, and when they both sat down, their knees were almost touching. Gin glanced at the door, which Tuck had shut behind them.

Suddenly, the office seemed very small indeed.

"So. Here's what we know," Tuck said, regarding her closely. "That bike's a 2006, but it hasn't been registered in three years. Secondly, it belongs to a Marvin Morgensen."

"Not Griffin Rudkin? Could he have bought it from his shop, maybe?"

"Rudkin's shop wasn't in business in 2006, and Morgensen has owned it since it was new."

"But—I have no idea who that is. Why would he come after me?"

"I don't know. Morgensen lived in Clarion County his whole life before moving to Trumbull. He was born in Perry township and grew up around there. Joined the service after graduating from high school, then came here after serving in the army and went to work as a mechanic. Eventually opened up his own shop—mostly emissions testing, small jobs. Not all that successful. Never married, kept his nose clean for the most part, though he was picked up a few times for peeping about twenty-five years ago. Liked to show his goods to young girls, apparently, though after the cops talked to him a couple of times, he seems to have stopped. And there's one more thing—apparently he's been involved, off and on, with a local group of reenactors."

"You've got to be kidding," Gin gasped. "You mean, he could have access a to Civil War uniform?"

"I don't know if I'd go that far," Tuck said, taking another page from the sheaf of papers. It showed a group photo that had run in the newspaper, two dozen men—and a few women—posed on a field in costume, holding replica weapons and flags. A man kneeling in the front row was circled, but the quality of the photograph was poor enough that it was next to impossible to make out his features. "All I could dig up for sure is that he was present in two events, and only because he was listed in the captions. I couldn't even say for sure that it's the same Marvin Morgensen, though I didn't turn up any others in a three-county area. He wasn't on the official rolls of any organization I contacted. So maybe he was an occasional participant, or the guest of a member."

"Interesting," Gin said, suppressing a shudder. "So you're saying he's the guy who ran me off the road? Some—some creepy mechanic who occasionally liked to dress up and play soldier?"

"Maybe. But that isn't even the weirdest part. Morgensen disappeared in 2013. He just didn't show up to work one day.

His car was in his garage, there were dishes in the sink. He didn't even take his phone, left it lying on the kitchen table. The case went nowhere. He hadn't been in any trouble—squeaky clean record."

"But that doesn't make any sense. Why would he come back now?"

Tuck picked up the folder from the desk and fanned out the contents, mug shots of four different men. "Especially when there's a good chance he's been lying in the ground for the last three years."

"Wait." An electric shiver of excitement and fear raced through Gin. "You're saying you think that the body buried up at the worksite could be Morgensen?"

Tuck tapped the closest photo—a man with greasy dark hair falling over his brow. "I'm saying it's a hell of a coincidence. On the other hand, I've got four possibles, if I go back five years and focus on a thirty-mile radius. If we open it up beyond that and look at men aged twenty to fifty who disappeared anywhere in the county—well, then we're back in the dark all over again."

Gin felt her hopes slipping away. "When I was at Cook County, we'd get cases like this once in a while—where because of the conditions of decay, we were never able to figure out the identity of the body. There's only so much you can do with bones, for instance. People think that the potter's field is an outmoded concept, but the truth is that hundreds of people die every year whose identities will never be known."

"And a lot of them aren't ever even found. If your boyfriend hadn't decided to build right there—if someone hadn't decided to come along and torch it—if, if, if. You get my drift."

"Have you had any other leads on the arson?"

"Nothing new. With no data from the security system, all the investigators can do is look at what was left after they got the fire put out, which isn't much. I've checked on all the firebugs the department knows about, but the record keeping around here . . . I'm not trying to criticize Chief Crosby. Folks here clearly have a lot of respect for him. But I will say that paperwork wasn't his strong suit."

"Wait—why wasn't there any data?" Gin asked. Jake had installed security cameras as soon as they broke ground.

"Someone turned the cameras off," Tuck said, holding her gaze.

Was he implying that it was Jake? Was that possible? And if Jake had shut off the cameras . . . why?

"We'll be talking to Crosby and his crew about that, obviously," Tuck said, leaning back in the chair and setting the sheaf of papers back on the desk, apparently satisfied that she hadn't known this detail already. "Of course, it could have been the arsonist. The cameras weren't exactly hidden, and they weren't hardwired."

Gin winced, knowing that the battery-operated cameras had been the more economical choice. She wondered if Tuck was aware of the financial pressure Jake was under.

"I just . . ." Gin thought fast. "I thought I could give you a little insight into how folks think around here," she said, latching onto something he had said in an attempt to change the conversation. "It's true that Chief Crosby was old school. It doesn't surprise me that he didn't keep up with his records, not to mention technological advances in law enforcement. And maybe, as the town continued to change and the problems facing Trumbull changed too, that was a mistake. But you have to remember that people here still think of this as a small community. Relationships matter. Tradition matters."

"Try telling that to the drug dealer who sets up shop across from the high school or the crooks from the city who've been hitting houses during the day when people are at work. I hate to break it to you, Gin, but the twenty-first century's well under way even here. Trumbull's already got its fair share of the plagues of modern society—heroin, meth, gangs . . ."

"And I don't think people are trying to ignore that," Gin said. "I just think that you might want to make sure the community knows you care."

Tuck grimaced. "You mean I have to have coffee with every old lady who calls in a suspicious stranger in the neighborhood? Ride in a convertible in the Fourth of July parade? Sorry, that's not going to happen."

Gin allowed herself a small smile. He had a point: she couldn't picture Tuck Baxter with a bib around his neck at the annual Lions Club spaghetti dinner and doubted he'd be receiving an invitation any time soon to the parks department poker game. "Maybe there's a happy medium in there somewhere," she said. "Rome wasn't built in a day. Maybe Trumbull—the new Trumbull—can't be built in a day either. You might want to talk to my mom," she added impulsively.

"I've spent a fair amount of time with your mom already," Tuck said drily. "She was nice enough all through the interview process, but once I was hired, she read me the riot act on my first day. She told me I didn't have to like her, but I'd damn sure better respect the authority of her office."

"I can't believe I'm saying this myself," Gin admitted. "Until recently, I never thought I'd come back to Trumbull. I thought I'd miss city life—not to mention the state-of-the-art facility where I worked. And as for my mom . . . well, I know firsthand how tough she can be. But the thing is, Mom really believes in this place. If you show that you care about Trumbull's future, she'll be your best ally."

"I'll take that under consideration." He leaned back in his chair, drumming his fingers on the armrests. "Now that you've told me how to do my job, Gin, how about a piece of advice for you?"

"I'm listening."

"That little trick we pulled up in Squirrel Hill—smart people don't try to get lucky like that too often. Keep breaking rules, and it's going to come back and bite you."

"Says the guy who got forced out of his last job . . ."

"I never said do as I do," Tuck said. "Just do as I say."

"Is that an order?" she snapped, her irritation tempered by other, confusing emotions. "Or a suggestion?"

Tuck's eyes narrowed, and his lips parted as though he was going to make a retort. Instead, he clamped his mouth shut and glowered at her.

"I'm sorry," Gin said. "But I've always had trouble being told what to do."

"That's abundantly clear. Unfortunately, your stubborn streak only adds to your appeal."

"My . . . appeal?" Gin faltered.

"Come on, Gin. There's . . . *something* . . . between us, and you know it every bit as goddamn much as I do. Now, we can ignore it, and that's probably a good idea, and I can keep things professional every day of the week. But I'm not going to stand here and pretend that you don't drive me crazy every time I see you. Even when you're being a pain in the ass. *Especially* when you're being a pain in the ass." He leaned forward and gently pushed a lock of her hair back from where it had fallen over her eyes. "I know you're taken. But the day that changes—hell, the *minute* it changes—all bets are off between you and me."

For a moment, Gin could only gape at him, barely remembering to breathe the charged air between them. Then she staggered to her feet and pushed back her chair, backing toward the door. "I—I have to go."

Tuck stood too, his eyes on her, not a shred of apology in his gaze.

Gin put her hand on the doorknob and realized she'd nearly forgotten her coat. She grabbed it off the chair and flung open the door, rushing down the hall with her face flaming, hoping to make it to her car without running into anyone else.

She welcomed the rush of cold air when she got to the exit, pulling on her coat and keeping her head down. She hurried to her car and slammed the door behind her, pausing to catch her breath as she started the engine. For a moment, she waited for the car to warm up, watching her breath cloud the frigid air as her pounding heart finally slowed.

Tuck Baxter, who had the power to threaten everything Jake cared about, wanted her.

And she couldn't deny that there was a part of her that wanted him back.

17

When Gin was halfway home, a thought that had been nagging at the back of her mind came to the fore.

She'd been trying to banish thoughts of Tuck Baxter, the way his gaze seemed to go straight to the core of her, by focusing on Jake: going over their interactions over the last few days, trying to figure out what she could have done differently, where the two of them had gone wrong to allow distance to come between them.

And she'd gotten stuck on the dinner party. It should have been the perfect evening for the two of them—a chance to relax with friends, for Jake to let go of his worries for a few hours. And for a while, it had seemed to be just that, the two men avoiding dwelling on the building site and sharing wine and laughter. Until the end of the dinner, when talk turned to the presence of solvents as a possible source of the fire—and Gus's presence on the site during the wee morning hours of the fire.

He hadn't said anything about the cameras.

She went over the conversation in her mind: Gus describing seeing the smoke, his insomnia, and his habit of going on site early to guard against copper theft. It had seemed reasonable at the time—but as she replayed it in her mind, she couldn't help remembering the way Marlene had watched her husband as he spoke. If it wasn't fear on her face, it was something close. Did she know her husband was lying? Had he cautioned her not to say anything to contradict him?

And what might he have been asking her to cover up?

The couple was expecting a baby, a baby that it sounded like had been a long time coming. How far would Gus Sykes go to provide for it?

Or . . . Gin felt tendrils of unease as she remembered an old case, when a body of a woman who was seven months pregnant was brought in, beaten nearly beyond recognition, the baby's life extinguished along with her own. What if Gus had threatened his pregnant wife—or worse? If he was involved in something illegal on the building site, he'd managed to convince Jake otherwise. Domestic abusers were often charming, successfully hiding the violence they committed behind closed doors. If Gus was such a man, and he took out his frustrations on his wife, the loss of a job could be disastrous. Which would also give him a motive for the copper thefts that he seemed to know so much about.

Gin pulled over to the curb and did a quick search on her phone. Gus and Marlene Sykes were easy enough to find; their address was over in the Galleria, a newer subdivision of affordable townhouses built on the site of the former steel company headquarters that had been one of her mother's key redevelopment efforts.

Before she could change her mind, Gin headed over to the neighborhood, unsure what she was looking for. She had a ready-made excuse—the pan in which Marlene had brought homemade banana bread to the dinner party was in a bag in her car. If she could strike up a friendship with Marlene, maybe she could learn more—specifically, whether Gus had any reason to want to burn the project down.

She parked in the development's visitor lot next to the little pocket park overlooking the river, where the city had put in a play structure shaped like a barge. Half a dozen children played while their parents looked on.

Number nine was an end unit bordered by a hedge that had shed its leaves. A couple of spindly, bare trees seemed to cling to their support posts, waiting for the spring that was still months away. In the yard, a plastic bag had blown up against the fence. A single strand of Christmas lights hung from the porch rafters.

Gin walked to the door, pausing on the porch. Inside, she could hear the faint strains of country music and the sound of someone moving through the front room.

Seconds after she rang the doorbell, the music was turned off. The silence stretched until Gin started to think no one was going to answer the door.

But a moment later, it opened, and Marlene was standing there in an oversized sweat shirt and leggings, her hair pulled up in a simple ponytail. Even without all the makeup she'd been wearing the other night, she was a striking woman, but her face was puffy and her eyes were red.

"I thought you were the religious cult guy," she said. "He's been going door to door, trying to convert people."

"I'm sorry," Gin said. "I should have called. I just—I've had your pan in the car, and I was over on this side of town doing errands, and I thought I'd just bring it by. We had such a lovely time the other night."

She held out the bag containing the pan. Marlene stared at it for a moment before taking it. "I'm kind of a mess," she said. "But I could use the company, and I've just made another pot of coffee. Will you come in?"

"You're sure I'm not intruding?"

"I promise you're not. I'm going stir crazy here."

Inside, the house was warm and pleasantly decorated, with framed inspirational sayings on the walls and colorful pottery lined up in a hutch.

"I was going to look for a job when we got up here—I'm a certified property manager. But with the holidays coming up, no one's looking. So I've been trying to keep busy until the new year. But Gus is worried about money, especially now that the project's been shut down, so he took some side work, and I hardly see him at all."

Marlene's appearance had suffered since the other night. Her hair was lackluster and straggly. Her nails were ragged, her skin sallow. Gin searched her skin for signs of a beating but didn't see any; unfortunately, some abusers knew how to hurt their partners while hiding the damage.

"Marlene," Gin said gently, knowing she would have to ease into the delicate topic. "A move can be a huge stress. I should know—I didn't think I'd be here more than a week or two when I came back. And while I've loved being near my family again, it's really hard to pull up roots so abruptly. And I have friends, a community, meaningful work. I'm sure you'll have all of those things in time, but for now, it's no wonder you're feeling a little blue."

"Oh, my gosh, that's so true," Marlene said. Tears welled up in her eyes again. "I really didn't invite you in here just so I could feel sorry for myself. I thought—I mean, you were so nice the other night—I just thought maybe . . ."

She reached for a tissue and dabbed at her eyes.

"What is it, Marlene?" Gin prodded.

"I thought it would be so nice to have a friend here. Someone I could talk to—I mean, *really* talk. Not just to say hello, like I do with the other women around here."

"I'm happy to," Gin said carefully. "Is there anything in particular that's on your mind?"

Marlene stared at her for a long moment before finally blurting, "Have you ever done anything you regretted so much that you can't get a moment's peace?"

Gin raised her eyebrows. This wasn't what she'd expected. "I—I'm sure I have," she said. "Feelings of guilt and regret are only natural when we make a mistake. But you've got to remember that you're only human."

"Oh. Well . . . I deserve to feel bad. I wasn't raised that way—I'm ashamed of myself."

"Would it make you feel better to tell me what happened?" Gin asked, wondering if it had been a bad idea to come here. "You truly don't need to feel like you need to confide in me."

"It's not, like, illegal or anything like that!"

Gin gave her what she hoped was a reassuring smile. "I never guessed that it was."

"It's just . . ." Marlene stared out the window. "I don't have anyone to talk to, I don't have any friends here. Everyone I know is back home. And the worst part is that it's my fault. Me and Gus didn't come here because he got laid off. I mean, that's what he told Jake when he interviewed. But the truth is that Gus left a good job to come here." She took a deep breath. "I got mixed up in something last year. With—with a guy. One of our neighbors, him and Gus used to watch football together. Sometimes the four of us had dinner, only they had kids and we didn't, which can be—well, you know, especially because we'd been trying for so long. The thing is, last winter when Gus was working overtime, and Max, he and Denise were fighting a lot and . . . Oh, God, I don't even want to say it."

"I see," Gin said. It wasn't her place to judge; she'd certainly done things that she wasn't proud of.

"No, wait, that's not even the bad part. I mean, not the worst part. Gus found out because he read my e-mails. And he said he couldn't stand to stay in that house, not when he knew, you know, that Max was still right next door. He was so angry, you can't even imagine. We decided to come up here, our counselor said we needed to treat it as a clean break. No more talk about the past, no blaming, no dredging it up again. And Gus agreed. I mean, he's still mad, of course, but I deserve it after what I did."

"When you say he's still mad at you . . ."

"Oh, don't take that the wrong way. I mean, he loses his temper sometimes, but everyone does. It's nothing compared to what I've done to him, the way I betrayed him. See—Max, he came up here. A few times, since we moved here. I tell him not to, and we agree it's over, and he has to come up this way for business, and he texts me and I try, oh, I try so hard to say no. But Gus is gone so much, and I'm so lonely, you know? And we can't go to a motel because neither one of us could put it on our credit cards, because he's married too. And there's no way I'd bring him here.

"Last week he called because he had to be up here for a morning meeting. And this time, I said I'd meet him because . . ." Tears streaked down her face, and she grabbed another tissue. "I was going to break it off for real because of the baby. Gus thinks it's his, and I wasn't going to ever tell him the truth, because it would destroy him. He's proud, you know? Max left home super early in the morning, and I took a chance too—I go to the gym in the morning a lot of times before Gus gets out of bed, so I knew he'd think that's where I was. We met at the building site a little after four in the morning—I knew the code to the door because it's the same as our ATM pin; it's what Gus always uses. Max and I left our cars on the road down below and came up the trail. We were only there an hour, maybe a little more—and I told him we were done. I told him we could never see each other again."

"Wait a minute—are you telling me that you were there the night of the fire? Marlene . . . did you start the fire?"

"No! I swear I didn't. It was still dark when we left. I went first, because Max thought we shouldn't leave together, in case anyone saw us."

Underneath Marlene's obvious feelings of shame and guilt, Gin couldn't help noting that she'd done some careful planning.

"Did you turn the trail cameras off?"

Marlene's face froze, and she stammered, "I—I don't know what you're talking about, I—"

"I'm not trying to get you in trouble," Gin assured her. "But you said you knew the door code. It would make sense you'd have known about the cameras too. And it would explain why they were off that night. I'm just trying to piece together what happened, since both Jake and Gus are having to answer for what went on that night."

Marlene stared at her hands in her lap for a moment. Then she glanced up, looking even more stricken. "Yes," she said quietly. "That was me. I turned them off. But Gin, I saw something. It almost gave me a heart attack, honestly, as nervous as I was. There was a pickup parked around the bend, off the road—it had pulled into that flat area where the rock slide was. Somebody got out of the truck, and I ran into the woods where they couldn't see me—but I could see them, a little, through the trees. They went around behind the truck and got something out of the back that I couldn't see. A box, maybe, or a crate. They carried it up the hill."

"What did the person look like, Marlene?"

"Well, it wasn't Jake, that's for sure." Marlene dabbed at her eyes and wouldn't meet Gin's gaze. "Too short. I think . . . I think it was Gus."

18

When Gin got home, Jake's truck was in the drive, and wood smoke trailed from the chimney. Jett came loping around the house, a feather in her mouth, wagging her tail. A moment later, Jake appeared, his ax over his shoulder and his face sheened with perspiration.

"Have you been working out your frustrations again?" Gin asked tentatively.

Jake grimaced. "I guess you could say that. Or maybe I can get a job felling timber. At least we won't have to start burning the furniture for heat."

He wouldn't look at her, his jaw set as hard as the granite outcroppings along the ridge. Jake had been stubborn as a teenager, and the years had only seemed to make him determined to go it alone when things got tough. He couldn't—wouldn't—let her in, couldn't expose what he felt was his weakness, even to her.

An image of Tuck Baxter came unbidden to Gin's mind, and she felt her face flood with shame. What had she been thinking? When Tuck had brought up his attraction to her, she should have shut it down firmly and quickly. She had to do better, to focus on healing the damage in her relationship with

Jake. She loved him—had loved him forever—and she wasn't about to give up on him now, no matter how hard he tried to push her away.

"You don't have to go through this alone. I'm here, remember? We should be facing this together."

He glanced at her, then quickly away. "Your last offer of help involved you opening up your checkbook," he said. "That's not going to happen. Not now, not ever."

Frustration shot through her. "How can you turn me down like that, without even considering it? What if I told you that I would like to consider it *our* money? That when I think about the future, it's always a future with you?"

Other than those exquisitely tense moments in Tuck Baxter's office . . . She hadn't been thinking about Jake then, had she?

She forced the thought away as Jake heaved a sigh and set down his ax, finally turning to face her. "It's easy to make offers like that," he said bitterly, "when you've never had to wonder where your next mortgage payment was coming from. Or how the guys who work for you are going to put shoes on their kids' feet."

"Okay, I'm sorry!" Gin erupted, suddenly unable to keep her frustration in check. "But I'm sick of having to apologize for the way I was brought up. My parents have money—it's true. I didn't ask for it, and I've never taken a cent from them since I finished school."

"Yeah, that's kind of what I'm getting at," Jake said. There was a coldness to his voice that Gin had never heard before. "You've been a success your whole career. Everyone respects you. You've got publications and awards and shit—I don't even know what else. I'm just a guy with dirt under my fingernails. When you get sick of playing house here with me, when you want more of a challenge than a few hours of consulting work a week, what then? You going to give me an allowance while you commute to the city? Or do you want me to move some-where closer to your job with you, and I'll just keep house and have dinner on the table when you get home?"

"Jake!" Gin exclaimed, shocked. She had no idea his anger ran so deep. "Those are—if we ever—decisions like that would need us both to treat each other with respect and—and you can't keep shutting me out if we're ever going to—"

"I'm not the one shutting you out," Jake shot back. "You can't—won't—even talk to me about the case. Hell, you're working for the county. The people who are trying to shut me down, if you haven't noticed. I have to wonder, sometimes, how much you could care about me if you can't remember whose side you're on."

"I'm trying to *help* you!" Gin protested. "Meanwhile, I find out you've been talking to a bankruptcy lawyer without even discussing it with me first!"

A bleak expression settled onto Jake's face. "I hate to break it to you, but this is just the way it goes for regular folks. Some-times you can't buy your way out of your problems."

He picked up the ax and started walking away. Jett looked worriedly between the two of them and whined before trailing after him.

Gin stood rooted in place for a few moments, fuming. He was determined to go it alone, which meant that she could either accept the cold, empty silence between them for how-ever long it took Jake to snap out of his funk—or she could leave. There was a third option—the most difficult, the one that would require the most of her.

She could keep trying to convince him to let her in. But until Jake saw a way out of his current problems, there was no way he would be receptive. Which meant that their relation-ship was riding on the investigation.

And Gin only knew one way to help with *that*. Which was to bring all of her skills—analytical, scientific, and

investigative—to the case. Where Jake was impulsive and passionate, she could be calm and thorough. Where he saw closed
doors, maybe—just maybe—she could see a way to make
sense of what had happened at the building site.

Calmer, finally, she made her way down the hill. Maybe it
would be wiser to simply take what she knew to the police and
let them deal with it . . . but Gin knew that if she didn't share
what she'd discovered with Jake, he would see it as a betrayal.

She found him at the sink, staring out over the snowy
woods, a glass of water in his hands. Hearing her come through
the front door, he turned and looked at her with an anguished
expression. "I'm sorry," he said. "I'm an idiot. It's just that I
don't—I can't—"

"Some things happened today," she said. "Things you
should know about."

She stayed on the other side of the bank of cabinets sepa-
rating the kitchen from the dining area, the distance between
them emphasized by the expanse of stone and hickory. She
told him about the events at the bar and the motor pool,
downplaying Tuck's role in both discoveries. He listened with
increasing agitation, erupting when she told him about Marvin Morgensen.

"What the hell am I supposed to make of that?" he burst
out. "A total stranger may have tried to kill my girlfriend, for
no reason?"

"Jake, Tuck thinks that Morgensen might be the dead man
on your land. We still don't know who was riding his motorcycle that night."

"And that's supposed to make me feel *better*?"

Gin sighed. "Look—at the moment I'm here, with you, safe
as can be. But I'm still not finished telling you what happened
today."

Jake rubbed his eyes incredulously, cursing under his
breath. "Okay," he finally muttered. "Tell me the rest. All of it."

So she told him about the visit to see Marlene Sykes.

"No, not a chance," Jake said, practically before she'd finished repeating what Marlene had said. "Gus would never do something like that. He'd never try to hurt her—or anyone else."

"But how well do you really know him?" Gin pressed. "I mean, he's only been working for you for less than a year."

"It's not about how long I've known him," Jake said. "Look, how do you think my business has survived as long as it has? I'm a damn good judge of character. It's true that when I hired him I was going by my gut more than anything. But you show up with a man at the crack of dawn and work side by side in all kinds of weather, day after day, you get to know him pretty quick."

Gin wasn't as trusting. She'd seen too many family members shocked by the secrets their loved ones kept until their dying breath. There had been the husband who never knew his wife's infertility was caused by uterine scarring from chlamydia. The priest who'd died of opioid abuse, whose parishioners thought he had a seizure disorder. The woman who'd compulsively ingested cigarette ashes for over a decade.

In Gin's professional experience, often people knew only the sides that their loved ones wished to show them. It was entirely possible for people to hide the things they did, their secret passions and fears.

"Just for the sake of argument, talk this through with me, okay?" she said. "They were living in Steubenville, right? They had a whole life there. Jobs, a home, family nearby. He left it all behind so that they could make a fresh start. Only, Marlene didn't stop her affair as she had promised. Don't you think that could push him over the edge after he gave up everything for her?"

"Look. We can talk about this all day long, and it's not going to change the fact that I'll never believe Gus would set fire to the work we did. We both put our hearts into this project. And besides, he was going to earn a hefty bonus when those houses closed. It's in the contract. Why jeopardize that?"

"I'm not saying it was planned," Gin said. "It could easily have been the heat of the moment. An impulsive decision he made when he discovered that his wife was still cheating on him. And the fact that she was doing it inside the house he had built with his own hands—that could have been the trigger."

"Then why didn't he simply try to kill her at home? It would have been a lot easier to cover it up."

"I think it was a spur of the moment decision, like I said. Maybe all he meant to do was get proof of the affair, at first. He hears her get out of bed. He follows her—he's careful, so she never knows. Maybe he sees her turn off the security cameras. He waits to be sure, and he sees them in the house, sees their cars parked down below. What he doesn't realize is that they were just talking; Marlene tells him it's over, they leave. He thinks they're making love, and it drives him to do something crazy."

Jake gaped at her. "So you're asking me to believe my partner, my *friend*, flew into a jealous rage and burned down everything we worked for. Do you also think he tried to run you off the road and kill you? And what about the body— do you think Gus is responsible for that as well?"

"I never said that," Gin protested. "I have no idea how it's all tied together—or if any of it's related to anything else. But I'm trying to help you here. The county's ready to close the case. We only have a few days to stop them. At least I'm trying to do something, rather than sit here and wait for disaster to strike."

Jake shook his head slowly. "I don't know, Gin. I guess I can understand how you drew the conclusions you did. But you're *wrong*. And I want you to promise me something: Don't say anything about this to the cops, not for now. Not until I figure out how to talk to Gus about . . . all of this."

Gin nodded reluctantly. "Okay. I . . . promise."

Maybe he was right. Maybe she was being too hasty. She believed that Marlene had seen *someone*—but it wasn't necessarily her husband. Quite possibly, her guilt and shame had predisposed her to make assumptions.

"Good," Jake said. "Look, give me a little time. I'll take Gus out for a beer, find a way to bring it up with him."

"All right. But I can't just sit here and do nothing. I'm going to go look up those reenactors, the ones up in Munhall."

"Gin—you don't have to drive all the way to Munhall just to find reenactors. They're all in town to protest the site. They're having a big get-together at McNally's tonight." He dug in his pocket and came up with a dog-eared, bright-yellow flyer. "They were spreading these around town today."

Gin looked over the flyer, a photocopied hand-drawn invitation to "Learn How We Keep History Alive!" It advertised half-price well drinks for ladies and a halfhearted suggestion to "Bring all your FRIENDS."

"Well, do you want to go?"

"Not especially," Jake said gloomily. "But it beats sitting at home. Besides, the drinks are cheap enough even for me."

* * *

The turnout was surprisingly large. A few patrons wore Civil War regalia, and an earnest man with long silver sideburns was wandering around with a petition, but most people seemed to be ignoring the event's purpose and simply having fun. Many of the partiers seemed to be local people taking advantage of the opportunity to have a little fun on a weeknight, but one cluster of people were toasting each other with sloshing mugs of beer and singing what Gin took to be historic ditties.

When Jake came back from the bar with their drinks, Gin propelled him over to the singers, who'd given up on harmonizing and were moving on to a drunken game of darts.

She approached the table, introduced herself to the two men remaining seated, and asked if she and Jake could join them.

"Absolutely!" the drunker of the two shouted. "Here, I've got another one. Raise your glasses, boys . . ."

He threw his arm around Jake's neck and started singing.

> *"Here's to the American eagle,*
> *That gray old bird of prey,*
> *Who eats on Northern soil,*
> *And shits on Southern clay!"*

"Bravo," his companion said mildly. "Hey, Pete, how about you go see if you can get that hot reporter to interview you?"

"Great idea, Doyle," his friend said, belching loudly before lurching off through the crowd.

"Sorry about that," the man said, shaking hands with each of them. "My name's Doyle Grynbaum. I swear we're not all like that. Most of us are simply amateur historians." He leaned across the table as if sharing a confidence. "Some of us don't even dress up, but don't let that get around."

"My name's Gin, and this is Jake."

The man's eyes narrowed in recognition. "Aw, shit. You're Jake Crosby, the developer."

"Is that a problem?" Jake said coldly.

"No, not for me, it isn't. In fact, I feel bad about what's going on up there. I didn't join the protest, just so you know. I mean, I'm pretty jazzed about the possibility of a significant find, but not everyone wants to shut you down, man."

Jake relaxed next to Gin. "Well . . . thanks. I guess you know the investigation has me in a jam. I just want to get through this."

Doyle nodded. "I'd offer to buy you a drink, but I see you have a full one. No hard feelings though, okay?"

"I have a few questions, if you don't mind," Gin said.

"Hell, fire away. Least I can do."

"I was curious about something. I know some reenactors carry replicas of Civil War weapons, and some collect authentic antique pieces. And I read online that some of these old guns actually still work. I was wondering about ammunition . . . does anyone make historically accurate bullets or musket balls?"

She held her breath, wondering if she'd gone too far, but Doyle seemed intrigued by her question. "I wouldn't be surprised. I mean, I haven't seen it myself, but people make all kinds of things. You should come to one of our events—you can buy historically accurate insignia and footwear and even underwear."

"I'll keep that in mind."

"Yeah, people do get a little crazy about this stuff. I got to say, I'll be really surprised if the body does turn out to be authentic."

"Yeah? How come?" Jake asked.

"There haven't been any other artifact discoveries near here. To find a soldier buried in his uniform, away from a known camp or conflict site? I don't see it."

"There's the teeth thing too," Jake said, warming to the conversation now that he'd found an ally. "To me, that signals that someone wanted to avoid identification through dental records, which of course they didn't have back then."

Doyle raised his eyebrows. "Yeah, but there's other reasons he might not have had his teeth."

"What, like really bad dental hygiene?"

"Actually, a favorite method of avoiding the draft back in those days was to knock out your front teeth."

"But—why?" Gin asked. "How would that make someone less suited for the service?"

"Pretty simple—you have to have at least four opposing front teeth to open a gunpowder pouch," Doyle explained, miming the motion. "But that only applied to infantrymen. If you were in the cavalry, you'd use a revolver, so you wouldn't need gunpowder."

"Damn," Jake said. "That would suck—go to all that pain and trouble and get drafted anyway."

"And then there was battlefield dentistry," Doyle continued. "They had this device called a tooth key that pretty much ripped it right out of the skull—without any anesthesia in most cases."

"But that would just be for diseased teeth, right?"

"Sure," Doyle said, "but I haven't told you the weirdest one yet. Like you said, in the nineteenth century, dental hygiene wasn't exactly very advanced. People started losing teeth to decay and disease in adolescence, and it was common to end up in your forties with only a few left. So what do you do if you're wealthy and vain enough to want a cosmetic replacement?"

"Dentures?" Gin suggested. "I've seen pictures of old wooden ones. I can't imagine they were very comfortable."

"Or sanitary," Jake added. "I bet there wasn't anything like Polident for wood back then."

"Well, if you could afford it, and if you had the right connections . . . you could buy dentures made from human teeth."

Jake turned a slightly greenish shade. "You've got to be kidding."

"No, not at all. The practice started at the Battle of Waterloo, and there were even ads in the paper for one hundred percent human dentures. They cost a fortune, as you might imagine, which was all the motivation scavengers needed to raid battlefields for fallen soldiers. They'd sell the teeth, and they'd be boiled and the root chopped off and then set into an ivory plate."

"They did that here in the US?"

"Well, it wasn't nearly as common during the Civil War," Doyle admitted, "but I've run across a few mentions in my reading."

"Something else," Jake said, changing the subject. "If someone owned an authentic uniform, would they wear it to a reenactment?"

"Not usually for the actual battle," Doyle said. "People don't understand how physical it can get. You can end up with bruises, cuts—friend of mine got knocked out cold last summer. But for the ceremonies, the dinners—sure, they might bring them out. Same for parades and historical festivals."

"I have to say," Jake said, "you seem pretty normal. I guess I had this impression that most reenactors were zealots."

"Yeah . . ." Doyle scratched his mustache. "You know, there's this whole perception that we're a bunch of lonely, socially maladjusted geeks. I mean, the truth is that reenactors come from all walks of life. We've got Sunday School teachers; we've got bikers. We've got a former Miss Ohio; we've got a family with seven kids who are all involved. But I've also known guys who took it a little further than I guess you'd call normal."

"How far?" Jake asked.

Doyle grinned. "Well, further than me, I guess. Everyone's perception of weird is based on themselves being the norm, right? I mean, I probably put a few hours a week into this, tops. Less time than a lot of guys spend on golf or fantasy baseball. I highly doubt it had anything to do with my divorce. I've tried like hell to get my daughter into it, but she draws the line at watching from the sidelines. I'm hoping my son might want to come along when he's old enough, but if he turns out to be into band or football or chess or something, it won't kill me. But some of these guys? They've got their gear in every room of the house. They stay in character for the whole weekend. They eat, breathe, and shit this stuff."

"Could you give me the names of some of the really involved people?" Gin asked.

"I could do you one better," Doyle said. "I'll introduce you. There's going to be a casual dinner tomorrow night, since so many people are in town. Why don't you come along?"

"I'd better not," Jake said. "I kind of want to keep an eye on the site. My foreman's there now—tomorrow's my turn."

"Well, how about you, Gin?" Doyle asked, winking. "We're always short of chicks. Got any cute friends who might want to come?"

Gin smiled. "I just might."

19

Tuck called the next morning around eleven. Jake had left to do an estimate for a job he was bidding, and Gin was reading the news on her phone while she sipped the last of the coffee.

"I've been here since six," Tuck said. His voice was brisk, professional, with no trace of the dangerous attraction that nearly derailed their last interaction. "I've put calls in to everyone I know up there, even Wheeler, but no one's getting back to me. I think they're tired of telling me to get lost. So I decided to dig around some more on my own."

"What did you find out?" Gin asked, adopting her own businesslike tone. "Anything helpful?"

"I'd rather discuss it in person," Tuck said. After a beat, he added, "And that's not a ruse to get you alone. Look, Gin, I apologize for some of the things I said the other day. I . . . should have handled that better."

"I accept your apology," Gin said stiffly, trying to ignore the complicated mixture of relief and disappointment that flooded her. "I'll even pick up lunch."

Gin took a quick shower and dressed in leggings, shearling boots, and a long, soft blue sweater. She blow-dried her hair, letting it fan out over her shoulders, and added a light application of makeup. Not, she sternly reminded herself, because she was going to see an attractive man who'd shown interest in her—the opposite, in fact. She'd lead by example and prove it was possible for them both to put the uncomfortable moment behind them and have a professional relationship.

The day was unseasonably warm and sunny, and the snow had melted off the roads and was dripping from the trees. A big droplet landed on her cheek as she stepped out from under the porch overhang.

She felt unaccountably better than she had in days, despite the fact that nothing was resolved. The night out with Jake had done them both good. And she'd texted Rosa, inviting her to the dinner that Doyle had told her about; though she doubted she could learn much more from the reenactors to help make her case, she was looking forward to the outing with her new friend.

She stopped off at the High Test Grill, an outpost of a popular Pittsburgh burger chain, picked up a couple of bacon blue cheese burgers and a mound of curly fries, and arrived at the police station a little after noon. Tuck was standing at a file cabinet, flipping through old files; when he saw her, he pushed his reading glasses up on his forehead and motioned her to follow him.

"They're like piranhas around here," he said, shutting the door to his office. "If they see that you brought food, there'll be a revolt."

"Maybe you should pay them more so they can afford lunch."

"Your mother's already threatened to squeeze my departmental budget," Tuck shot back. "Talk to her about it."

They took a break from the banter to eat. Gin made it halfway through her burger before giving up, then licked the salt from her fingers, only to catch Tuck staring. She felt her face flame with embarrassment and crumpled up her trash. So much for her vow to ignore the mutual attraction—things were clearly going to continue to be complicated between them. But they were adults, not kids, and they'd simply deal with it.

"So what's this new development you're going to share with me?"

Tuck wiped his hands on a napkin and threw it at his wastebasket, banking the shot off the wall. "I found some handwritten notes that Lawrence Crosby made back in the nineties. It would have been a hell of a lot easier if he'd bothered to digitize them—or even if his handwriting were legible. But long story short, he seems to have spent some time hunting down an angle on Marvin Morgensen that never panned out."

"What angle?"

"After those peeping incidents I told you about, something got under Crosby's skin. He seems to have followed him pretty closely for a couple of years. At some point, it became clear that he suspected Morgensen could be the Shopgirl Rapist."

"What? You mean the guy who did all the rapes in the nineties?"

"First one in 1992. Last one they think is linked was in 1996. He was nearly caught then—probably why he stopped. His last victim wasn't like the others—she was a fighter, and she managed to rip off his mask and gave the cops a good enough description of him that they were able to release drawings." He tapped his keyboard and brought up a police artist sketch of a middle-aged man with poor skin, a bulbous nose, and dark hair receding in furrows on either side of his head.

"And this is Morgensen," Tuck said, laying a photograph on the table next to the drawing. "Found it in the files from when he was picked up for peeping. Put a tie on the guy in the drawing and we'd have a possible match. Granted, the margin for error is considerable."

"What did Chief Crosby find that led him to believe it could be the same man?"

"Well, it's pretty hard to find a cohesive narrative in his files. There were literally half a dozen notes written on the back of other reports, on pages he tore out of a yellow pad, and in one case, on the back of a paper placemat from a diner. He did do a pretty thorough background check at one point, but it didn't turn up anything unusual."

He handed Gin several yellowing, stapled pages. She flipped through the information, but it just contained copies of his birth certificate and social security records, army enlistment and discharge dates, and lists of addresses and employers.

"It didn't help that Crosby didn't date anything, so I can't even construct a timeline of his investigation. But basically it seems to have boiled down to a couple of factors: he was able to place Morgensen near the scene of three of the rapes, using witness accounts. He'd done some digging into the peeping accusations, tracking down several young women who thought he might have followed him. The youngest was sixteen, incidentally. Also, from the notes, it looks like he made a trip to Clarion County, to Morgensen's hometown, and talked to the sheriff there. Doesn't help that he's dead now too."

"And what was the third thing?" she said. "You said there were three."

"Yeah, well, not that it would hold up—and I'm not sure I even believe it—but Crosby seems to have had an intuition about it."

Gin smiled wistfully. "He was kind of known for that."

"So I'm coming to understand," Tuck said wryly. "In between telling me every day that Chief Crosby did things differently and making sure I understand how much they'd prefer to be working for him than me, my guys have managed to make it really clear that he was a genius *and* a savant."

"Did he base his hunch on anything?"

Tuck picked up what looked like a receipt from a hardware store. On the back, she saw a few lines of Lawrence Crosby's familiar handwriting and felt a tug of sadness.

"He apparently went to see him after work one afternoon. Didn't take formal interview notes, so I'm guessing it was the sort of 'friendly chat' that's disappeared in this era of body cameras and cell phone videos."

"You mean he might have been coercive?"

Tuck shrugged. "Times were different then. Hell, I would have been a twenty-six-year-old cop in 1994—practically still a rookie. We all wanted to be hard chargers. Our training officers would tell us to forget what we learned in the academy. There was an unspoken feeling back then that if you talked to a guy off the record, you might not be able to use anything he said in court but you might be able to pick up something that could lead you to harder evidence."

"So what did Lawrence write there in his notes?"

"There's a date—June 25, 1994. An address that matches up with Livingston Hospital, where one of the victims was working at the time. And here, it's like shorthand for comments Morgensen made to him. 'Candy striper . . . came on to him . . . had it coming.' My guess? Crosby probably engaged him in conversation, went back to his car, and wrote down what he remembered. He wouldn't have taken these notes while talking to Morgensen, especially if he went on some other pretense."

"You mean . . . like Lawrence didn't tell him he was a cop?"

"He might have gone in and pretended to need an oil change or something, engaged him that way. No way to tell now."

"None of that necessarily means he did anything."

"No, it doesn't. And eventually, Crosby dropped it—no cop can continue putting resources toward a lost cause forever. But for him to pursue it this far tells me that he was convinced."

"Did you talk to anyone else?"

"Yeah, I went to see a guy who used to be a deputy."

"Did he remember the case?"

"His memory's starting to go, at least about events that long ago, and he couldn't help. There's another cop who Crosby mentioned in his notes back then—she's in Ohio now."

"Are you going to follow up with her?"

Tuck gazed at her with bemusement. "What, like right now? Because I'm picking up my daughter after school in a couple hours, Gin. And then I'm looking forward to fish sticks and tater tots for dinner, then working on math homework over a cup of hot cocoa with marshmallows . . . and after Cherie goes to bed, a beer and falling asleep with Netflix."

Gin felt her face get hot. "I didn't say it had to be right now. I only—"

"Yeah, I know. You just want to make sure I make it a priority, right? Not to be insensitive, because I know that you've got a personal stake in the outcome, not to mention a frightening incident that took place a couple of nights ago, but I need you to believe me when I say that I'm committed to doing right by you. But not just you—by the whole town."

"I appreciate that."

"Do you?" Tuck's voice gentled. "Look, Gin, the other night . . . I've already apologized, and I stand by that. But I just don't want you to misunderstand. I think you're a remarkable woman. It seems to me that you're caught between a rock and a hard place here. You're trying to fit in back home, but you spent a hell of a long time learning to adapt to a city pace. I did a little digging—call it background investigation."

"You investigated me?"

Tuck shrugged. "I did a few online searches and made a couple of calls. You're not exactly difficult to trace, Gin. Let's just say that I got an education in forensic pathology—you're obviously well respected in your field. But my old friend who's a pathologist in Philadelphia made damn sure I understood that you don't get where you got without putting in a lot of late nights and weekends."

"I'm . . . dedicated." Gin tried to shrug off his words. "But anyone who wants to get ahead in a competitive field would do the same. I mean, you must have worked hard to get where you are, right?"

"I was in line for lieutenant," Tuck said, without a trace of vanity. "It could have gone either way. And you're right; I was gunning for Wheeler's job once she moved on. But things didn't pan out. Look, neither of us came to Trumbull by choice. But I'm finding that I'm better suited to it than I expected. Time with my daughter, a house with a backyard *and* a view, and neighbors who bend over backward to get to know us—hard to put a price on that, Gin. Question is . . . How does the tradeoff look to you?"

Gin thought of the way Jake had looked at the bar last night, more relaxed than he'd been in a long time. For a moment, they had recaptured the easy rapport they'd shared all those years ago. She'd loved Jake in high school, and she'd never stopped loving him.

But one night out wasn't going to erase the weeks of tension between them—or bridge the divide that Jake's financial troubles had created, a divide Gin could not cross alone.

As for family, while she was grateful to be living closer to her parents, she found herself putting off visiting them. Her mother had been hinting at a future that included grandchildren; she'd begun asking Gin how serious things were with Jake. And Gin was torn between wanting to buy into the fairy tale her mother still believed in for her and wondering if she could ever be a good enough mother.

But she couldn't tell Tuck any of that.

"I don't think about it in those terms," Gin said, aware that she was evading the question. "I don't feel like I'm giving anything up. I've got interesting work."

"All right," Tuck said, straightening a paper clip on his desk, not meeting her eyes. "I stand corrected."

His voice had lost its warmth, and Gin had an inexplicable urge to backpedal. She found that she didn't want the conversation to end.

But that was a dangerous urge.

"The only thing missing from my life right now," she said briskly, gathering up her coat and purse and standing, "is peace of mind. Look, I understand that you're seeking balance in your own life. But I just hope that there's still room in that equation for you to give this your best shot."

Tuck leaned back in his chair, his hands behind his head, and stared at her with an inscrutable expression.

"If you knew me better," he said, "you'd know that I never do anything unless I give it my all."

20

"I can't believe I let you talk me into this," Rosa said, tugging at the neckline of her top. At Gin's urging, she'd changed out of her tailored blazer and conservative slacks and into leggings and a soft draped jersey top that showed off her generous curves. Gin had chosen a deep-ruby sweater dress with a twist neckline and tall black boots, hoping she wouldn't look overdressed.

"It'll be fun," Gin promised, injecting a little extra enthusiasm into her voice. She'd spent extra time dressing for the outing after Jake called to let her know that he was going to be home late. He had hired a couple of guys from his crew to take overnight shifts keeping an eye on the construction site, but he was pitching in to keep the costs down.

She hadn't told Jake that she planned to do a little investigating at the event. And she didn't tell Rosa, either. After all, it was likely that no one remembered Marvin Morgensen, if it had actually been him in the news photo. But she couldn't give up without trying.

"You know I'm thrilled to have a night out of the house, especially with Olive babysitting," Rosa said as they headed out the door. "Antonio can't get enough of her. But I was sort of thinking we'd drive up to the city, have a glass or two of chardonnay, and maybe flirt with lawyers and executives. You know, like all the other single girls in town."

Gin laughed. "But that's just it—we're not like all the other single girls. Why settle for a bunch of boring rich guys when you can spend an evening with Civil War reenactors?"

"Why indeed," Rosa agreed, smiling.

The dinner was taking place at a popular casual restaurant. They walked through a lively happy-hour crowd at the bar to the back room reserved for the meeting. Inside, an attempt had been made to give the bland meeting room a festive air: each table had a centerpiece of thirty-six-star Union flags in vases of red, white, and blue carnations, and rows of tea lights around the banquet tables flickered and danced.

At least two dozen people filled the room, sipping drinks and chatting like old friends. As Doyle had promised, the crowd was diverse and lively. Clean-shaven, button-down professional men rubbed elbows with bikers in leather vests and complicated facial hair; an elderly, grandmotherly woman in a velour tracksuit held court with several tattooed young women in miniskirts and heavy black boots.

Doyle spotted them standing in the doorway and hurried over. "Wow, you came!" he exclaimed. "I was afraid things might have gotten a little out of hand last night."

"I hope you don't mind that I brought a friend," Gin said.

Doyle's cheeks turned pink as Gin made the introductions, and he vacillated between grinning and staring at Rosa. She didn't seem to mind.

"I'll tell you what, Doyle," Gin said. "I hate to take advantage of your kindness yet again, but I thought I'd take you up on your suggestion and see if I can talk to some of your members who've been active for a while. But Rosa doesn't really know anyone here, and I was wondering if you'd mind telling her a little bit about the organization."

"Oh, sure!" Doyle bobbed his head enthusiastically. "Rosa, we've got a tab going, could I get you a drink?"

As the pair went off to find beverages, Gin congratulated herself on her matchmaking—and then focused on her own task.

She took the photograph of Morgensen from her purse, printed from an online news article from when he went missing, and approached a group of older men standing near the spread of appetizers. They made room for her to join the conversation and listened politely as she introduced herself and explained that she was doing an article for an online news outlet and that she'd been given Morgensen's name by a source. She said she hoped to interview Morgensen for background information, a story she'd concocted as the easiest way to try to gather information without having to explain how the connection had been made.

"I'm delighted that the media are taking such an interest," an elderly gentleman in a plaid sport coat said. "I really wish I could help. But I'm afraid I didn't start attending regional events until last year. There are a lot of people here who'd be happy to talk to you, I'm sure."

"Oh, that's very kind," Gin said, hoping that the lie she'd prepared would sound convincing. "But my story has an angle that only he can help with—he was apparently descended from a soldier who died right here in this county."

Gin moved on to several other people but met with similar responses. A few of the attendees thought Morgensen looked familiar from various events, but no one knew him well.

Until she started talking to a pair of sixty-ish women in owlish glasses, who so resembled each other that they had to be sisters, a fact Gin confirmed during introductions.

"Oh, I remember him," Tanya exclaimed. "Marty something-or-other. Remember, Tina, he came to the holiday party that one time?"

"I don't remember."

"Well, that's understandable, because he spent the whole time pestering Danielle Sigal. Couldn't take his eyes off her. Remember, he tried to get her out on the dance floor, but she turned him down. It was disgusting, really—he was old enough to be her father."

"Oh, I vaguely remember . . . kind of a homely fellow, receding hairline?"

"And the waistcoat that didn't fit!" Tanya crowed. "That's exactly the one."

"This Danielle Sigal," Gin said. "Is she still active in the organization, by any chance?"

"Is she ever," Tina gushed. "She's just a doll, sweet as can be. She's got wonderful energy."

"She's here tonight," her sister, Tanya, added. "Would you like to meet her?"

Gin followed in the women's wake, taking a detour past the buffet table with paper plates full of canapés to a small group of people sitting at a table in the back.

"Danielle, honey," Tina said. "You shouldn't be hiding back here. Why aren't you out there dancing with all of the other young people?"

"Oh, I would be, but I threw out my back during a firing drill." A young woman got up with obvious effort, holding onto the chair back for support, keeping her weight off her left leg, which was encased in a brace. Her hair fell forward from a barrette, covering half her face, which was dotted with acne; she was probably trying to disguise the worst of it. "You know how you're supposed to keep your left foot in place and step diagonally with your right so the musket goes in between the soldiers in front of you? I keep getting it backward—if it had been a real battle, I think I would have accidentally killed that gym teacher from Wexford."

"She would have had it coming," Tina said. "She refused to die when Laura told her she was hit."

"Laura was General Banks," Tanya confided. "She likes to have a lot of bloodshed up front. But nobody wants to spend the whole battle lying face down, so some people cheat."

"I never realized the battles were so hotly contested," Gin said.

"Oh, you don't know the half of it. Danielle, this is Gin," Tina said. "She's writing a story for the Internet."

For a few minutes, they all chatted about the attention the discovery of the body was bringing to the reenactment community and how the protests had turned into a miniconvention, with events planned every day that week.

"You going to the moonlight battle, Danielle?" Tina asked.

"Wouldn't miss it," the girl said shyly from behind her heavy curtain of hair.

"There's going to be a staging of the Battle of Dranesville at the fairgrounds two nights from now," Tanya explained. "It's mostly just for fun—there's going to be a full moon, and Dranesville was a minor battle without many casualties, which means mostly there will be a lot of standing around and drinking."

"See you there!" Tina and Tanya excused themselves to go find refreshments.

"How do you like living in Trumbull?" Gin asked after the sisters had moved on.

"Oh, it's great," Danielle said. "I love the arts revival that's going on downtown. I work as a nurse's assistant, but I'd love to have my own ceramics studio someday."

"My mother would be thrilled," Gin said, smiling, then explained her mother's arts initiative.

"That's awesome."

"I wonder if you can help me with a different matter," Gin said, changing the subject. "I had actually set up an interview with someone who was supposed to meet me here tonight. I was wondering if you might know this man."

Danielle took the photograph and held it up, peering closely in the dim lighting. She pushed her hair back impatiently, revealing a tiny bandage near her hairline. "That's Mr. Morgensen!" she exclaimed. "Sure, I remember him; he used to come to a lot of the events back when I first joined. He helped me get started, took the time to talk to me about where to find gear, especially since I was on a budget—he introduced me to some people who had things they were giving away or selling cheap. He gave me tips on how to act at the battles too—there's a whole etiquette, you know? Anyway, one day he just stopped coming. Someone said he moved back home to Kansas."

"It sounds like he showed a real interest in you." Gin took back the photo.

Danielle smiled fondly. "I mean, there's so many great people in this group. But he just went out of his way to help, you know?"

The girl certainly fit the profile of the Shopgirl Rapist's other victims, according to the articles Gin had researched that afternoon. All of the victims were between seventeen and twenty-two years old, and all were attractive and outgoing. Psychiatrists interviewed for the articles had speculated the young women had rejected their attacker sexually before becoming his victim—that he was acting out of rage.

Maybe he'd never gotten around to making a move with her—perhaps he'd been so spooked by Chief Crosby's interest in him all those years earlier that he truly had quit harassing women for good. Or maybe Danielle was so naïve that she hadn't been aware that his interest was inappropriate.

"Did he spend time with you outside of the organization?" Gin asked, trying to make the question sound casual. "When it was just the two of you?"

"Oh, he was always offering to show me his own collection of memorabilia, but it never worked out. I work strange hours, you know? I really hope nothing bad happened to him. It would just be too sad."

"Just one more thing—did you hurt your face too? During the firing drill?" She nodded in the direction of the tiny bandage.

"This?" The girl's hand went to the side of her face. "Yes, we only shoot blanks, of course, but it can still cause a kick. I wasn't ready for it—I need to be more careful." She mimed the firing of the long rifle, showing how she would have rested it on her shoulder.

"Anything for authenticity, right?" Gin said wryly. They continued chatting pleasantly about the various elements of the staged battles for a few moments, but when a few people Danielle's own age came over with mai tais, Gin made her excuses.

Let the girl enjoy the evening, she thought. There wasn't anything to be gained by explaining how close she might have come to being one of Marvin Morgensen's victims.

*   *   *

"You're having a good time?"

Rosa leaned in close enough that Gin could smell her perfume. "He's terrific, Gin. Did you know that he's got a teenage daughter *and* a four-year-old?"

"No, I just met him the other day."

"He asked me if I'd like to bring Antonio apple picking with him and his kids next week."

"Are you going to go?"

"Absolutely, if I can find someone to stay with Mom for the day."

"I will," Gin said. "If you think she'd be comfortable with me."

"Oh, I couldn't ask that of you . . ."

"Of course you can! We're friends, Rosa." The truth of the statement sunk in, and Gin smiled. "I'd actually really enjoy it. We can watch HGTV together and eat popcorn for lunch."

"She'd love that."

Doyle came back, balancing two glasses. "One Arnold Palmer for the lady. Sorry, Gin, can I get you something too?"

"No, I think I'm going to call it a night soon."

"Did you have a good time? Meet anyone interesting?"

"I did, actually. Although . . . perhaps not as interesting as the two of you."

* * *

While she waited for the old Land Rover to heat up, Gin checked her messages. Jake had texted around nine o'clock:

Meeting Gus for a beer, home soon

That was good . . . wasn't it? Maybe Jake just needed to blow off a little steam, put his problems in perspective with a few drinks and some live music. And maybe he would figure out a way to talk to Gus about Marlene.

A frisson of fear snaked through Gin, thinking of the two men together, drinking, late at night. Jake clearly didn't find her fears credible, but it was hard to stop imagining Gus setting fire to the very site where Jake had invested his hopes and dreams. And a man who would do something like that . . .

A man who discovered the woman he loved was having an affair with someone else—someone who might be the father of her child—might be moved to do a lot of things. Some men might confront the problem head-on; others would go on a bender, maybe internalize the pain.

Gus, if his wife was to be believed, had symbolically destroyed the lovers' bond by burning down their love nest. But had he actually believed that the pair was still inside the house?

Could Gus truly be a murderer? Gin thought about the man who'd visited their home, who'd worked alongside Jake for months. Gus was soft-spoken, but he was also obviously passionate. When he spoke about starting a family in Trumbull, about saving for a larger home to accommodate more children, he had an intensity about him that was hard to ignore.

If his wife had desecrated that dream, what was he capable of?

Gin shook her head, frustrated with herself. Maybe it was the glass of wine she'd had, but she was letting her imagination get ahead of her. Jake was capable of taking care of himself—not to mention a good eight inches taller than Gus and considerably more fit. And besides, no matter what Gus had done when confronted with the reality of his wife's infidelity, it didn't make him a threat to anyone else. If he and Jake were talking it out tonight, all that was likely to happen was that Jake would try to help him find a way out of the situation he'd gotten himself into.

When Gin got home, she took Jett for a quick walk, then changed into her flannel pajamas and made a cup of tea.

She curled up on the couch with her laptop and scrolled through Facebook, searching for Marlene and Gus. Gus didn't appear to have an account, but after a few attempts, Gin found the correct Marlene Sykes and spent some time reading through her posts.

She grew increasingly confused the further back she went. The meek, lonesome wife who'd been wasting away in Trumbull had apparently led an entirely different life in Steubenville. In nearly every picture, Marlene was surrounded by friends, dressed in flashy clothing and made up to the hilt. She posed with girlfriends, waiters, store mannequins, dogs—she was a master of the selfie, alternating between coy puckered lips and sexy smiles and off-camera gazes.

There were pictures with Gus too, but they diminished in frequency in recent months. In some, they looked like any other couple, holding hands or posing in front of scenery, or with various nieces and nephews and groups of friends.

There were a great many photographs with a particular woman named Karin, who Gin surmised was Marlene's best friend. She clicked over to Karin's profile and discovered that she owned a shop that specialized in the style of clothing Marlene had worn the night of the dinner: bright, close-fitting, trendy items.

Gin went through the photos a second time, slowly, trying to see if she could figure out who the secret lover was. Of course, it was possible that Marlene had deleted those pictures. Perhaps Gus had asked her to—or insisted—when they moved away to make a fresh start.

It didn't add up. Granted, Gin had spent only a few hours with the woman. The first time, Marlene had seemed distant, bordering on afraid. Yesterday she'd been despondent. Could this be evidence of a worsening depression? Mental illness could drastically alter a person's personality, if only temporarily. And Marlene had certainly suffered potentially precipitating events: the guilt and shame of her continuing infidelity, the loneliness and boredom of being far from home, and the shock of suspecting her husband of a terrible crime.

Gin tried searching for Gus Sykes online, not really sure what she was looking for. Evidence of prior crimes, perhaps, especially those that revealed a temper he couldn't control. But all she found were mentions on a family reunion site, his parents' fiftieth wedding anniversary announcement, and an out-of-date LinkedIn profile from when he was looking for work.

Gin closed her laptop and took her teacup to the sink. It was almost ten; she decided she would read in bed until Jake got home.

Halfway up the stairs, her phone chimed.

Had too much to drink. Gus and I walked back to
his place. I'm going to sleep on their couch. See you
tomorrow. Love you

Gin paused, looking out over the narrow window Jake had installed at the stairs' landing. She had a view of the entire valley from here, the meandering black curves of the river, the bridge lit up prettily like a string of Christmas lights, and the cars traveling along the road on the other side.

Of course she didn't want Jake to drink and drive. And no matter what the truth was about Gus Sykes, she knew it was silly to worry about Jake spending the night in his house.

She had just hoped for a while now to spend some time relaxing with Jake, putting their cares aside, enjoying each other's company. Going to the reenactors' party at the bar didn't count because they hadn't been alone the whole evening. Tonight, he'd begged off coming with her to go to the jobsite—but then he'd ended up getting drunk with a friend.

Gin thought of Tuck and his plan to spend tonight with his daughter. The image was sweetly domestic; it wasn't hard to imagine, given how Tuck melted whenever he was around Cherie. There was something incredibly appealing about a man who loved his children.

If Gin was honest with herself, there was something incredibly appealing about Tuck, period.

She thought of the way he'd watched her leave his office, replaying his words in her mind. "If you knew me better," he had said, "you'd know that I never do anything unless I give it my all."

Had he been talking about her? Or only about the case?

She turned away from the window, impatient with herself. So Jake hadn't come home tonight—that wasn't an excuse for mooning over another man.

She undressed quickly and turned out the light, no longer in the mood to read. But sleep didn't come easily. And as she tossed and turned, she had to work very hard to stop herself from thinking about Tuck, alone in his own bed, just a few miles away.

21

In the morning, she left the house before Jake returned home, not bothering to leave a note. She stopped to put gas in the Range Rover and bought a large Styrofoam cup of coffee. Then she put the address of Marlene's friend's clothing shop in her phone.

Traffic was light, and she arrived in forty minutes. Steubenville was a town of several thousand people, with a picturesque main street that belied the statistics Gin had found online. One would never guess the rates of drug use and unemployment from the old-fashioned streetlamps, the charming shop fronts, and the festive strings of holiday lights. But based on the news articles she'd skimmed, no fewer than a dozen meth labs had been shut down in the neighboring countryside in the last two years—and posters for support groups and treatment centers were tacked up in some of the shop windows.

Gin felt a little apprehensive as she parked and walked down the street toward the dress shop. The story she'd invented—that she was considering a career change and needed interview clothes and her new acquaintance Marlene Sykes had recommended her friend's shop—seemed like a shaky one once she arrived in front of the shop windows. The store appeared not to carry anything appropriate for a job interview. The mannequins all wore clothes in tight-fitting styles and eye-popping shades, many featuring suggestive touches like cutouts and sheer panels, slits and bare necklines.

"Come on in, it's freezing out there," a voice called as she hesitated in the doorway. Gin recognized Karin from Facebook as she emerged from behind the counter, patting her teased blonde hair, a welcoming smile on her face. Marlene's friend was more attractive in person, she decided, without the theatrical poses that she struck for many of her online photos. "Are you looking for anything in particular today?"

"Well, a job interview, actually," Gin said, attempting to ad-lib. "My friend Marlene said you might be able to help."

"Marlene Sykes?" Karin asked in surprise. "You drove all the way here from Trumbull?"

"Well—Marlene convinced me that you'd have what I was looking for. The position I'm interviewing for is to be an events manager at a high-end nightclub. I'll be meeting with clients and vendors who are expecting me to look like I belong there. I know I can do the job, but I've never been very good with fashion. All I know is that my wardrobe could definitely use some color and style."

"I think I can help with that. What sort of work did you do before?" Karin asked politely, beginning to sort through racks, pulling out items for Gin to try.

"Oh, I was a—I worked as a receptionist for a medical examiner's office, actually," Gin said. Sticking close to the truth might keep her from tripping herself up, but saying the words out loud made her feel unaccountably self-conscious.

"That's fascinating!" Karin exclaimed. "I love crime dramas—I bet you hear this all the time, but I always wonder if it's really like on TV. You know, solving murders and cold cases and all."

Gin grinned wryly. "Mostly I just dealt with the families and helped with records and schedules, but I have to say that none of the pathologists I worked for seem to think it was that exciting. In truth, being a medical examiner seems to have the same issues as lots of other jobs—lots of paperwork, long hours, and constant budget cuts."

"How did you meet Marlene, if you don't mind my asking?"

"My, uh, boyfriend works with Gus." Gin blushed, wondering how long it would take her to stop tripping over that word. "They came over for dinner not long ago."

"Oh, I see," Karin said. She seemed to be choosing her words carefully. "I'm glad she's making some new friends there. I know they haven't been able to spend much time together, given his hours."

"Yes, he and Jake have been putting in some long shifts at the jobsite."

Karin raised a well-shaped eyebrow. "Marlene says he barely comes home."

"Mmm," Gin said noncommittally. She wondered if Marlene had confided in Karin about her lover. If not, maybe she was exaggerating Gus's job responsibilities to deflect suspicion away from herself. "That's a shame. It must be difficult for both of them. Does Gus, um, handle the stress well?"

"Gus?" Karin laughed. "We used to call him The Rock—not like that actor, but because he never gets upset. He's, like, the most even-keeled man I've ever met. Tell you the truth, I was surprised when Marlene hooked up with him—she always had a lot of drama with men in the past. I guess I figured she liked it that way."

"But Gus is . . . devoted to her?" Gin had to be careful; if she went past idle curiosity to outright snooping, Karin was bound to notice.

"Oh, yeah. They're good for each other. I mean, sure—he doesn't do a thing around the house, and he can be kind of uptight. Of course, the way she spends money, they kind of balance each other out."

"She was saying she misses going out," Gin said, taking a chance. "I get the feeling she's got a little cabin fever."

"Well, yeah, she's a girl who needs a lot of attention." Karin smiled fondly. "Before she met Gus, she used to date a couple of guys at a time. She loved the excitement, but it got old for the rest of us, because she was always using me as an excuse for why she couldn't see one or the other—and then she'd cancel on me and sneak off with the other one. Which, I know, makes her sound awful, but it really was all in fun. I never thought she'd settle down." Karin shrugged. "Shows what I know."

"When the baby comes, she'll be in for a whole new level of settling down."

Karin looked at her in surprise. "She told you she was trying to get pregnant?"

"I, uh, thought she already was . . . ?"

"Oh, no. They're having the hardest time; she just can't seem to conceive. And Gus wants a baby *bad*. So they're trying. I keep telling her they should look into adoption, but—oh, listen to me, it's totally none of my business. Just the other day she was telling me I should be a shrink so people would pay me to hear my opinions." She laughed and pulled a lime-green blouse from a display. "Okay, how about I'll shut up, and we'll get you a room to try on all these cute things, okay?"

"Of course," Gin said shakily.

"I can totally see you in this," Karin said, holding up a fuchsia sheath dress with an asymmetric hem. "This shade is called peony. You know what? I think you just might be a peony kind of girl."

*　　*　　*

An hour later, Gin was heading back home, a shopping bag containing her new clothes on the passenger seat. She'd ended up purchasing the pink sheath dress and a pair of matching sandals, as well as a sweater and faux leather leggings. Karin had turned out to have a keen eye for fashion, and the clothes fit Gin so well that the effect was flattering rather than over the top.

Karin truly did seem to care deeply about Marlene—even if the two had clearly not been sharing all their secrets. Gin replayed the conversation in her mind as she drove. Why wouldn't Marlene tell her best friend that she was pregnant? The obvious answer was that she wasn't sure who the father was.

Or—

Maybe the reason she hadn't been able to conceive had to do with Gus, not her. If that was the case, and Gus discovered that Marlene was still seeing her lover, he might have been enraged that the baby wasn't his. Angry enough, maybe, to want to destroy both his cheating wife and her lover's child?

It was a pretty farfetched conclusion, Gin had to admit. Tuck would laugh her out of his office if she came to him without any evidence to support the theory. And Stillman probably wouldn't even take her call.

Gus had seemed so easygoing whenever Gin met him. "The Rock" seemed like an apt nickname. But she really didn't know him at all. And she couldn't even begin to guess what a man like Gus, a man who'd given up everything to make a fresh start with his wife, would do if he discovered he'd been cuckolded a second time.

22

When Gin pulled up the hill to Jake's house at a little before six, she was momentarily startled to see her mother's Lexus parked in the drive.

Then, with a sense of mortification, she remembered: when she'd had coffee with her parents the morning of the fire and the discovery of the body, she had invited Madeleine and Richard to come to dinner. She had *meant* to write it down—but then in the turmoil that followed, she had forgotten.

Grabbing her purse and opening the door, Gin's heart pounded with anxiety. Though the four of them had had dinner together several times, either at Gin's parents' house or a restaurant they liked that had opened up downtown, this was to have been the first time her parents came to dinner at Jake's house, the first time that Gin and Jake entertained them as a couple.

It was, in fact, the first time that Gin had ever invited her parents to dinner with a man. At the time, it had felt thrilling—a prelude to something deeper, she had hoped: nothing so formal as an engagement, but a subtle shift in the relationship.

Now instead, she had not only forgotten to tell Jake about the invitation, but she'd done no preparation. No shopping, no menu planning, no arranging flowers or putting fresh hand towels in the bathroom or setting the table. And to make matters worse, she and Jake had barely spoken in two days.

All in all, Gin had screwed up royally.

But as she stepped through the door, she could hear her father's voice, animated and full of life the way it was when he was telling a story. The house was filled with the aromas of garlic and herbs, and a classical guitar recording played softly in the background.

"Virginia!" Madeleine walked out of the kitchen, the sculpted planes of her face flushed with happiness. She was holding a nearly empty wineglass by the stem, and behind her, Jake was uncorking a second bottle of wine, and—shockingly—her father was bent over a cutting board, fastidiously slicing a carrot into rounds.

"Dad!" Gin exclaimed. "You've never cooked anything in your whole life!"

"And you've never forgotten my birthday, or your mother's, or our anniversary," her father countered cheerfully. "But today you somehow forgot that you invited your poor old parents to dinner." He gave the end of the carrot a decisive chop for emphasis.

"Oh, Dad . . . I'm so sorry, truly, it's just been such an incredibly busy—"

"Don't worry," Madeleine interrupted, tilting her glass so Jake could fill it. "Jake has the situation well in hand."

Gin met Jake's eyes. For a moment, neither looked away. Rather than the tense, distracted expression he'd been wearing for days, he looked relaxed and slightly amused.

"I'm so sorry." She tilted up her face for a kiss, then suddenly felt awkward and turned away. She had never kissed Jake in front of her parents. "God, I can't believe I forgot to tell you."

"Luckily, you're dating a culinary genius," Jake said. "One who's not above hiring some cheap labor to do the scut work while I put the finishing touches on . . ."

He turned dramatically toward the stove and flourished a sizzling sauté pan.

"*Mélange de fruits de mer al Crosby*," he announced.

"Oh, my gracious, that smells divine," Madeleine sighed. "How on earth did you come up with it on such short notice?"

"Eh, it's just whatever I had on hand. I had shrimp and cod in the freezer, and saffron and Arborio rice from when we made paella a few weeks ago, plus whatever was in the veggie drawer—you get the picture."

Richard raised his glass for a toast, wiping his free hand on the apron that Jake had lent him. "To the men in this family," he announced. "We're good-looking and highly intelligent, obviously—"

"And modest!" Madeleine interjected, laughing.

"—and surprisingly skilled in the kitchen, but our greatest accomplishment is finding women who are too good for us and put up with us anyway."

Everyone raised their glasses, the ruby wine glowing in the light of the pendant lamps, and Gin wondered if maybe, just maybe, their luck had finally turned.

*   *   *

They were finishing a dessert of frozen pound cake with a sauce Jake had whipped up from mandarin oranges simmered with rum, Madeleine and Richard arguing good-naturedly about a trip to Mexico they'd taken when Gin and her sister were eight and ten years old, when there was a knock at the door.

Jake looked at Gin quizzically. "Any other surprises up your sleeve, Gin? More guests you forgot to tell me about?"

"No," Gin said, getting up from the table and checking the time: 8:54 PM, late for a casual drop in. She peered out through the decorative square pane.

Bruce Stillman was standing there, holding his badge aloft.

"What on earth—" Gin opened the door.

"I'm here for Jake," he said before she could say a word.

Jake came to the door, pushing past Gin. "What the hell do you want now, Stillman?"

"I need you to come with me, Crosby," Stillman said. "We can talk about it on the way."

Her parents had also come to the door, Richard digging his glasses from his shirt pocket.

Jake didn't budge. "You talk to me about it right here."

Stillman sighed. "You sure that's what you want, Jake? Hello, Madeleine, Richard."

"What are you doing here, Stillman?" Richard said. "You're interrupting a private family gathering. Whatever you want, surely it can wait until tomorrow."

Gin knew that her father's outrage stemmed, in part, from the fact that he himself had falsely accused Jake in the past, a wound that had only recently healed.

"Just tell us what it's about," she pleaded.

Stillman kept his eyes on Jake. "It's about the insurance policy you took out right before the fire," he said. "And the two million dollars you stand to collect if they shut down your project."

"What the hell are you talking about?" Jake snapped. "My policy won't pay a fraction of that."

"We both know that's not true; only I just found out about it. Pretty clever, how the insurance payout comes no matter what happens with the dead guy. They can make the whole place a historic site tomorrow and start selling snow cones and dressing up in bonnets, and you will have already gotten out whole. I guess this entire mess is kind of your lucky break."

"I don't know what you think you know about my finances," Jake said, "but you're wrong. My insurance barely covers my tools and my truck. The money I've got tied up in there is mine."

Richard cleared his throat, and everyone turned to him.

"There's, ahhh . . . something I maybe should have told you," he said. "I tried to tell you the other day, Gin, honey. Madeleine and I . . . which is to say, really, it was me. I took out some insurance, Jake. On your business. When, er, things began to look serious between the two of you."

Gin gasped. The conversation she'd had with her father the other day, the one she hadn't let him finish—that was actually the second time he'd tried to talk to her about her relationship with Jake. There had been a rare invitation into his study weeks earlier, where he'd poured them each a scotch and asked how things were going with Jake. At the time, she'd found it charmingly old-fashioned. Richard had asked about Jake's business, his plans for the future, his ideas about growth, and whether he would ever move the business away from Trumbull.

And, just in passing, about his insurance coverage.

And Gin had admitted that Jake probably didn't carry enough insurance. She'd said it laughingly, affectionately even; it was proof of the reckless zeal Jake still had for his work. It didn't surprise her that he would put his money back into the business rather than into extra insurance. It was part of what made Jake who he was.

Other people, though—especially someone like her father, who was not only conservative and careful by nature, but who had helped found a medical center and sat in on countless discussions about insurance—might see Jake's choices as irresponsible. And Richard would never want to see someone gambling with his daughter's future.

"Dad," she gasped. "Did you . . . without even *telling* either of us?"

Richard shrugged uncomfortably. "It wasn't something I thought you'd ever need to know about," he said. "When the paperwork came through, I planned to sit down with you, son. I hoped you'd consider it a token of my faith in you."

It had been Richard's way of giving his approval, of blessing the relationship.

"Richard, I can't believe you never discussed this with me," Madeleine said.

"Well, now you know," Richard said, addressing Stillman. "So that's the explanation."

Stillman shook his head. "What I know is that insurance was recorded on Jake's company only a few days before the fire, and according to the guy I talked to at the insurance company, the payout could go as high as two million dollars. We'll want to talk to you too, sir."

"Wait, wait," Madeleine said. "I think we all need to take a step back here. Detective, please, you've got to see how ridiculous this is. You don't live in Trumbull, you can't know—"

"I may not live here, ma'am," Stillman said, an edge to his voice. "And I appreciate the fact that we've been wrong about your family in the past. But don't for a minute think that buys any free passes. I don't plan to screw up twice."

Jake's face had gone pale, and Gin put her hand on his shoulder.

"I'm so sorry," she said. "Go ahead with him now. I'll—I'll figure something out."

"Yeah," Jake said bleakly. "I'll call when they let me, I guess."

Richard kissed his wife, his shoulders sagging, and laid his hand on Gin's shoulder for a moment without meeting her eyes. Then the two of them followed Stillman out, and Gin and her mother were alone in Jake's kitchen. The pound cake sat sodden and forgotten on the counter.

"Oh, honey, what a mess," Madeleine said.

"I can't believe Dad didn't tell us," Gin said. "Or even you."

"That's the way he is. He feels like he has to carry the weight of the whole family on his shoulders."

"Even now, though? I mean, come on, Mom, you're the *mayor*. I'm thirty-six years old. And Jake . . ."

"Your father made things hard for Jake for a very long time," Madeleine said quietly. "And Jake has been remarkably forgiving. I'm sure your father simply wanted to respond in kind."

"And instead, he's made a mess of everything."

Gin went to the counter, where the coffee waited untouched. She got down two mugs and the sugar bowl and poured two cups.

"Oh, honey, I shouldn't. Caffeine at this hour will keep me up all night."

"Mom," Gin said, "neither one of us is going to be able to sleep, worrying about Dad and Jake. And besides, something happened earlier that I need to tell you about. Something that could explain what happened that night—and clear Jake too."

"You know something? But—but why didn't you say anything to Detective Stillman?"

Gin thought about the look of resolute confidence on Jake's face when he spoke of Gus, of the promise he'd demanded from her. She sighed. "I told Jake I wouldn't discuss it with the cops until he'd had a chance to look into it."

"Well, I think the fact that the police just took him in might change things, don't you?"

Gin took a sip of her coffee to avoid answering. Yes—any other man would probably consider his arrest an emergency.

But Jake wasn't any other man. He was stubborn as hell and loyal to a fault. He'd think nothing of spending a night in jail to protect the people he cared about.

Gin wondered if Jake and Gus had spoken about Marlene last night—and if so, if Gus had been able to reassure Jake of his innocence. She wished that she had had a chance to discuss it with Jake before now. Maybe he'd learned something that cleared Gus completely.

But maybe he hadn't. And if Gus was guilty, and Jake was sitting in jail out of a misbegotten sense of loyalty, then Gin had no choice but to intervene.

"Okay, Mom," she began. "Let me tell you about a very interesting conversation I had a couple days ago."

*   *   *

"We'll just go down there and explain it to Chief Baxter first thing in the morning," Madeleine said when Gin had finished telling her what she had learned about the relationship between Gus and Marlene Sykes. "He can contact the county investigators."

"Mom, don't be ridiculous! They're not going to listen to us now, not when they've got Jake in the crosshairs. And besides, Tuck can't do anything. It's not his case."

"They still have to follow up if he gives them a solid lead," Madeleine said stubbornly.

"I—I don't know. They seem determined to wrap this up as quickly as possible, especially given all the positive media coverage it's generated for the captain."

"Well, that's just fantastic," Madeleine said in disgust. "And to think I campaigned for Wheeler. You'd think she'd show some loyalty."

"Mom, she's just doing her job."

"It seems like no one's doing their job, or your father and Jake wouldn't be in the hot seat! We're just going to have to figure this out ourselves. Come on, let's think this through. Don't you think it's a huge coincidence that Gus happened to go to the site early on the same morning Marlene and her lover were there? Surely anyone could see that it doesn't make sense."

"I don't know, Mom . . . maybe he had his suspicions already, and he followed her there. Or maybe he really was worried about theft. I know Jake's been concerned, with all the copper theft and vandalism in the news." She paused and thought about what her mother had said. The coincidence *was* suspicious—or at least very strange. "Maybe . . . maybe there is an innocent explanation. I mean, maybe Gus had some other motivation that he's covering up, like you say—whether he was tailing his wife and hoping to catch her in the act or something else. But Mom, Jake *believes* in Gus. And he's a good judge of character, you know that."

Madeleine sighed. "Good people have been fooled before," she said quietly. "I just hate to see Jake go down for something that Gus did. Listen—if there is another explanation, and if Gus really is the man Jake believes he is, wouldn't he want to clear things up now? To help Jake?"

"Yes . . ." Gin said slowly. "You think I should talk to him?"

"Yes, but if he *is* lying—if he's trying to protect himself—you don't want to tip him off, right?"

"I'll go talk to him." Gin looked at her watch. It was nearly 10:00 PM—too late for a polite visit, but these were hardly ordinary circumstances. "I'll tell him Jake has been taken for questioning. If I can talk to him in person, I think I'll know if he's lying."

"That seems like a very dangerous idea. What if he tries to hurt you? To keep you quiet?"

"That's very unlikely, Mom—he'll just keep lying, if it comes to that. But at least I'll know, and then I can go to Tuck and—and—"

"And he can strong-arm his way back into the investigation?" Madeleine shook her head. "I know we're both upset about Jake, honey, but maybe the best thing to do is simply wait until morning, when we both have a clear head."

But Gin had made up her mind. She got up, bending to kiss her mother's cheek. "I'm just going to talk to him, that's all. And then I'll come right back. I promise."

"Be careful," Madeleine called as Gin went to get her coat.

But Gin's mind was already racing far ahead.

* * *

When Gin pulled in front of the Sykes' townhouse in the Galleria, she could see lights on in the upstairs windows. Someone was still awake.

She knocked firmly on the door, then knocked again after a few moments passed. She could hear voices, then movement from the living room. A moment later, the door opened, and Gus stood facing her, dressed in sweatpants and a Steelers jersey, his face lined and tired.

"Gin?" he asked. "Is everything all right? Has something else happened?"

Behind him, Gin thought she caught a flash of movement on the stairs, but then it was gone. "Everything's fine," she assured him, even though it was far from the truth. "I just—I wondered if I could talk to you for a moment? I know it's late, and I wouldn't have come if it wasn't important."

"Of course," Gus said without hesitation. "We were just upstairs watching TV. Can I get you a drink or something?"

"No, no, I'm fine," Gin said, following Gus into the house.

It had been cleaned since the other day, and Gin wondered if it was Gus or Marlene who had picked up the clutter and dusted the furniture and placed an inexpensive grocery-store bouquet of red carnations and holiday greenery on a lace runner on the dining room table. She took the seat that Gus offered, in an upholstered chair pulled close to the coffee table. Gus sat down on the sofa and waited expectantly.

And Gin didn't know where to begin. She glanced up the stairs, but the only door she could see in the upstairs hallway was closed. Maybe Marlene had gone to bed, or maybe she was already in her nightclothes and didn't want to join them. Perhaps she was annoyed by the intrusion.

Or terrified of what her husband might do if Gin confronted him with the truth.

Gin pushed that thought out of her head. She had to do this—for Jake, and for Marlene and her unborn child, if they were really in danger.

"Jake has been picked up for questioning about the fire," she began, willing her voice to stay neutral. "I'm afraid they're not going to let him go this time, not without some new information to clear him. I've just come to talk to you to see if there's something, anything, that you've thought of that might shed light on that night."

"Oh, God," Gus said, running his hand heavily over his face, shadowed with a day's growth of beard. "I was afraid something like this was going to happen. I kept telling him he needed to get a lawyer. Hell, I've wondered if I should get one myself, but what with the baby coming, and Marlene's medical bills—" He shrugged helplessly.

"About—about that," Gin said carefully. "I need you to know that I know about the affair."

Gus blanched. He started to say something, then stopped himself. Emotions battled on his face. Finally, he asked, "How did you find out?"

"Marlene told me," Gin said. She was taking a chance—if Gus was unstable, if he was furious enough with his wife to try to harm her, then there was no telling what he might do if he found out that she'd told others about her infidelity. And yet, he'd seemed concerned, even tender, when he talked about the baby.

It was confusing. Based on what Marlene had said, Gus was a jealous and impulsive man. Of course it was possible that his feelings were conflicted. Maybe he truly was trying to work things out with his wife in hopes that they could build their family together. Maybe he'd come to his senses after that single irrational act and, realizing how close he'd come to harming the woman he loved, vowed to forgive her.

If, after talking to Gus, she determined that he was a threat to Marlene, Gin wouldn't leave without ensuring her safety—even if it meant summoning the police. But she had to press on if it meant a chance at clearing Jake.

"I think—I think she might be suffering from a breakdown, Gus. I'm concerned for her well-being."

Gus jumped off the couch and started pacing. "This is all my fault," he said. "God, I'm such an idiot. If I could go back and change things—if I could only have known—"

He turned and faced Gin with a look of such pain and remorse that she felt her resolve weaken a little. "I wish I'd never met her."

"Never met . . . Marlene?" Gin asked, confused. There was a sound from upstairs, and they both turned to see Marlene standing on the landing, dressed in a silky robe, her hair cascading over her shoulders. She wore no makeup, but unlike the last time Gin had seen her, she no longer looked heartbroken and disheveled. Her eyes were clear and burned with intensity. Her fist was tightly closed around some small object.

She gave Gin a thin smile, raising an eyebrow, and started unhurriedly down the stairs. "Aren't you a persistent one," she said in a dreamy voice. "Never give up, that must be your motto. There's probably nothing you wouldn't do for Jake, is there?"

She stumbled slightly, and Gin wondered if she was drunk, but she grabbed the railing and kept coming down. She was humming, and it took only a second for Gin to recognize the tune of "Stand by Your Man."

The hairs on her neck stood up.

"What's going on here?" Gus demanded.

"I know about Marlene's affair," Gin repeated. "You went there that night—maybe to catch her in the act, maybe to confront her. Maybe you didn't intend to hurt them at first, though the accelerant in your truck is going to make that hard to prove. I don't know if you wanted to kill her or simply give her a message. But either way, you've put things in motion that have gotten way out of control."

To her astonishment, Marlene started to laugh. She'd reached the bottom step and sat down abruptly, her back against the wall, her robe spilling over her long pale legs. One slipper had come off, and she wiggled her foot.

"Look, I don't know what you're after here," Gus said angrily, "but Marlene never had an affair; *I* did. I fucked up—Mar even gave me a second chance and agreed to move here with me, but I . . . I . . . ." His voice ended in a strangled sob. He went to his wife and knelt down in front of her. "I only agreed to meet Cassie that night to end things for good. I realize you've got no reason to believe me, Mar. But if you can't find a way to forgive me, then how are we ever going to give the baby a decent chance?"

He tried to take her hands, but she swatted them away. Gin's mind swirled in confusion. "*You* had the affair, Gus?"

"Of course he did," Marlene said. She pushed her way past Gus and staggered over to the couch and dropped into it, just a couple of feet away from Gin. Gin followed, trying to take her hand, but she kept jerking it away. "He can't help himself. He's a horn . . . dog." She drew out the syllables and ended in another small giggle.

"Honey, you need to stop talking now," Gus said. "Listen, we can talk about this later. We can see that counselor if you want. But you need to forget about that night, okay?"

"You knew," Gin gasped, the pieces falling into place. "The whole time, you knew it was Marlene who was there that night." She turned to the woman, whose head was lolling. "*You* set the fire. You were trying to harm Gus and his lover."

Marlene simply stared at her. Her pupils were huge, and her breath was coming in increasingly ragged breaths.

"What . . . what's wrong with you?" Gus demanded, putting his hand gently under her chin. "Are you all right, honey?"

Gin was instantly on alert, chastising herself for not realizing that her affect was dangerously off. "Did you take something, Marlene? Listen to me. You need to tell me what you've done. The baby could be at risk of—"

"There is no baby," Marlene mumbled.

"Stop it," Gus said, his voice rising in panic. "Honey, please, tell Gin what you've done. You're not yourself, you're—"

She gave him a sad, resigned smile and allowed him to pry her fingers free one by one from the small bottle she was holding. "You were just so happy," she said softly. "When I told you we were having a baby. I thought it would fix everything. I thought it would fix *us*."

Gus worked the bottle free, and Gin snatched it from his hand. Reading the label, she felt her mind switch into professional mode, all the shocking new information receding to the background as she realized that her first task was to save Marlene's life.

"How many did you take, Marlene?" she demanded, putting her hand to the woman's wrist, feeling for the irregular, thready pulse. "Call nine-one-one, Gus. Do it *now*. Tell them she's ingested an unknown amount of hydrocodone."

"I can't, you know," Marlene slurred. "I can't have a baby. But it made him so happy. He brought me flowers and a baby name book, and I thought . . ." She shook her head, and a tear slid down her face. "But he went back to her."

"Stay with me, Marlene. Gus is getting help. Tell me how many you took, please? How many pills?"

Marlene slumped forward into Gin's lap, her limbs floppy and heavy. "It doesn't matter," she mumbled against Gin's neck. "It doesn't matter anymore."

*　　　*　　　*

"So it was *Gus* who met a lover there the night of the fire?" Madeleine asked, nearly two hours later, when Gin finally got back to the house. She and Gus had followed the ambulance to the hospital in her car, Gus nearly hysterical with concern and, Gin was sure, an overwhelming sense of guilt. She'd left him there in the waiting room with Detective Witt, who was undoubtedly going to take Marlene into custody as soon as she was recovered enough to leave the hospital.

"Yes, apparently. He says he'd gone there to break things off with the woman, but I guess Marlene doesn't believe him."

"And yet she tried to kill herself this time instead of him," Madeleine said, shaking her head. She was still sitting in the kitchen chair, where she'd been waiting by the phone ever since Gin left. "It sounds like she's got some serious issues."

"I'd say so," Gin agreed. "Although I don't know that she ever really wanted to burn him down along with the house. As crazy as it all seems, I think she really loves him."

"Well, at least now they've got to believe Jake," Madeleine said. "All he's guilty of is trusting the wrong people."

"I certainly hope you're right, Mom," Gin said, giving Madeleine's hand a squeeze. "I'm ready for our luck to turn."

*   *   *

Gin let Jake sleep in the next morning while she cooked a full breakfast of French toast, bacon, and sliced fruit. He'd gotten home around two in the morning, not long after Madeleine finally left, exhausted but relieved that the arson case finally seemed to be resolved. He'd fallen into bed practically midsentence and was asleep before Gin could even turn out the light.

He came into the kitchen just as she was taking the pan off the stove, stretching and yawning. After a week of gray, wintry weather, the sun had broken through shortly after dawn, and the house was bathed in its bright, cheery light.

"That smells fantastic," Jake said. "I guess I'll forgive you just this once for trying to take over."

Gin handed him a plate and smiled. "You can have your apron back," she said. "I'm happy with cleanup duty."

"How about we take the day off and forget all about the construction site, Civil War reenactors, and anything that doesn't have to do with you getting back in my bed and out of those clothes?"

"Sounds like a deal, mister," Gin laughed. "Do you want me to do the dishes first?"

"Only if you plan to do them in the nude," Jake growled. "Get over here, woman, and bring me some coffee."

*   *   *

The second time Gin got out of bed that day, Jake was gone, it was already late afternoon, and the house was comfortably warm and silent. When she came downstairs, Jett whined for her dinner, and Gin realized that they'd forgotten to feed the old dog. Jake had left a note saying he had gone into the office to return e-mails and work on a proposal and that she shouldn't wait for him for dinner.

"Guess it's just the two of us," she told Jett as she settled in for her meal. "How about a nice easy run and then a bath? One of us smells like she needs one."

An hour later, she was toweling off the dog, gently wiping suds from her ruff, when her phone rang. She saw that it was her father and set down the towel to answer: he rarely called, relying on her mother to maintain family communication. Gin had talked to her mother briefly around lunchtime when she had gone downstairs to heat up some leftovers, and she was sure that Madeleine had passed along her account of the events that had transpired last night.

"Hi, honey," her father said. "Everything good over there?"

"Sure, Dad. We had a—a lazy kind of day."

"Well, after last night, it sounds like you needed one. Your mother talked to Chief Baxter, by the way. They're going to charge that woman in the arson case. Jake doesn't have anything to worry about. At least, not on that front."

Ah, there it was—her father was feeling guilty. "I'm relieved, of course, for Jake," she said. "And I'm glad that Marlene Sykes admitted the truth. But I hope that she'll get some help while she's awaiting trial—I think at least some of her behavior may have been exacerbated by stress and possibly a major depression or other mental illness."

"Of course, of course," Richard said, sounding distracted. "Listen, I, uh, well . . ." He cleared his throat, sounding uncharacteristically uncertain.

"Are *you* all right, Dad?" Gin asked. "It can't have been much fun, being questioned along with Jake half the night."

"Oh, I'm fine, just fine. It's just that I, well, I had a lot of time to think, sitting there waiting for Stillman and his crew to talk to me. And I came to a few conclusions. Well, one important one, anyway."

"Oh, really?" Gin asked, pretty sure where her father was going. He was a fair man and a moral one, but apologizing had always been difficult for him.

"Yes. You see, I think I may have, er, underestimated both Jake and you. When I took out that insurance policy, I overstepped. I made something my business that has nothing to do with me—and worse, I ended up making both of you feel like I don't have faith in you to run your own lives."

Gin allowed herself a small smile, glad her father couldn't see her in this moment. Maybe now, finally, her father would realize that she didn't need him—or Jake, for that matter, or anyone else to provide for her or rescue her or fix her mistakes.

Still, it was kind of nice to know that he was still ready to do all of that and more for her.

"It's okay, Dad," she said. "I know it came from a place of love. And in a way, it's proof that you've truly accepted Jake as part of my life. That means a lot to me."

"All right," Richard said gruffly. "You know, I've always dreamed that someday you'd come back home. I think people just have a natural connection to the place they were born."

"Thanks, Dad," Gin replied. "I'm glad to be home."

But something he'd just said nagged at her mind, making her replay the last few sentences of their conversation.

"Hang on, Dad . . . what did you just say?"

"Just now?" Richard asked, sounding bewildered. "Just that your mother and I are glad you're back home with us."

"No, the part about . . . people having a connection to where they were born."

"Well, I was thinking of your mother, actually, since she's spent her whole life here, but—"

"No, wait. You made me remember something." The nagging feeling rapidly blossomed into full-blown excitement as the pieces fell into place.

"What are you talking about?"

"Just . . . that girl." As Gin's mind raced ahead, she struggled to explain to her father. "Danielle. I think she might have been lying."

"Honey, I don't have any idea what you're talking about."

"I met this girl, this young reenactor, at a party a couple of nights ago. She knew the guy who owned the motorcycle that, umm . . ." She paused, realizing that she hadn't told her father about her accident, not wanting to worry him. "Anyway, she met a man named Marvin Morgensen at a reenactor event. Apparently Chief Crosby investigated him for a series of rapes years ago."

"Slow down, honey," her father protested. "I can hardly keep up."

"Well, it's just that this girl, Danielle, she said Morgensen had been friendly to her when she first started coming to the reenactor meetings, and then one day he just disappeared. But Dad, she said he went 'back home to Kansas'—that's what you reminded me of, because Tuck Baxter told me that Morgensen spent his whole life in Pennsylvania. She was trying to throw me off his trail, to convince me that he'd simply moved away."

"I'm afraid you've lost me," Richard said. But Gin couldn't take the time to stop to explain it to him. Pieces were falling into place all at once, and the picture that was emerging wasn't a pretty one.

Danielle had said she had hurt her back during a drill, and that was why she wasn't out on the dance floor. But she had been wearing a brace on her *leg*, not her back. It was an over-the-counter brace, and she'd wrapped her knee as if she'd torn a ligament. She'd obviously done it herself, which suggested that she hadn't gone to see a doctor.

And then there was the bandage on her forehead. Danielle had worn her hair clipped to one side, and Gin had assumed she was hiding a breakout, as she herself had once done at that age.

Until Danielle had said she'd hurt herself when she fired a blank round from her rifle.

"The problem is that it's typically the shoulder that's injured from the kickback when a round goes off," Gin said, talking herself through the things that didn't add up, the problem that had been nagging at the back of her mind for the last two days. "I've never heard of anyone hurting their face that way."

"Gin, honey, you're not making any sense at all," her father said. "This girl you met, who hurt her leg or her back or her face or whatever—what does it matter?"

"Because what if she'd hurt herself in a *fall*?" Gin let her words hang in the air for a moment. The rider who had struck her had landed on his side. Or maybe *her* side. The helmet she'd been wearing could have shifted violently, bruising or abrading her skull, which would account for the bandage near her hairline. And Danielle's leg injury could certainly have been explained by the crash as well.

"Sweetheart, are you all right?" her father asked, his voice full of concern. "It sounds like you haven't even given yourself a chance to recover from everything that's happened. Before you get started on a new case . . ."

"It's fine, Dad." Gin couldn't spare the time to explain it all to her father. The person who had run her down was small—unusually small for a man, but not for a woman. Gin didn't know what the connection was yet—but she was convinced that Danielle Segal was lying to her about *something*. That she had been trying to prevent Gin from learning something she didn't want her to know.

The bike belonged to Marvin Morgensen. If Morgensen had been the Shopgirl Rapist—what if Danielle *hadn't* escaped him at all? What if she had actually been one of his victims? What if he had preyed on her, pretending to help her learn about reenacting . . . then somehow got her alone and raped her?

"It's just that there had to be a reason why this girl didn't go to the police," Gin mused, aware that she was further confusing her father but needing to walk it through out loud. If Danielle had sought help, and the investigators had done a rape kit, it would have been a pretty straightforward matter to get a DNA sample from Morgensen.

But maybe she had been afraid the evidence wouldn't stick. Maybe Morgensen had threatened her, cautioned her not to say anything.

"Danielle might have felt that it would be pointless to report him," Gin said, excitement building inside her. "Maybe she decided to go after him herself. It's like the Lincoln Alley Killer, Dad, remember him?" Two of the victims of the grisly serial killer had ended up on Gin's table nearly a decade earlier.

"He took the ears from his victims," Richard said. "What does that have to do with anything?"

"Do you remember how they finally took him down?"

"One of his victims escaped, didn't she? And she was able to give a good enough description to the police artist to iden- tify him."

"Because he didn't finish her off," Gin agreed. "And she actually stabbed him with the ballpoint pen. Nearly killed him. Well, what if that happened with this girl? If Morgensen stuck to his pattern, he would have tried to come on to this young woman that he met in a meeting. If she turned him down, and he became enraged, he might have taken her to some hidden location and raped her. But what if she somehow was able to get the upper hand—if, during the attack, she actually *killed* him?" An explanation for everything that had transpired was emerg- ing from her racing thoughts. "It might not have even been on purpose—it might have happened in self-defense. After, she might have panicked and tried to get rid of the evidence." The motorcycle might have been part of it—if Danielle had felt that it could tie her to Morgensen's murder somehow, she might have found a way to take it. She could have had it for years; it would have been easy enough to keep hidden. "And then, when Morgensen's body was found and the news reported that I was helping with the autopsy, she decided that I was a threat."

"You're saying that the body found on Jake's jobsite was connected to all of those rapes?" Richard asked. "But they were years ago, weren't they?"

"The media made it sound like I was on the verge of solv- ing the whole case," she said. "They said I'd never failed to identify a body since I started consulting to the county."

"But that's true," her father said. "You're much too humble, honey."

"But that's just news media hyperbole, only Danielle wouldn't have known that. Maybe she thought she had to stop me."

"Those rapes were years ago," Richard said. "I'm still struggling to understand how they're connected."

Gin ignored her father and focused on Danielle. Even if Morgensen had stopped, even if he had somehow managed to live a clean life, he might not have been able to resist when a girl who perfectly matched his profile turned up. Especially since Danielle had put him in a mentoring role by seeking him out for help with the reenacting. She might have appeared compliant or even submissive.

Gin had pulled up the old news articles around the rapes. The profile was remarkably consistent. Morgensen had gone after girls who were attractive but not beautiful—sorority girls, estheticians, retail workers—but they were all young and white with long hair and traditionally feminine style of dress. And in each case that the victim was able to describe the events leading up to the attack, there was a moment when his demeanor seemed to change—when he went from calm to frenzied and furious. Generally, it had been when Morgensen's victims rejected him, when his fantasy of romantic involvement was shattered.

What if, as Danielle became more and more interested in reenactment, Morgensen interpreted her growing interest as sexual attraction? At some point, he might have made a move, which took Danielle off guard. Her rejection would have been instant and quite possibly humiliating.

"That could have set him off," Gin reasoned, mostly to herself. But if Danielle had somehow managed to kill him during the attack, it would have been considered self-defense. Only, Gin had worked with rape victims during her residency. In the hours following their rape, it was all too easy for girls to believe they somehow were complicit, that they should have read the signs differently, that the attack was somehow preventable. Depending on Danielle's background and lived experience, she might have even believed she deserved it. If she had been operating out of shame and fear, she might have truly believed that her only option was to cover up what she had done.

To dispose of the body.

But that left the teeth. Even if Danielle had had the fortitude to get the body to the woods and to dig the hole, was it really plausible that she'd knock out his teeth? *And* dress him in the historic uniform? *And* shoot his dead body with a musket?

There were a lot of improbable details in the scenario that Gin had come up with. But at the very least, there was the problem of Morgensen's birthplace, along with Danielle's leg brace, the bandage on her face, and her limp. Not, perhaps, enough to go to the cops.

But enough to go talk to her.

"Dad, thanks for listening to all this. But I've got to go."

"But honey, I still don't understand what this entire conversation has been about! You think you might know who killed the man who was found on Jake's work site? But surely you don't plan to go and talk to them—isn't that dangerous?"

"I know where to find her, though," Gin said. Tonight was the "moonlight battle" that the women had been talking about at the reenactors' dinner. "And it's a public place. Don't worry, Dad—I'll be perfectly safe."

23

As she got into the Range Rover, Gin called Rosa. When her friend answered, Gin could hear the sounds of shouting and laughter in the background.

"Would you happen to be at the moonlight battle, Rosa?"

"How did you know?"

"Lucky guess. Plus, Doyle looked like he never plans to let you out of his sight the other night. I think he's truly smitten."

Rosa laughed. "You should come! There's this group playing harmonicas and drums and actual *fifes*. They're really good."

"I was actually wondering if Danielle Sigal was there."

"Oh, the girl with the long hair and the leg brace? She was here—but I think she went home already. She said she has to work early tomorrow."

"Oh—thanks, Rosa."

"Are you coming over?"

"No, I don't think so. But you have fun, okay?"

She barely heard Rosa's good-bye over the cheering in the background.

Gin debated for a moment. It was still fairly early, so she ought to be able to come up with a plausible pretext for a visit—and a chance to talk to the girl alone. She did a quick search on her phone, deciding that if the girl's address wasn't listed, she'd give up and return home.

It came up immediately: 24 Old Gordon Road.

Gin knew the road, which hugged the hill to the south of town. It had fallen into disrepair in the seventies and been replaced by a four-lane route that cut off much of the steepest part. The original workers' housing had largely been demolished, save half a dozen tiny cottages that were still inhabited.

She found number 24 at the end of the row, separated from its nearest neighbor by several overgrown lots. She pulled into a gravel turnout and walked up to the door, encouraged to see that lights were still on in the house.

Within seconds of knocking, the door opened, and Danielle Sigal peeped out. She was dressed in sweats, her hair in loose waves over her shoulder.

"You're the lady from the other night, aren't you? Gin, was it?"

"I'm sorry, I know it's late—I saw the lights on, and I really need to talk to you."

The girl looked spooked, small, and afraid. "What about?" she said uncertainly. "Did something happen at the battle?"

"No, no, nothing like that. I just . . . it's something else." Gin tried to communicate with her body language that she was no threat, offering a soft smile. "Could I just come in and talk to you for a few minutes?"

"Okay, well, sure. Could you just—could you just give me one second, please?"

Before Gin could respond, the girl gently shut the door. Moments passed, making Gin wonder if Danielle was ever coming back. But eventually the door opened again, and Danielle stepped aside to let her enter.

She had changed into jeans and a long sweater that practically engulfed her small frame and put her hair up in a ponytail, but Gin was distracted by the state of the room. Danielle had obviously tried to tidy up for her guest—papers had been hastily mounded on the table, and empty dishes had been stacked on the counter of the sink visible from the living room.

The effort had made little difference.

Danielle lived in the squalor of someone well on her way to becoming a hoarder. There was barely a path through the room, and every piece of furniture was stacked high with books and papers and clothes and junk. Clothes spilled out of cardboard boxes lined up two deep along the wall. The dining room table was covered, with only a square big enough for a single person to eat a meal in front of the television, which sat unsteadily on top of more boxes. Even the hall was filled with bookshelves and dressers and boxes, leaving a space barely wide enough for a person to ease through sideways.

"I'm sorry for the clutter," Danielle said quickly, barely meeting Gin's eyes. "It's just, I'm going to be selling a lot of this. I just have to, um, get some time to go through it."

"Oh," Gin said. She'd worked on a few cases of hoarders who'd been discovered dead inside their homes, and while the investigations had little to do with her department outside of confirming the cause of death—usually natural causes—she had done some reading on the propensity to hoard. Often, though not always, it had its roots in some trauma or loss; the hoarding became an ineffective coping mechanism for the anxiety, depression, and grief.

All of which supported the theory that Danielle had suffered a breakdown after being raped.

Gin spotted a framed photograph that had been carefully dusted and set on a crocheted doily on top of a relatively clutter-free table. In it, Danielle wore a scarlet graduation gown and cap. Her hair was shorter and darker, and she was beaming with pride. Her hands rested on the shoulder of a seated woman who could be her mother or an aunt or even an older sister—the resemblance was striking, though the woman couldn't have been forty. She was very thin and dressed in a long plain skirt and blouse.

Danielle saw Gin looking. "That's me and my mom at my high school graduation. She, um, died a few months later."

"Oh, I'm so sorry," Gin said. "Did she live near here?"

"Yes, ma'am. It was just me and her. She didn't have much family left—not that were speaking to her, anyways."

"Red suits you," Gin said, unsure what else to say.

"Our mascot was the Red Devils."

"Oh, from Sturgeon? What year did you graduate?"

"2012."

Gin did a quick recalculation; that meant the girl was only twenty-two or -three at the most, younger even than she had guessed.

Which also meant that she had been still a teenager when she met Morgensen.

"And you've been working since high school?"

"Yes . . . I'm hoping to start community college in a year or two, once I save a little. All my mom left me was this house, and I don't earn that much in my job. That's why I'm starting my online business. I'm going to sell vintage clothes, you know? There's a big market for that." Idly, Danielle touched a filmy orange print garment piled on top of an open box. "I'm going to specialize in the seventies."

"That's great," Gin said. The idea wasn't a terrible one, but it was clear that the girl had no idea where to start. Unchecked, the collecting could eventually force her out of her home. "I wonder . . . is there somewhere we can sit down to talk?"

"Oh, sure. Come on in the kitchen."

Danielle dashed ahead and started unloading more junk from a chair so Gin would have a place to sit. The odors of rot, mold, and dust rose into the air, but she didn't seem to notice.

"Would you like a soda? I have some in the garage."

Gin could only imagine what the garage looked like, and she quickly declined. "I've been thinking about something ever since we talked the other night. Danielle . . . I know I didn't tell you this when we met, and I'm sorry to have misled you, but I have a medical background. I'm a physician, actually." She waited to gauge Danielle's reaction, but the girl's expression didn't change. "I've dealt with any number of people who've suffered serious trauma. Assault . . . abuse . . . rape. The effects can be devastating."

At the word *rape*, Danielle flinched as if struck and then seemed to retreat into herself, crossing her arms tightly across her chest.

"And it seems to me," Gin continued, "that you might have suffered something similar. That you were . . . taken advantage of by someone who you trusted, someone who you thought cared about you. I know that you spent a lot of time with Marvin Morgensen several years ago when you joined the reenactors."

Despite her efforts to remain composed, Danielle's mouth began to wobble, and tears welled in her eyes. She made a soft gasping sound, and her body began to tremble.

Alarmed, Gin rebuked herself for not bringing someone else along with her, someone trained in counseling victims of sexual assault. The last thing she wanted to do was deepen Danielle's trauma. But her reaction proved that Gin was on the right track. If she could establish what had happened to Danielle before contacting the detectives, maybe she could help smooth the way to make sure that she was handled with sensitivity.

Gin leaned forward, keeping her body language as non-threatening as possible. "I believe that Marvin Morgensen took advantage of that relationship," she said, gently but firmly. "That once he was certain of your trust, he treated you in a most inappropriate way. That he . . . harmed you. Afterward, he may have told you that no one would believe you if you tried to tell what happened. He may have convinced you that somehow you invited his attentions. Maybe you even believe that what happened was your fault."

"Nothing that happened was my fault!" Danielle said. Her face twisted up in an ugly rictus of rage and pain. "I wasn't even there. I never asked for anything, ever!"

"You . . . of course not," Gin said. Maybe Danielle had blanked out the traumatic events—maybe her mind had taken over to protect her psyche, revising her memories, blotting out those that were simply too painful to revisit.

It wasn't uncommon, in horrific attacks, for the victims to bury their memories. Sometimes the events could be reconstructed through therapy, but the process could take months, even years.

And if Danielle had blocked the rape, perhaps she had blocked the rest as well—if she had killed Morgensen, she might honestly have no memory of it. Her mind's frantic attempt to stay a few steps ahead of the painful truth could easily have been the trigger to begin hoarding, to try to fill the yawing chasm inside her.

Gin reached across the table and took Danielle's hand. Her skin was waxy and cold, her muscles tense.

"Marvin Morgensen hurt you," Gin said. "I want to help you."

"He never hurt me," Danielle said, a strange, grim smile twisting her lips.

"Oh, honey, it's understandable that you have complicated feelings about the man who raped you."

Danielle gave an anguished cry and flung Gin's hand away with such force that it bounced off the table.

"Marvin Morgensen isn't my rapist," she sobbed. "He's my father."

24

G in recoiled in shock. If Morgensen was Danielle's father, then . . .

"Oh, my God, your mother," she gasped.

"Marvin raped her. She was only seventeen years old," Danielle said dully. "She was working at a dry cleaner. He worked at a car dealership down the street, and he always talked to her when he came in to pick up his shirts. She said he was always really polite—he barely spoke to her at all other than to say thank you. Until one night he waited for her behind the building. He knew she took a shortcut home—he'd been watching her."

"Oh, Danielle. I'm—I'm so sorry." The pitiful inadequacy of the words were not lost on Gin.

"Why?" Danielle glared at her, her voice suddenly sharp. "You didn't do anything. It's not your fault."

"No, of course," Gin stammered, thrown off by Danielle's volatility.

"There's one person on this earth who was responsible for what happened to my mom that day. One person who wrecked her life. You want to see something?" Danielle's voice was growing increasingly angry and agitated.

"All right," Gin said, as calmly as she could, trying to keep up. All along she'd been thinking that Danielle was Morgensen's victim, which would have been an anomaly in the pattern of rapes, coming so long after the attack before it. Tuck had been right all along, but Gin—trained by her profession to draw conclusions from the evidence in front of her—had ignored him.

Danielle got up and went into the living room. Gin could hear her moving around; there was the sound of papers falling to the floor and boxes being pushed aside.

In a few moments, she was back. Clutched in her hand was a large fabric-bound yearbook.

"My mom was her class *president*," she said, opening the book to a dog-eared page. There, in the center of several rows of senior portraits, was a picture of a beautiful young woman with an impish smile and hair styled in perfect nineties waves. "She had a scholarship to Penn State. She wanted to be a teacher."

"What happened to her was terrible," Gin said shakily. "But it doesn't mean that you have to—"

"She almost didn't have me, you know," Danielle said matter-of-factly. "She said she thought she couldn't stand to see his face every day in her baby, if I took after him. But she just couldn't have an abortion. And she always said that I was my own person with my own look. But I had to resemble him at least a little, or else why would she have killed herself?"

"Oh, honey," Gin said, her heart breaking for what the poor girl had endured. "I'm sure your mother loved you with all her heart. But she was ill, after what happened to her. She had a sickness, the disease of depression."

"Oh, *stop*." Abruptly Danielle raised her other hand, which she'd kept hidden behind her until now.

She was holding a gun.

"Danielle . . ."

"Just stop trying to psychoanalyze me, okay? I hate that."

"All right," Gin said carefully. The muzzle of the small handgun was waving erratically, Danielle snuffling and wiping her face with her sleeve. "I'm sorry I brought up what must be a really painful subject. But Danielle, it doesn't have to be like this. You don't have to live with this kind of pain. We can get you the help that you—"

"Don't *judge* me," Danielle snarled, whipping the gun around to point directly at Gin's heart. "Don't you dare!"

"I'm not judging," Gin said, a little desperately. Coming here had been one of the stupidest decisions she had made in the whole case. Tuck had warned her to step back, and Stillman had tried to keep her out since the whole mess began. Why couldn't she have listened?

"Don't *lie*. I see how you look at me. I see you looking at my house, my things. Not everyone has the chance to go to medical school. Not everyone has their whole life bought and paid for. I looked you up. I know who your parents are. You think that just because you're rich you get to come back here and all the doors open for you." She was sobbing now, rocking back and forth slightly and clutching her stomach with her free hand.

Gin had to keep her talking somehow, had to keep her from impulsively pulling the trigger. They were surrounded by mounded trash; next to the kitchen table were stacks of boxes filled with what looked like newspapers and old magazines. They might make a shield if she could get behind them, but there was nowhere to run to, no way to reach an exit without putting herself in the line of fire.

"It was you who tried to run me off the road, wasn't it?"

"I watched you with those girls," Danielle said. "I came to your practices. You never even saw me. All those girls with their expensive things. My mom couldn't ever afford the fees for me to play sports."

"You were there? In the gym?"

"I've been everywhere," Danielle said, her voice going high and manic. "I never realized all the things I could do. The power I had."

"The power you had . . . to do what?"

"Whatever I want. Whatever needs to be done. To make people pay for what they did."

"You mean Morgensen . . ."

"Shut up!" Danielle snapped. "Don't say his name; don't keep saying his name."

"But he was the one who hurt your mother," Gin said faintly.

"My mom never told me it was him. All the years I was growing up, she wouldn't say his name. She couldn't go to the police because the police don't care. They let rapists walk around free, and they do it again and again and again. That's what happened with M—with *him*."

She was crying so hard she could barely get the words out. Gin knew she was dangerously distraught but couldn't think of any way to calm her other than to keep her talking.

"Your mother didn't report the rape because she felt that no one would help," she said, employing a basic technique of patient inquiry, repeating back what Danielle had said in slightly different words.

"And then he'd come after me, to punish her! That was her biggest fear—that he'd come for me if she ever said who he was. But I figured it out. I mean, there was only one dry cleaner in town and only one car dealership nearby. And all I had to do was pretend like I was looking for a car. They had these plaques on the walls. You know, with like top salesmen for every month, way back to when my mom was young. I wrote down the names, and then I just looked on the Internet, and it came up where he had been arrested for doing disgusting things, so I knew it was him."

"Why didn't you go to the police then?"

"She wouldn't have wanted that," Danielle said, shaking her head. "And they wouldn't have done anything, anyway. Not after all that time passed. Besides, I didn't even go looking until after she died."

Gin took the opening that Danielle had provided; she knew that hoarding behavior often followed a traumatic loss. *Just keep talking*, she thought; the longer she could distract Danielle, the better her odds of figuring out some way to get the gun away from her. "Tell me about when your mother died," she said gently.

Danielle shuddered, wiping her eyes with the back of her free hand. "One night she asked me to come into her room. She never let me go in there because that was where she kept her bottles. She didn't want me to see her like that. But she wasn't drinking that night. She *wasn't*. And she asked me if I would be all right, and I didn't know she was going to kill herself. I didn't *know*!"

"Of course you didn't," Gin said, some part of her heart breaking for the girl. She would have been eighteen, barely graduated from high school, living a hell that no one knew about.

"I said I would, and then she said I should never trust any man who tried to talk to me. She said it would be better for me to keep to myself, to stay single. And I said I would. But what she was really saying . . . He *took* her from me, don't you see that? He made her do what she did."

"What your mother's rapist did was . . . unconscionable," Gin said, but hearing her own words, she knew they could never describe the magnitude of the pain he had caused.

Abruptly Danielle seemed to get control of herself. She angrily swiped away her tears and refocused her aim. "It doesn't matter," she said, smirking. "I took care of him."

"You found out he was a reenactor," Gin said. "You got to know him. Gained his trust."

"It wasn't hard," she said. "And besides, I like the meetings. Everyone's nice, and it's not all like, you know, parties with people my age, where all the men just want one thing."

Gin tried not to react to the strange mix of naïveté and suspicion that Danielle harbored. Had she ever had a close relationship with someone her own age?

"You made friends," she said. "You enjoyed the socializing."

Danielle nodded. "It made it easier, you know? I couldn't be all obvious. I took my time, and after we were introduced, I would just make sure to end up next to him at the drills and meetings."

"You pretended to be interested in him?"

"I went to his house. Not the first time he invited me, but . . . after I'd known him for a few months. By then I had a lot of friends in the group, so it wasn't hard to make it seem kind of natural. I had asked to see his old uniforms, and he invited me over. I had my mom's old car, so I drove myself. He went upstairs and came down wearing his best uniform. Then I asked him to let me see his guns. He had all this stuff, he said it was worth a lot of money, but I didn't care. He let me hold this one that he said was worth thousands of dollars. I asked him if it actually worked, and he said he paid a guy to make sure it did; he bought real ammunition from him. It was so easy; he just stood there grinning at me thinking—thinking I was going to—oh, my God, that made it *easy*." She looked directly into Gin's eyes, and her voice went ice cold. "I shot him and I watched him die. I watched him fall down, and the whole time he was staring at me, I told him who my mom was, and that was the last thing he knew."

Gin was trying to decide whether to make a grab for the gun, but she was afraid she'd lost her opportunity. She should have lunged forward when Danielle was distracted; now she seemed almost eerily calm.

"What made you decide to bury him where you did?"

"Mom and I used to go up there," Danielle said. "We knew it was private land, but there was a back way where you could hike up. Mom used to say it was the best view in town, and it was free. We used to take picnics."

"What about his teeth, Danielle?"

The girl rolled her eyes at her in disgust. "I was just being thorough. Mom always said that if you were going to do something, you might as well do it right. I did it right there in his living room. Went out to the garage and got a hammer. I had to put a plastic bag under him, but it wasn't hard."

Gin felt a faint wave of nausea, imagining the girl at her grisly task. She'd seen the fragmented skull; she knew the force Danielle would have had to put into each blow, fueled by all the rage and pain that Morgensen had caused her.

"I took other things too," she said, almost defiantly. "After I got rid of him? I sneaked back on foot to make sure I hadn't left any evidence. I took a bunch of his reenactment gear—I have it in a box here somewhere. And I took his motorcycle." She grinned. "My mom's car was a pile of junk. And that motorcycle was almost new. He had so much . . . and she never had anything."

"But how did you know how to ride it?"

"The boys that lived next door all rode dirt bikes when we were growing up. It's not hard. Of course, I've had to keep it in the garage most of the time, since I couldn't register it." Her hand that was holding the gun twitched convulsively. "I guess I'll never ride it again, though."

"Because the police have it, you mean."

"It would have been fine," Danielle said angrily, "if you hadn't showed up. The way they talked about you on TV, they made it sound like you could identify anyone."

The news reports after the body had been found . . . the reporter had seized on the fact that the medical examiner's office had brought in an expert, emphasizing—even exaggerating—Gin's role in the toughest cases, her experience in the aftermath of the Bosnian war.

"Okay, enough talking," Danielle said crossly. "I'm sorry about this, but you're not going to mess everything up for me now. Look away, okay? I don't want to have to look at your face when I do it."

She was going to do it. She was going to kill Gin, just like she'd killed her mother's rapist.

Gin took one last, desperate look around the kitchen, looking for something, anything, that she could use to stop Danielle. But there were only the walls of trash, the barriers that could never make the girl feel safe enough.

"Please," she whispered. "Please don't do this."

"Turn *around*!"

Gin was frozen, unable to accept that these were her last seconds on earth. She thought of her parents, of the unimaginable loss they had already suffered; she thought of Jake, of how much they had endured together to come this far. It wasn't fair.

There was a crash, a yell, and the sharp report of gunshot. Instinctively, she threw her arms over her face and ducked, rolling to the floor in a ball.

Screaming.

And then a voice she recognized.

Maybe she was already dead, or dying, her mind making one last desperate connection before blacking out forever. Because she could swear that he'd come for her.

25

Gin woke to a strange sensation of choking. She gasped and felt an unfamiliar pain in her throat. She tried to blink her eyes open, but they didn't want to obey. She could hear voices, mechanical sounds, a chair being dragged across the floor.

She knew these sounds. She was in a hospital.

She forced herself to stop fighting, suddenly aware that the thing in her throat was a breathing tube. She struggled to lift her hand and got as far as wiggling her fingers. She heard the shift in the mechanical sounds as the machines responded to her body coming awake.

"She's coming out," an unfamiliar voice said. "Get Rafferty."

The next few moments were a blur, both familiar and strange. During her residency, Gin had performed dozens of surgeries, but she'd never been the one lying in bed, helpless and vulnerable.

The tube was eased out, and Gin struggled for her first few breaths on her own, gulping in air despite the soreness. Her eyes adjusted to the bright lights overhead, and she moved her toes, her fingers. A male doctor leaned over her, but all she could see between his cap and mask was warm brown eyes behind horn-rimmed glasses.

"Mom . . ." she gasped, her voice a raw whisper. "Jake . . ."

But the next face she saw was neither one of them.

"I'm here." Another cap, another mask, and a voice strained with worry and fear.

Tuck Baxter took her hand between his. "Goddamnit, Gin, you scared the hell out of me."

She blinked, and the blurriness left her vision. "Was it you?" she croaked. "Did you come for me? At Danielle's?"

His expression betrayed a complex mixture of emotions. "Yes. But I didn't get there in time. Crosby got there first."

"Oh, my God—is he okay?"

"Yeah. I guess he tackled her, and once she saw that she wasn't going to win, she let him take the gun from her without a fight—she just curled up on the floor, shaking and babbling about her mom. Jake called nine-one-one, and then he tried to stop the bleeding. The bullet went in a few millimeters from the scapula and between two ribs, which was lucky—none of your bones were shattered. He'd got it under control by the time the paramedics showed up. By then, Danielle got her shit together and hightailed it out of the house, but we picked her up a few blocks away."

Even in her groggy state, Gin felt a rush of sadness for the girl, whose need for psychiatric treatment would have to be met from within the justice system now; she might never fully recover from the trauma she'd been through. "How did Jake know where I was?"

"I guess he called your mom, looking for you, and she told him you were going to see Danielle." He shook his head in frustration. "Gin . . . you should have called me. You should never have tried to take her on alone. You don't have any idea . . ."

His voice trailed off, but he was standing close, close enough that she could see the stubble on his face, the dark circles under his eyes. His hands were warm and strong around hers. The electric attraction that coursed between them was here even now, even under the glare of fluorescent lights, with her hair matted with her own blood, with the weight of all of his responsibilities heavy on his shoulders. It would have been easy—so easy—to give in to the comfort he offered, the promise of strength.

Instead, she gently pulled her hand away and dropped her gaze. "When can I see Jake and my parents?"

*   *   *

The emergency surgery, which had been performed to remove the bullet that had migrated after entering her body and threatened to block her axillary vein, had almost certainly saved Gin's life. With the bullet gone, her prognosis was excellent. However, the doctors wanted to keep her for observation for at least another day, given the threat of infection.

"I told them to keep you for the rest of the week," Jake fretted. "Just to make sure." He and her parents had taken turns sitting with her throughout the day, Richard and Madeleine taking the afternoon shift while Jake went to check on a few things for work. Now he was back, and they had gone home to get some dinner and some sleep, promising to return in the morning.

Gin's meal had been taken away nearly untouched, and Jake had pulled a chair up next to her bed and turned it around, straddling it so that he could reach around and hold both her hands without putting any pressure on the wound site. Outside, night was falling over the view of the river valley, stars twinkling against a background of pale, wispy clouds and a sliver of moon.

Gin laughed sleepily; the pain medications had made her woozy. "For such a tough guy, you're remarkably fearful of doctors," she said.

"It's not the doctors; it's the place," Jake said, looking around the room with a shudder. "I hate hospitals. Doc Rafferty seems okay, though I'm going to tell him I'll kick his ass if he doesn't give you top-notch care."

As if on cue, a nurse came in with a tray bearing a cup of water and Gin's medication. "You going to kick my ass too?" the nurse teased while Gin swallowed the pills and sipped water. "Tell you what, let's wait to brawl until Gin's had some rest. I recommend you go home and get a little rest yourself and check back in with us in the morning. I think there's a good chance you'll be able to take her home tomorrow."

Jake waited until the nurse was gone. Then he took Gin's hand, holding it tightly as he leaned against the bed.

"We need to talk," he said.

"Oh, yeah?" Gin said. "What about?"

"About you and me. About the way it's going to be from now on."

Something stirred inside Gin at his terse words. "That sounds like you're about to give me orders."

"I am. And so help me, you're going to follow them. Gin—I've waited too goddamn long to get you back. I'm not losing you again."

"I'm not going anywhere . . ."

"Not *physically*, maybe. But I know you, Gin. I'd wager I know you better than anyone on this planet."

Gin opened her mouth to say something—to argue, perhaps—and then shut it. He was right. No one saw into her soul the way Jake did; no one else had walked through the same fires with her that he had.

"So?" she said instead, with a pout that masked raw fear. Because what if this was the moment that Jake demanded that she put it all on the line? That she commit—forever, this time?

"You're living with me," Jake said, not quite meeting her eyes. "I want you to start acting like it."

"I *do*!" Gin protested. "My clothes are in your closet, I have my mail forwarded—"

"Get rid of that apartment in Chicago," Jake said, biting off the words. "I don't want to hear about how you 'can always go back if things don't work out.'"

Gin flinched, recognizing the words she'd spoken only a few weeks ago after some minor disagreement had given her cold feet. But she hadn't known he'd been listening that closely. Hadn't known he'd cared so deeply.

She swallowed. "Okay."

Jake nodded curtly. "I'll drive the truck up if you need to bring anything back. But really, why bother? Get new stuff. We'll get stuff together. *Our* stuff—not yours and mine."

"All right," Gin said in a small voice. For some reason, the more Jake demanded, the more willing—eager, even—she was to comply. "Is there anything else?"

"Damn right there is." Jake squeezed her hands so hard it almost hurt, but she was pretty sure he wasn't even aware he was doing it. He stared at a spot on the sheet, not meeting her eyes. "I don't ever want you offering to bail me out again."

"You mean . . . financially?"

"Yes. Financially—or any other way, either. Look, I may not be able to buy you diamond rings and trips to Paris—not yet, anyway, not while I'm still trying to get my business off the ground. And maybe another guy wouldn't ask you to wait. But I want you there for all of it. *All* of it, Gin—the hard times and the good ones too. None of it means anything without you."

Gin felt tears stinging her eyes. Jake had never been so unguarded, never voiced the things she knew he felt so powerfully but kept buried deep.

"That's all I've ever wanted," she whispered.

"Good," Jake said, letting out a sigh of relief. "That's settled, then. For the love of God, woman. Try not to scare me like this again. Let's have a few months just to enjoy each other without any drama. Do you think we can make that work? Please?"

"I think we can," Gin said, a smile taking over her face.

"Good. Because if you don't behave, you're going to have some explaining to do."

Gin didn't miss the dangerous edge to Jake's voice—an edge that promised that boundaries were going to be pushed and provocations rewarded.

"I see," she murmured, blushing.

Jake bent and kissed her gently on the forehead. "For now, you just take care of yourself. Do everything the doctors tell you. I'm going to go see when we can get you out of here. And Gin . . . I love you."

"I love you too," Gin said, her eyes fluttering closed over the approach of fevered dreams.

*   *   *

Gin woke again when an orderly brought her lunch, which she made an effort to finish. She was eager to get home, and the nurse had announced that she'd be released as soon as the final paperwork was prepared. But as the sun streaming through her window gradually faded, it turned out there was one more surprise in store for her.

"Knock knock," came a tentative voice at the door. Then two blonde heads of hair peeped shyly around the corner: Olive and Cherie escorted by Brandon.

Cherie came first, standing very solemnly at the edge of the bed, her hands clasped behind her back. Her eyes were wide and owlish, but even Olive looked apprehensive. Gin looked down at the various tubes connected to her and smiled. "It's not as bad as it looks, I promise," she said.

"Dad says 'don't touch,'" Cherie blurted. "He says you're a little bit broken, but they're going to fix you."

Gin liked that—*a little bit broken*. She smiled, wondering if that was how Tuck saw her, then decided that it was a label that applied to just about everyone now and then.

"Your dad helped make sure of that," Gin said lightly.

"Your father is a stone-cold badass, Cherie," Brandon said teasingly, "but Mr. Crosby was the one who saved Gin from the bad guy."

"We made you something," Olive piped up. "Do you want to give it to her, Cherie? Or do you want me to?"

"The girls have been working on this all morning," Brandon said. "Tuck let Cherie stay over last night, and well, they've been shut up in Olive's room with the door locked. They made me promise not to peek—wouldn't even come out for donuts."

Cherie accepted the folded paper that Olive was holding and carefully spread it out on the bed next to Gin. It was a handmade card, decorated with crayon and glitter and beads and stickers, and in the middle, it said, "I Love You, Gin." The "I" had been crossed out and "We" had been written above in a careful hand.

"We made it *together*," Cherie said proudly. "And then we made grilled cheese sandwiches, and I got to use the heart shape cutter."

"Tell you what, girls," Brandon said, winking at Gin, "I seem to remember there's a soft-serve ice cream machine in the cafeteria. If I can get one of you to bring me back a scoop of chocolate in a cup, you guys can get whatever you want. And get some for Gin too. Sound like a deal?"

"Deal!" the girls cheered in unison. Olive accepted a ten-dollar bill from her father, and with a backward glance and a smile for Gin, the girls raced out of the room.

"Forgive my little ruse," Brandon said, "but I kind of wanted a moment of privacy to ask how you are. You know . . . how you *really* are."

"Well, I'm going to have an interesting scar for bikini season next year," Gin said wryly. "But I'm actually feeling pretty good. All things considered, I'd say I was pretty lucky."

Brandon raised an eyebrow. "You're tough, Sullivan; we already knew that. I kind of meant . . . how about you and Jake? You guys can't seem to catch a break."

Gin smiled. "I think we're going to be okay," she said. "I mean, I've given up predicting what life will bring next week, much less next year. But Jake's going to take a couple weeks off while they wrap up the investigation, and then he hopes to rebuild by next summer. And earlier today, Dad was talking about renting a cabin for Christmas for the four of us—cross-country skiing and roasting chestnuts. I don't know how he'll talk my mom into taking the time off, but it sounds like fun."

"That's great, Gin," Brandon said sincerely.

Another knock on the door was followed by Rosa entering bearing a paper sack and a huge bouquet of brightly dyed carnations. "Mom sent tamales," Rosa said after Gin introduced her. "She doesn't trust the hospital food."

"This is going to be a regular gourmet feast!" Gin laughed as Brandon and Rosa squeezed into the small room. "Tamales and ice cream . . . that hits all the major food groups, right?"

"*Barriga llena, corazón contento!*" Rosa said.

"Sorry, Rosa, I don't remember my high school Spanish," Brandon said.

"It means 'Full stomach, happy heart!' It's one of my mom's favorite sayings."

"I'll toast to that," Gin said, lifting her plastic cup of water high.

Amid the laughter of her friends and the delicious aromas of the food, Gin closed her eyes for a brief second and let gratitude wash over her—for her health, her family, and Jake. For the children in her life and those that might come, someday. And for the twisted path that had brought her, finally, back home.

Epilogue

On a crisp winter morning a few weeks later, Gin drove out to the construction site with a thermos of coffee and a basket of muffins that her mother had baked. She parked behind Jake's truck and adjusted her shoulder sling before getting out of the truck. The wound was healing well, according to her doctors, but now and then, a twinge of pain reminded her of how close she had come to dying at the hands of a girl who'd known nothing but sorrow.

Jake walked toward her across the foundation of the burned house, the only thing to survive the fire. He expected the new permits to rebuild to be issued by the middle of January, and in the meantime, his crew had their hands full with the other two homes. The Ashers had bought a custom home in Fox Chapel, trading Monongahela River views for the Allegheny, but they'd recommended Jake to a handful of friends, and a couple was coming to take a look the Sunday after Thanksgiving.

"Hey, beautiful," Jake said, lifting a corner of the napkin on the basket. "All those for me?"

Gin playfully lifted the basket out of reach. "No fair," she said. "I can't fight back."

"You'll be healed in no time." Jake put an arm around her waist, and together they walked up onto what would be the back deck, eventually. "And when you are, watch out—I've got plans for you."

"I'll take that as a promise."

Jake offered her a paint bucket to use as a seat, but Gin preferred to sit on the edge of the platform so she could swing her legs while she looked out over the valley. Sunlight glinted off the water, and wispy, lazy clouds floated high above in the dazzling blue sky. There was little traffic on the road in the distance because today was a holiday.

"Mom said to tell you that if you're late, she's locking the door and feeding your plate to Jett."

Jake laughed. "Your mom is a formidable woman. Who's coming, again?"

"Well, besides Mom and Dad and us, there's Rosa and her mom and Antonio, Doyle and his kids, Brandon and Diane and Olive and Austen, and half the city council. It'll be the first time she's managed to fill that enormous dining room table in ages."

"Yikes. I think I'll just sit at the kids' table."

Gin punched him playfully with her good arm. "No chance, mister, you're carving the turkey. Dad says he's passing the torch—or the carving knife, as the case may be."

"Wow." Jake seemed genuinely taken aback. "That's a lot of responsibility."

Gin rolled her eyes. "Well, if that's too much of a commitment, I guess we could go back to you dropping me off at my folks' house and making out in the driveway after dates."

"Hmmm. Let me think about that." When Gin slugged him again, he pulled her into his lap, wrapping his arms around her waist.

It was thrilling and a little bit scary to look down over the edge of the deck, past the steep, rocky cliff, to the road far below. A fall would be perilous—but Jake would not let her fall.

Today, the first Thanksgiving she'd spent at home in nearly two decades, Gin decided to try to simply savor every moment. The scent of burning leaves mixed with the fresh breeze off the river, and she could hear a dog barking in the distance and birds calling to each other in the branches. She felt the stubble of Jake's beard along her neck and the beating of his heart against her back.

Of all her senses, though, it was the sense of gratitude that she felt most of all. For this day, this man, the family and friends at the table. The good food and good conversation and good wine to wash it all down, and—much later—the good, honest, simple home that she would return to with Jake.

Nothing in life was certain, and nothing was promised. She and Jake had found their way back to each other, only to discover that each of them had changed. The ease and simplicity of their young love was gone, perhaps forever. But in its place, they had been given another chance.

"I almost wish this moment could last forever," she sighed, letting her eyelids drift closed and leaning back against Jake's chest.

"I don't," Jake said. "Because then we'd never know what comes next."

Nothing lasted forever. Pain, joy, anger, sadness, and pleasure. Each had their season and their time. And on this day of thanksgiving, Gin was grateful for the bounty.